Life's Two Live

Also By

Sherry L. Snelgrove

Decision Criteria
Another Man's Treasure

Life's Two Live

Imagine The Possibilities

Sherry L. Snelgrove

iUniverse, Inc.
Bloomington

Life's Two Live
Imagine the Possibilities

iUniverse books may be ordered through booksellers or by contacting:

iUniverse
1663 Liberty Drive
Bloomington, IN 47403
www.iuniverse.com
1-800-Authors (1-800-288-4677)

ISBN: 978-1-4759-3355-0 (sc)
ISBN: 978-1-4759-3356-7 (e)

Printed in the United States of America

iUniverse rev. date: 8/3/2012

DEDICATION

To Bev, Sandy, Debbie and Wil.
You mean more to us than we can say.

PROLOGUE

If the human brain were so simple that we could understand it, we would be so simple that we couldn't.

Emerson M. Pugh

The human brain is the most precious three pounds on the face of the Earth, yet the most underutilized.

It's often compared to a computer. Even so, this mass of muscle and synaptic connections defies replication with more power and ability than any technological marvel ever constructed.

Yes, our most complex organ is truly an amazing masterpiece. It *consciously* responds to calculate the square root of a number, but *unconsciously* manages our senses allowing us to appreciate a colorful sunset. It also gives us dreams…and nightmares.

The brain's two hemispheres are comprised of several unique parts, each with a designated purpose. The cerebrum allows us to decide what to wear for a leisurely day at the park with the family. The stem keeps the heart beating while the pituitary releases hormones that convert a delicious picnic lunch into energy. We stand upright when playing with our children because the cerebellum controls balance. As the hot summer sun bears down, the hypothalamus prompts sweating which regulates our body temperature. Small bunches of cells called amygdales control our emotions allowing us to enjoy the day and regret when it's over.

For years scientists have examined the role each component plays. Although much has been learned, questions still remain. Why are some better at math than others? What causes criminals to commit horrendous acts of violence? Where does a concert pianist get the talent to play so beautifully?

What if these independent islands of reason, emotion and reflex could be further developed? Would our abilities be enhanced if the biological bridges linking them were strengthened? Could these distinctive neighbors function more effectively together as one?

Everyone's born with different cognitive skills which are continually influenced by life experiences. But how much brain capacity does one actually use? Some scientists estimate only ten percent. Unfortunately, we may never fully realize its vast potential.

Then again, one never really knows! Can't you just imagine the possibilities?

CHAPTER 1

No windows exposed the sixteenth floor boardroom to the surrounding New York City landscape. Bright fluorescent lighting illuminated the room.

An executive group—six men and a woman—sat stoically around the large conference room table. All were impeccably dressed in expensive dark suits. The silver-haired Chairman of the Board occupied a seat at the head of the table. He would control the agenda and oversee the committee's fiduciary responsibilities. Portraits of previous chairmen hung in a row along the back wall, respectfully paying tribute to the pharmaceutical company's tradition of leadership.

In the middle of the mahogany table sat a gleaming silver coffee service, its contents pervading the room with an aromatic scent. Several board members filled their delicate china cups, then helped themselves to a tray of flaky, warm croissants and perfectly sliced fruit. Others sat comfortably in their seats waiting for the meeting to begin. Quiet conversation filtered throughout the room.

Charles flexed a sore calf muscle strained during a morning workout. But the wrinkles etched across his forehead weren't the result of stiffness in his leg. He was concerned about various operating issues facing the company.

"Good morning," the Chairman spoke in a firm tone. "We've a full agenda so let's get started." The room fell silent as the group quickly settled down, directing their full attention to him.

The committee diligently reviewed the company's quarterly financial results before debating the merits of future marketing programs. They then approved management succession and corporate compensation plans. The last item on the agenda dealt with various product development activities, including the discontinuation of a compound labeled NRC8890.

For over a year the company had performed extensive laboratory testing on the new compound to determine its effects on animals. The analysis was conducted to find out how the experimental drug was tolerated and if there were any undesirable side effects. All were basic protocols mandated by the U.S. government before approving the compound for human trials.

Addressing the Chairman, Charles asked, "Can we please review the conditions for which NRC8890 was targeted and how it works?"

"Certainly. I'm neither a physician nor a scientist but can offer a layman's explanation." He began. "The drug's meant to treat neurological disorders. More specifically, the brain's made up of billions of cells connected by bridges called synapses. Thoughts are carried through cells as electrical charges. When a charge reaches one of these synapses it releases neurotransmitters that travel to an adjacent cell. If the synapses are damaged or if neurotransmitters aren't released, the information can't reach the next cell. NRC8890 is believed to strengthen these connections."

"So this could be a treatment for Alzheimer's disease or Autism."

"Possibly. With Alzheimer's the brain's damaged by a buildup of plaque accumulating between the cells, or in some cases tangles within the cell itself. These conditions are believed to cause the death of brain tissue." The Chairman glanced around the table to ensure everyone understood before continuing. "Savant Syndrome, which is a form of Autism, is different. It's caused by deficiencies or injury to the left hemisphere of the brain."

"Doesn't the right side take over in that situation?"

"It does, but the left half controls logic. And that's the issue. If the creative right hemisphere overcompensates and becomes dominant, the ability to reason and function is diminished. Our researchers hope to find a way to repair the damaged portion."

"How does the compound impact these conditions?"

"One of the most promising aspects of NRC8890 is that it might actually regenerate lost tissue. If it works, brain cells ravaged by Alzheimer's could be revived. Regarding Savant Syndrome, an individual's left hemisphere could be stimulated or repaired to achieve balance with the right."

Charles probed further. "What about other neurological conditions? Could the drug be beneficial to other mental maladies?"

"Maybe. We won't know until further research is conducted."

Charles shook his head and leaned forward. "But the Food and Drug Administration didn't approve the I.N.D." An Investigative New Drug Application is submitted to the Food and Drug Administration along with the testing results. The F.D.A. reviews the data and if the compound is deemed safe, the application is approved and Phase I Clinical Trials on human beings may begin. Both are critical steps in a long and tedious regulatory process designed to ensure new drugs are both safe and effective before receiving approval for the market.

"That's correct," the Chairman reluctantly responded. "According to the F.D.A. our tests didn't demonstrate the compound was safe. The lab animals used in the experiments displayed inconsistent and in some cases very serious side effects. Consequently our application was denied."

"What exactly do you mean by inconsistent? And what kind of side effects are we talking about?"

The Chairman leaned back in his chair and took a deep breath. "Some of the animals responded quite well with no adverse impact. In fact their reaction to the compound yielded some remarkable behavioral changes."

"Please elaborate," a board member sitting near the head of the table asked before lifting his coffee cup for a sip. The overweight man then reached for another roll. His pudgy red cheeks exposed a lust for food.

"A small percentage of the laboratory mice developed some extraordinary learning skills. Their behavior and interaction with the other test animals was also significantly enhanced."

For a few moments the committee sat in silence, absorbing the information.

The Chairman continued, "Those particular subjects became dominant within the test group." He paused then smiled and humorously added, "They became in a sense, the leaders of the pack."

The group chuckled at the descriptive explanation, temporarily lightening the mood in the room.

The levity was soon broken when someone seriously asked, "What about the others? How'd they respond?"

"In many, there wasn't any noticeable change. However some became very agitated and unstable. Others simply perished."

"How prevalent were the deaths?"

"Enough to stop the experiment," the Chairman admitted.

"What a shame. The financial opportunities associated with NRC8890 are tremendous," another board member stated in a concerned tone. "That's one of the most promising compounds we have in development." He laid his expensive Montblanc pen on the table and reached up to rub his eyes.

The Chairman agreed. "We all know what's at stake. This latest setback along with our patent expirations on several products, well...." He added in a serious tone, "If new drugs aren't discovered or those being tested don't survive the development process, the company will face some very difficult times. I believe everyone here understands the financial gravity if our product pipeline fails."

"What other compounds are currently being tested?"

"We have some potential products under development. There are two in Phase III trials with very positive outcomes so far. While these drugs will be important, neither is considered novel with any new properties. If approved they'll only join a host of similar products already in the marketplace. Just another 'me too' alternative for the consumer to choose from." The Chairman pointed out, "They'll certainly help but aren't expected to be financial blockbusters."

"How soon can the company submit the New Drug Application for those products?"

The Chairman replied, "The trials are expected to be completed over the next couple of months with their applications filed shortly thereafter. If everything goes well they could be in the marketplace within a year."

The lone female board member spoke as a pair of reading glasses dangled from a delicate gold chain around her neck. A thin layer of L'Oreal foundation attempted to cover several deep lines cutting down her aging cheeks. "What about the other compounds in Phase I and II? Any potential breakthroughs there?"

"It's still early. Very difficult to determine how the testing will go. We're probably several years away from really understanding their profiles and whether they're effective and safe. I'm sorry but that's only a long-winded way of saying...we just don't know yet."

The room became still as the group sat around the polished table digesting his sobering words along with their flaky croissants.

"Do we have any other options with NRC8890? Can we conduct some additional testing and resubmit the data to the F.D.A.?"

"Regulatory Affairs is working with the folks in R&D to evaluate our options. I don't have an answer for you, but odds are we won't be successful." The Chairman looked toward the Corporate Secretary who was diligently scribbling notes. "For now let the minutes reflect that NRC8890 is on hold."

"Does the company have any other strategic alternatives?"

"Let's not get ahead of ourselves. The company's entire future doesn't depend on this one compound. We're not in a live or die situation, not yet anyway. Just keep in mind that we may have to look at some different paths. Remember, we still have a modest cash reserve at our disposal. However, if news from our pipeline continues to deteriorate, maybe the best option for the stockholders is to sell the company." The Chairman took another deep breath. "Well, it's been a long but productive meeting. Are there any other items for discussion before we conclude?" He glanced around the table.

No one spoke.

"Very well then. If there's nothing more, the meeting's adjourned. Thank you all."

As the executives began filing out of the room the Chairman unexpectedly asked, "Charles, do you have a minute to speak privately?"

"Absolutely. What is it?" He returned to his seat.

"It's about NRC8890."

"What unfortunate news for the company. Everyone had such high expectations." He stretched his aching calf muscle.

"It could be devastating," the Chairman confided.

"Has news about the Fed's denial of our application been released?"

"Not yet. Public Affairs will be handling the communication and any questions that come in."

Charles shook his head. "Once the analysts get wind of this the stock price will take a real hit."

"I realize our shareholders aren't going to be very happy. With the lost revenue from our patent expirations, the company's going to be under intense pressure over the next few years to effectively manage the business."

"You mean cost reductions, employee layoffs?"

"We're not running an orphanage here. Eliminating unnecessary expenses is unpleasant, but that's our job. That's what leaders are paid to do. If we don't, the shareholders will find someone who will."

"It's a real shame."

The Chairman nodded. "That's why NRC8890 is so important. Not only would it have been a financial boon for the company, but think what it could have meant for society. That compound could've impacted mankind like no other in the history of medicine. We're talking about a possible paradigm shift in medical treatment, not to mention the overall field of scientific knowledge. It's unconscionable not to pursue it."

"Too bad there's nothing more we can do."

The Chairman looked reverently at the portraits lining the boardroom walls as if asking for guidance then returned his attention to Charles. "Maybe there is."

The two men locked eyes.

"But if we can't conduct clinical trials on humans…."

The elderly Chairman interrupted. "I know it seems impossible but squandering this opportunity just isn't acceptable. Sometimes one needs to take a risk, especially if the benefits are substantial. What if NRC8890 is capable of doing what we believe? Think about the possibilities."

"I suppose, but it's out of our hands. We can't proceed."

"Let's not throw in the towel just yet, Charles. There may be, shall we say, other alternatives."

"What are you implying? Continuing the trials would be unethical, not to mention illegal."

"But think about what's at stake here, and the people it could help."

Charles sat frozen as the words struck a nerve. He reflected upon a terrible accident from the past.

Courtney lay motionless in bed. The girl's head was wrapped in white gauze starkly contrasting a blackish, bruised face. Needles and wires protruded from the small battered body as a ventilator forced her lungs to expand. Thump-a-whoosh. Thump-a-whoosh.

"We've done all we can," the doctor assured the family. "Your daughter's suffered extensive head trauma. The rest of her body can recover, but I'm afraid there's evidence of brain injury."

His thoughts returned to the boardroom as hope surged. Was it possible? Could this new drug be a medical breakthrough, one that could actually benefit her? What if it was true? Prodded by guilt, he dared to grasp at the possibility.

"Well, if the potential's as great as you claim, maybe we shouldn't dismiss these other options so quickly," Charles finally concluded.

"Good, I'm glad you're keeping an open mind." The elderly Chairman cleared his throat before reaching for a telephone on the conference room table. "Pam, there's a gentleman waiting in my office. Would you please escort him to the boardroom? Thank you."

A few minutes later the door opened and a trim man wearing a perfectly-fitted suit entered. He confidently stepped toward the two executives. His expensive Ascorti pipe emitted a smoky haze and an air of conspiracy throughout the darkly-paneled room.

CHAPTER 2

A nondescript side street ran through a low-income section of south Atlanta. The rental home sat amid some patchy grass on a neatly rectangular lot. Since its construction in the 1950's, a parade of owners had modernized the house over the years. Clean and affordable, the cozy six room dwelling suited the Shealy family.

In the bathroom, an attractive, middle-aged face stared out from the mirror. Gwen ran a brush through her short, brown hair. The woman's skin was flawless except for the dark circles underneath her big, green eyes. The single mother tried wiping the shadows away. *Maybe a little concealer'd help.* While reaching for a makeup bag, she glanced at her Timex…6:35 a.m. *Lord have mercy, no time.*

The nurse tied the waist band of her blue uniform pants before grabbing a matching smock. She swung a faux-leather purse over her shoulder and hurried away to the kitchen.

Buzzzz. Tyler's morning alarm was always set for 6:40 a.m. He yanked the comforter from the bed and tossed it to the floor. The fitted sheet was tautly pulled over the mattress to eliminate any wrinkles or creases. The pillow was fluffed twelve times and placed precisely two inches from the headboard. He then arranged the comforter to ensure each side hung exactly six inches from the floor. The Savant's aversion to odd numbers was temporarily pacified, allowing him to move on to the next stage of his morning ritual.

The nineteen-year-old grabbed one of eight identical white T-shirts hanging in his closet. A neatly folded pair of jeans was pulled from the dresser. He placed a pack of Juicy Fruit gum in the pocket before laying the pants and shirt on the bed. Then he waited. When the bright red digits on the alarm clock flickered to 6:48, the teen marched into the bathroom and squeezed a line of Crest onto his toothbrush. He brushed exactly one hundred strokes, showered, dressed and was able to leave the bedroom. His routine was finally completed.

Gwen was finishing a cup of coffee. "Morning Hon."

"Morning, morning." Tyler stared straight ahead never making eye contact. His long, curly brown hair was still wet as he walked across the kitchen floor, his untied shoestrings clicking against the cool linoleum. He retrieved a box of cereal and began counting out three hundred Cheerios, the only cereal he wanted. Gwen once purchased Post Alpha-Bits but when the Savant became compulsively occupied with creating words from the whole-grain letters, she realized it was a mistake. He never ate.

Gwen picked up her lunch bag. "Your granddaddy will be up soon."

"Granddaddy. Granddaddy," he repeated.

"I'm off to work now so...."

"No. No," Tyler interrupted before wiping his runny nose.

"What?"

"No!" He poured milk over the cereal and began eating one Cheerio at a time.

"It's okay, Granddaddy will be here with you. He's sleeping now but...."

"Coming now. Coming now. Not later, now."

"Hon, he's still sleeping."

"Now!" Tyler repeated.

Ernest Shealy unexpectedly lumbered into the kitchen. The man was thin and fairly short with weathered, wrinkled skin from a lifetime on the farm. Random sprouts of gray hair protruded from his balding head while a pair of thick-lensed eyeglasses perched on the bridge of his nose.

"Morning Daddy, didn't know you were up."

"Couldn't sleep so I got up."

"How you feeling today?"

"Purdy damn chipper," he stated through a toothless grin. The old man had left his dentures soaking in a cup on the nightstand.

Tyler chimed in, "Chipper. Chipper Jones. Number ten."

"You got that right, Boy. He's number ten all right."

"Number ten. Atlanta Brave's third baseman," Tyler mumbled while picking out a single piece of cereal.

Gwen took two medicine bottles from the cabinet, one Namenda and the other Aricept. "Here you go, Daddy. Why don't you go ahead and take your pills now, don't want to forget again."

"After I eat."

"If we do it right off you won't miss a dose. Remember, we talked about this before."

"Said after I eat, Gwenny! Gonna eat my damn breakfast first."

"I know but…." The woman relented. "All right go ahead and eat." She poured more coffee into a 7-Eleven travel cup and waited.

Ernest was getting worse. She didn't use to worry about leaving him with Tyler, but that wasn't the case anymore. As his Alzheimer's progressed, he'd grown more forgetful. Now it seemed her autistic son was watching after him instead.

The old man dumped milk into the bowl. "Damn cereal smells like wet dog." Gripping a spoon with his withered hand, he leaned over and shoveled it in, gumming each soggy mouthful.

Gwen held out the pills.

"What's that?"

"It's your pills. You take them every morning."

Ernest begrudgingly popped the medications into his mouth, washing them down with milk from his cereal bowl. "Happy now?"

"Thanks Daddy."

A loud squawk from the far corner of the room pierced the air. Budgie, a Parakeet, was perched inside a wire cage suspended from a hook attached to the wall. "Daddy. Daddy," the bird screeched in a high-pitched tone.

It had been a gift for Tyler several years earlier. "Every young'un needs a damn pet," Ernest had argued. But because of Tyler's allergies, Gwen didn't want him to become attached to a cuddly puppy or kitten only to lose it later. Besides, she just didn't have time to care for a bigger animal.

Despite her protests, the battle over the bird was lost and one was purchased from the local PetsMart. Tyler was fascinated by the parakeet's green and yellow feathers. The store clerk explained the brightly-colored creature was from the Budgerigar species of parakeets, Budgie for short. That immediately became the bird's name.

"They're real easy to care for," the salesperson proclaimed. "And they live a good long while. Smart too, most can say lots of words. Course some talk more than others, just like people I suppose. Lots of folks go on and on and never buy nothing, then others…."

The bird quickly learned several phrases. Tyler would say a word and Budgie would repeat it. They'd go back and forth until one or the other got tired. It was cute but annoying. Surprisingly the Savant performed all the daily chores, religiously feeding, watering and cleaning the pet's cage.

Ernest poured more Cheerios into his bowl.

"I'm leaving now."

"Where you goin', Gwenny?"

"Going to work, just like I do every day."

"No!" Tyler interjected loudly. "No work. Mom no work."

"Hon, if I don't get going I'll be late. I need to get paid."

"Win lottery. Win Lottery. Pick seven, mega payout. No work."

"We can't afford that. We'd never win anyway. The lottery's just a tax on the stupid."

The teen rushed to the door, preventing her from leaving.

"What are you doing?"

"No work, no work."

"Good Lord, I've got to go. Why don't you finish your breakfast? I'll see you tonight when I get home."

"Boy, get your tail on over here and sit down. You and me'll finish eatin'," Ernest urged.

Tyler grabbed her arm and held steady. "Don't go. No work."

She looked into his green eyes and saw the same emotionless, blank stare. But the strength of his grip and the intensity of his words were different. Although accustomed to his autistic behavior, she was surprised by his actions. "Hon, what's this all about?"

"Get hurt. No work."

Not wanting to upset the erratic Savant further, Gwen reluctantly conceded and returned to the kitchen. Tyler sat down at the table and resumed eating.

Ernest pushed his glasses up the bridge of his nose. "God damn it, guess you ain't goin' no wheres, Gwenny."

"I don't know what's got into him. He's so insistent."

"Mom no work. Get hurt."

"What do you mean I'll get hurt?"

"No work. Mom get hurt."

"You keep saying that. How'll I get hurt?"

"Car. Car."

"I'll be careful, I promise."

"No! No!" he demanded adamantly, hitting his fist on the table.

"Hey Boy! What the hell you doin'?" Ernest challenged.

"That's all right Daddy, don't upset him any more. I'll just wait until he calms down."

She fumbled inside her purse for a cell phone and called Latrisse, a friend from work. "I'm...uh...I'm running a little late this morning, got something going on here."

"Don't ya worry none. I take care'a things til ya git here."

"Be there as quick as I can. Appreciate you covering for me, I owe you."

"See ya when I see ya, Baby Girl."

Tyler got up to retrieve a pencil and paper then began drawing. After several minutes a map emerged of her exact route to work. A small square box represented their house with a grid of streets leading to the nursing facility. Amazingly, the diagram was perfectly drawn to scale.

The Savant dragged the pencil along Rex Road pausing where it intersected with Dinsmore Avenue. He jabbed the lead into the paper leaving a dark smudge. "Mom hurt here. No work." He circled the black mark and without looking up repeated, "No work."

Each morning Gwen made a left turn at that particular location. She'd stop at the intersection, look both directions and then step on the gas pedal hoping another vehicle wasn't speeding around the dangerously blind curve.

Ernest belched and wiped a drizzle of milk from his chin. "Where you goin' anyway, Gwenny?"

"Nowhere now."

The minutes crept by as Gwen cleaned and put away the breakfast dishes, still confused by the drawing.

Her cell phone buzzed.

"Hello."

"Oh my Baby Girl, I so glad to hear ya voice."

"Sorry I'm not there yet, Latrisse."

"Don't fret 'bout that, I just glad ya all right."

"What are you talking about?"

"Guess ya ain't heard. There was a bad wreck, real bad. At that God-forsaken intersection ya always talkin' 'bout. What is it now? Rex and…oh shoot what's the other one? I so shook up can't think straight."

An icy chill ran down Gwen's spine. "Rex and Dinsmore?"

"That's it. One'a the nurses come in and said she heard 'bout it on the radio. Big ol' truck come bustin' 'round a curve and rammed a car. Squashed it like a tin can. Radio said it was tore up so bad the driver was killed right off. Just started worryin' that maybe…. Thank goodness ya okay."

Gwen's mouth became bone dry as she thought about Tyler's warning. Was it an ominous prediction or just a random feeling? It'd happened before.

"Baby Girl, ya still there?"

"Yeah, I'm here. Need to call you back."

Did Tyler really foresee the terrible accident? Would she have been involved if not heeding the warning?

She looked at him. "How…how did you…?"

"Bye," he stated, looking away.

"What?"

"Bye. Go work now. Get paid. Bye."

Still shaken by the teen's premonition, Gwen left. Thirty minutes later she arrived at Golden Years Nursing Home.

The single story building was surrounded by a plethora of azaleas lined against the brick structure. Although a low fence surrounded the grounds it still looked inviting, even welcoming from the outside. Hurrying through the back door Gwen was hit by an ever-present odor. Golden Years was a well-run facility, generally clean and properly maintained. However, it was next to impossible for a facility housing over a hundred sick and elderly individuals to smell good. The odors of uncontrolled bladders and bowel movements circulated throughout the building, sometimes owning the hallways and infiltrating neighboring rooms. No amount of disinfectant or deodorizer could mask the distinctive scent of incontinent patients in diapers or on bed pans.

Gwen rushed to put her bag lunch in the employee's lounge, then approached the nurse's station to check the patient roster. Scanning the names she noted that long-time resident, Mr. Dickson, had survived the night.

"Baby Girl!" Latrisse, the robust, well-endowed woman came toward Gwen. Her beautiful ebony skin shimmered in the artificial light. The certified nursing assistant was strong as an ox and had a huge, caring heart. Her shrill voice shot down the corridor, "Sho glad ya here."

"Thanks for covering for me. I'm blessed to have such a good friend."

"Ya git everythin' straightened out at home?"

"As much as possible."

"Let's meet in the break room for lunch and talk."

Gwen walked down the hallway toward a set of double doors. She punched in a security code which unlocked the entrance to the Alzheimer wing…and the sad scene inside. Some patients were bedridden while others remained mobile, but none were in control of their mental capacities. Many were left by families who couldn't handle the physical or emotional strains involved with their care. A few had no one, or at least no one who cared, and were institutionalized as they awaited death.

The residents were congregated in a large open room with a gray tiled floor and brightly painted walls. There were several windows allowing sunlight to enter. Some of the patients sat in wheelchairs or on colorful couches and chairs. Others just wandered aimlessly from one corner to another.

Two men with silver hair sat facing each other, chattering constantly. Their words were a jumbled mass of gibberish.

A woman listlessly shuffled along, pushing a child's doll stroller back and forth across the floor. Every few steps she stopped and reached up. But nothing was there.

Another patient stared blankly across the room, gazing through a maze of unknowns, searching for an escape. The vacant shell of a human being, who in a distant past led a vibrant life, now only had emptiness and confusion in his eyes.

In the middle of the room was a large table where oversized puzzle pieces lay scattered about, each waiting to be fit together, not unlike the random thoughts floating around in their minds. A few patients sat at the far end of the table using crayons to scribble pictures, all resembling sketches from a kindergarten classroom. One of the walls was adorned with their artwork.

Another wall was decorated with family photographs. Sadly most weren't recognized as their once familiar faces had vanished into the black hole of Alzheimer's.

The staff at Golden Years was trained to handle the special needs of dementia. Nurses roamed about talking with each resident, pointing and repeating the names of objects like "doorknob" and "picture". They read children's books and constantly wiped drool from the chins of those who forgot to swallow.

Gwen paused to reflect upon the group whose souls had been drained from their bodies. *This is what's in store for Daddy,* she sadly thought. *How awful it must be.* But only those trapped within their conflicted and frightening worlds could ever truly understand.

Shards of sunlight pierced the window pane and pooled on the gray tile next to a man in a wheelchair. Confused, he stared intensely at the spot trying to decide whether to move away or toward it. Random, irrational thoughts fired one after another like flashs from a camera.

He looked up and searched the faces congregated in the room.

That old woman pushing the stroller across the floor, what was she reaching for?

Those two men at the table in the middle of the room, what were they saying? He couldn't understand them.

All were strangers.

He once again stared at the pool of sunlight on the floor. Most memories were gone. His mind was an empty box waiting to be filled with letters, photographs and other mementos from life's journey. He peeked up and saw two more unfamiliar faces, a nurse and another woman wearing a bright red blouse. The lady in the colorful blouse was holding a bag.

Blessed with a fleeting moment of memory, he muttered, "Red's my favorite color."

They spoke quietly, then turned toward him. Gwen pointed as the other woman's face tightened. She forced a smile.

They're coming over here, the elderly Alzheimer's victim thought, becoming anxious. *Why? Who are they? What do they want?*

Something stirred. He struggled to penetrate the fog but the debilitating disease pushed him back into the quagmire of forgotten memories.

They stopped next to his wheelchair. Gwen laid a comforting hand on his shoulder. "I've got a surprise. There's somebody here to see you."

The woman wearing red stood in the pool of sunlight, her feet bathed in its glare. She spoke, forcing him out of the daze. "Hi Da…. Hello, how are you?"

The good manners which defined his character in better days surfaced. He extended a hand in greeting. "Hello, Ma'am."

She hadn't seen him for more than a year. Moving to Texas had made trips home infrequent. When Alzheimer's was diagnosed, residing a thousand miles away became a convenient excuse. There, the woman didn't have to watch him deteriorate into someone she didn't know, and who didn't know her.

An unrelenting conscience finally compelled a visit. *He's your father. No matter how hard, you have to see him before it's too late.* She boarded a flight home, not knowing what she'd find or how to deal with it once there.

"You look good," she tentatively offered. The man's outward appearance was just as she remembered, aside from the sad emptiness in his eyes. She searched them for an indication he'd remember. Maybe some sliver of recognition. She smoothed the red blouse which had been a gift, hoping to jar his memory and help him recall.

Like a child pressing her nose against a frosty window on Christmas Eve trying to catch a glimpse of Santa Claus, the woman persevered. She desperately wanted to see through the icy pane for a trace of the father who tirelessly read Dr. Seuss's <u>Green Eggs and Ham</u> at bedtime. Who'd muddle through 10th grade algebra, always coming up with the correct answers. The husband who tirelessly cared for his sick wife, never leaving her side while she was alive. The kind man who never said a spiteful word about others. Someone who loved working in the garden and grew bigger, better-tasting tomatoes than anyone in the county. Who stood at the screen door and called his beloved black cat in at night, then playfully swiped at it with his foot as the animal passed.

I need to see him, know he's still there somewhere, she thought. But the old man's detached eyes remained glazed, completely blocking the window to his heart. An impenetrable wall had formed between them.

"I brought you a present." She produced a package from inside the bag. It was wrapped in silver paper with a shiny white bow.

"Thank you." He took it and began tugging at the tape. "I'm sorry, but I don't know your name."

"I'm…I'm Marilyn."

"Marilyn? That's a real nice name." The last bit of paper was finally torn away from the box. The wheels inside his damaged brain spun as if stuck in a pit of mud. "I used to know a Marilyn."

She flinched. "Is…is that so?"

Lifting the lid from the box he stared inside. "Real nice, thank you."

"I knitted it myself."

"I'm sorry, I don't think I know your name."

"It's Marilyn."

"I knew a Marilyn once."

The woman's eyes began to water. She was a stranger to her father.

He ran a hand over the softness of the wool but didn't take the garment from the box.

"Here let me show you, it's a scarf to keep you warm." She lovingly placed the brightly colored wrap around his neck. "There you go, do you like it?"

"Real nice," he repeated. "Red's my favorite color."

"I know," she sadly replied.

* * * * * *

Gwen met Latrisse for lunch in the employee break room. She pulled an egg salad sandwich and granola bar from the paper sack.

"Hey, Baby Girl. Looks like ya had a rough mornin'," Latrisse observed.

"No more than usual."

"Ahh, I sorry." The nursing assistant put a forkful of leftover mulligan stew in her mouth. "Easy to git that way 'round this place."

"Some woman came by to see her daddy, first time in over a year."

"Ya know that happens all the time. Lots 'a folks put they kin here and forget 'bout 'em til they die. Then the buzzards show up wantin' to git whatever money's left."

"That's a little cold, Latrisse. Most just can't stand to see them waste away."

"Ain't no excuse and ya know it. Ya never do that." She swallowed the last bit of stew. "By the way, how's ya daddy doin'?"

"I'll need to do something soon. It worries me to leave him with Tyler anymore."

"Bless ya heart. What ya gonna do, Baby Girl?"

"Lord knows things will only get worse. They can't stay alone much longer."

"Can ya pay somebody to come stay with 'em?"

"On what I make, are you kidding me?"

"Ya daddy don't got nothin' saved up?"

"He and Mama worked hard but lived week-to-week. Never saved anything to speak of."

"Sho is a shame. Too bad ya can't git nothin' out'a that no-'ccount ex-husband."

"Hmmph! Gave up years ago trying to get blood from that turnip."

"What a jack-ass."

"Latrisse, please."

"Well, I just don't understand men who won't take care'a they babies."

"He couldn't care less. Got up one morning, said he was going to work. Instead the jerk cleaned out what little money we had in the bank and took off. Haven't heard from him since. Never once called to ask about his son."

"Ever try to find the no-good bum?"

"Talked to his family, but they wouldn't tell me anything. All just as bad as him, so I gave up." She took a bite of the granola bar then wadded up the brown paper bag. "Good riddance as far as I'm concerned. He's out of our lives and we're better off without him. Don't want anything of his. Even had Tyler's name changed to Shealy."

"Ya right 'bout that, Baby Girl. Better off without him...but not his money."

"Anyway, I'll probably be forced to put Daddy in a place like this soon. Sure he'd qualify for Medicaid but trying to put it off as long as I can."

"What ya gonna do with that boy?"

"Wish I knew." She brushed away the difficult questions. "Let's stop talking about my problems. What's going on with you?"

The black woman spent the next fifteen minutes telling anyone within twenty feet about her weekend. It was a welcome diversion.

After lunch Gwen noted a man dressed in dirty blue jeans standing in the hallway.

"Aren't you Mr. Dickson's son?"

"Yes, Ma'am."

"I've seen you around before."

"Uh, yes Ma'am. Someone called this morning. Told me Pop wasn't…wasn't doing real good. I'd been here sooner but…. Anyway, they told me I needed to come."

"I'll walk with you."

Wesley Dickson had entered Golden Years nursing home two years earlier. At first, a few friends and relatives visited and he recognized them. As his condition deteriorated, Mr. Dickson couldn't remember anyone or anything and most stopped coming. Now in the final stages of life he was oblivious to visitors, including his son.

As they entered the room, Gwen began taking care of his basic needs, emptying the catheter bag and making notes on a chart. "I know it's hard," she spoke quietly as the man stared at his dying father.

"Waiting? Yes Ma'am, it is."

Gwen took the man's temperature. "Does he have a lot of family?"

"I've got a sister, just the two of us now."

"She live close by?"

"No Ma'am." He stared down at the man's closed eyes and sunken cheeks. "Mama passed away a few years back. Thank God, this would've pained her something awful."

"Alzheimer's is a terrible disease." She strapped the blood pressure cuff on Mr. Dickson's limp arm.

"Yeah, it's tough to see him like this."

"You want to be alone?"

"That's all right, you can stay."

Gwen continued her nursing tasks.

"He's not going to regain consciousness is he?"

"We don't know."

"How much longer does he have?"

"That's out of our hands. Only the good Lord knows."

"Does it make me a terrible person to hope he goes soon?"

"Not my place to say, but I understand how you feel."

"Do you think he hears me?"

"You never know. Some folks believe they hear everything, even somebody in his condition."

He reached out to squeeze the dying man's hand. "I'm leaving now, Pop. I…I…. Bye."

When Gwen returned that afternoon, Mr. Dickson had passed. Although the medical chart recorded the time of death as 4:15 p.m., she knew he'd really died much earlier.

After work, Gwen trudged to the parking lot and climbed into a used Monte Carlo. It was sweltering hot and she immediately rolled down the windows letting the stagnant air escape. The compressor had been broken for several months, but she still turned the A/C knob hoping the air conditioner fairy had visited and fixed it. Unfortunately fairies don't exist and long, oppressive Georgia summers do. Hot air poured from the vents bombarding her sweaty body.

Taking the cell phone from her purse, she called home.

"Hello."

"Hey Hon, it's Mom. Everything okay?"

"Okay. Okay," Tyler stated mechanically as Budgie squawked in the background.

"Where's your granddaddy?"

"Sleep. Granddaddy sleep."

"Listen Tyler, I'm stopping by the grocery store on the way home. Make sure you watch out for him until I get there."

"Milk."

"What?"

"Milk. Need milk for Cheerios." He abruptly hung up.

A slight smile crossed her face. She loved the boy more than anything in the world but becoming a young single parent had been demanding. As a newborn, Tyler cried all the time. The doctors blamed colic. At one, he wasn't walking or talking. He didn't like close body contact and would stiffen and pull away when cuddled.

At times Gwen felt disconnected. Again the experts said not to worry. Children have unique personalities and develop at different rates.

Eventually Tyler progressed and seemed fairly normal. Then she received a call from a grammar school teacher asking for a conference. The youngster was beginning to demonstrate an abnormal propensity for math. He was advancing well above grade level and solving complex computations. His talent for memorization was unlike anything the teacher had ever seen.

However, there were concerns about his socialization. While other children played and enjoyed group activities, Tyler seemed content reading or playing on the class computer.

When the boy continued to withdraw, Gwen approached several doctors looking for answers. He was diagnosed with Autism. The child she'd given birth to, the little boy for whom she wanted great things would never be normal.

Life hadn't been easy, but she persevered and became a licensed practical nurse. Her goal was to attend school and eventually take the national licensing exam to become a registered nurse, a profession that would provide a good living and help care for an autistic child.

The road continued to be bumpy. Several years later, Gwen's mother was diagnosed with breast cancer and passed away. After living alone for a short time, a lonely Ernest moved in. The new arrangement worked well for everyone. She had someone to help keep an eye on Tyler and her father wasn't alone anymore. Then the family was dealt another harsh blow. Ernest developed Alzheimer's disease. At first his forgetful episodes were intermittent but recently they'd gotten much worse.

Because of the turmoil, her plan to become an R.N. was put on hold. Now it seemed nothing more than an unachievable dream.

After a quick stop at the grocery store, Gwen was finally on the way home to take care of her family, a task that was getting more difficult with each passing day. Despite the heat she shivered remembering an episode a few weeks earlier when she'd called home....

"How's Granddaddy?"

"Gone. Granddaddy gone."

"What do you mean, isn't he with you?"

"No. No. Not here."

"Tyler, go see if he's outside. Go now."

After waiting for what seemed an eternity, Tyler finally picked up the receiver. "Granddaddy gone. Not here. Granddaddy gone."

Gwen hurried home to find Tyler standing on the front step and Ernest nowhere in sight. They drove around the adjacent neighborhoods searching frantically, finally spotting him standing alone on a sidewalk.

"Thank God! Daddy, you all right?"

"Had to get my damn pills," the man responded matter-of-factly.

"I picked them up yesterday. Don't you remember?" The prescription cost $256.00 and the $97.22 left from his Social Security wasn't enough to cover it. Gwen wrote a check, virtually eliminating the remainder of her account until payday.

"Can't say I do."

"C'mon Daddy, get in the car. You need to be careful. You're a long way from home."

Tyler unexpectedly chimed in. "Seven thousand, three hundred, ninety-two feet."

"What on God's green earth are you talking about, Hon?"

"Granddaddy away. Seven thousand, three hundred, ninety-two feet."

On the drive home Gwen curiously checked the odometer. They'd traveled one and four-tenths miles...or seven thousand, three hundred, ninety-two feet. Somehow Tyler's autistic mind knew the exact distance.

"I'm home." Gwen carried the small bag of groceries into the house and began putting the items away. She noted a loaf of bread oddly stuck in the back of the refrigerator next to a pitcher of sweet tea.

Ernest entered the kitchen and sat down at the table.

"What'd you eat for lunch today, Daddy?"

"Sandwich."

That explains the bread, she thought. "What kind?"

"Damn, I don't know, can't remember." He paused then asked, "Where's Esther?"

"Mama died several years ago," she reminded him.

"That's right." The old man shook his head and sadly looked down.

"It's all right, why don't you go in the living room and watch television?" She guided him into a recliner. "I'll start supper in a little bit."

Tyler was at a small table surfing the internet on their old desktop computer. Amazed it still worked, Gwen kept waiting for the day it'd finally crash leaving him with nothing to occupy his lonely existence.

The official website of the Atlanta Braves was displayed across the monitor. The well-known tomahawk symbol with the words "Atlanta's Pastime" were scrolled along the bottom. The teenager was obsessed with the team. Not in the same way as most fans, although he loved watching the games. Tyler was fixated on the mathematics and numbers of the sport and could recite every statistic for every player, past and present. Batting averages, on-base percentages, number of R.B.I.'s, he'd memorized them all.

"You doing okay, Hon?"

"Okay. Okay," he mumbled through a mouthful of Juicy Fruit gum.

"Looking at the Braves, huh?"

"Braves move to Atlanta 1966."

"Is that so?"

"1966," Tyler confirmed. "Good team. Braves good."

"They sure are."

The Savant began spouting off a string of statistics about the team. "Braves won western division 1969. Good pitching. Top starting pitchers, Phil Niekro—E.R.A. 2.56. Pat Jarvis—E.R.A. 4.43. Ron Reed—E.R.A. 3.47. George Stone—E.R.A. 3.65."

"Umm, can you tell me again what E.R.A. stands for?"

"Earned run average. Earned run average."

"Oh that's right, now I remember."

"1969 Braves. Hank Aaron—44 homeruns. Rico Carty—.342 batting average. Orlando Cepeda—.428 slugging percentage. Felix Millan—652 at bats. Started All Star Game."

Realizing Tyler could and would go on all night if not distracted, she interrupted, "Do the Braves play today?"

"Braves game tonight. Play Cubs. Chicago Cubs."

"Maybe you can watch after we eat?"

"7:35. T.B.S.," Tyler stated. "7:35." He sniffed then coughed loudly.

"Is your asthma acting up?" During his early teens, allergies began triggering asthma attacks. The episodes weren't frequent but were quite scary when they did occur.

"No. No asthma. No."

"I need to change clothes, be right back. Keep an eye on Granddaddy, will you?"

She went into the bedroom and took off her scrubs replacing them with a pair of shorts and a tank top.

Then she headed back to the kitchen. "Be an angel and help me fix supper."

Tyler shut down the computer and obediently followed.

"Grab that box of mac and cheese from the sack on the table."

"Mac and cheese," he repeated.

Ernest sat in the living room watching Vanna White turn letters to a puzzle.

"Wheel…Of…Fortune," Tyler chanted slowly before sneezing.

"Yup," Gwen confirmed. "It's been on for a long time."

"Originally aired on network television in June 1975. Syndicated in 1983," Tyler parroted the origins of the program.

"If you say so, Hon," she stated, accustomed to his memorization of trivial facts.

"Up the creek without a paddle."

"What are you talking about now?"

"Up the creek without a paddle," he repeated. "Puzzle. Wheel… Of…Fortune. Up the creek without a paddle."

She glanced toward the television where the partially completed phrase, _ P _ H _ C _ _ _ _ W _ _ H _ _ _ A PA _ _ _ _, was sprawled across the screen.

"Oh." Gwen opened the package of macaroni and cheese and poured the pasta into a pan of hot, boiling water. "Ain't that the truth."

CHAPTER 3

The road meandered through Stone Mountain State Park. A mixture of ancient oak and tall, slender pine trees blanketed the grounds. The hazy murk of a nearby lake peeked through the forest as the car crept forward. A paddlewheel riverboat navigated the lazy water, its double decks full of tourists enjoying the scenic ride. A huge gray mountain of granite stood off in the distance and provided a unique but picturesque backdrop.

As the car rounded a bend, the entrance to the Evergreen Conference Center and Resort came into view. The elegant complex with its luxurious amenities seemed oddly out of place within the rustic park.

Dr. Barry Johnston entered the main lobby of the hotel to visit with a potential business partner from New York. They had spoken several times on the telephone, finally agreeing to meet and consummate their deal.

The physician's khaki pants were sharply creased and his polo shirt sported a small green alligator on the left shoulder. Designer walking shoes were recently purchased for his visit to the park.

The man was extremely intelligent, a trait which helped fuel his arrogance. Johnston's thinning black hair was combed straight back to conceal an ever expanding bald spot. Although intellectually gifted and confident, he remained a bit self-conscious about that particular feature.

Johnston scanned the spacious lobby. A polished hardwood floor provided an earthy yet elegant foundation. The lobby was bustling with activity as guests hurried about to beat the crowds and be first in line for the park attractions.

A couple with two young sons walked past. "Daddy, we gonna ride the train today?" the younger boy asked excitedly.

"I told you we would."

The older sibling chimed in, "How 'bout the sky car? You promised we'd take it to the top of the mountain. You promised!"

"We will, Son. There's plenty of time to do both."

"I don't wanna ride it!" the smaller child cried out.

"Don't whine," his father scolded.

"You chicken?" his brother taunted, flapping his arms up and down like wings. "Bawk, bawk, bawk."

"I ain't afraid, just don't wanna."

"Scaredy cat, scaredy cat."

"Shut up! Mama, make him quit."

"That's enough both of you or we won't do anything!" she warned, prompting the boys to stop squabbling.

Barry Johnston stepped aside as the family hurried toward the front entrance to begin their day at the park. He watched as the older boy resumed his taunting, while the father admonished the younger for whining.

Sympathetic, Johnston reflected upon his childhood. Jack, a brother, was born five years prior to his own unexpected and somewhat unwelcome arrival. Their father worshipped the older boy but never missed a chance to point out Barry's shortcomings. He was continually met with negative remarks and subtle reminders of disappointment. While Jack could do no wrong, Barry constantly tried to impress a father whose praise never came.

The lad turned to his mother for comfort and support. Hardened from years of marital neglect she began drinking and eventually withdrew from the family. Barry was once again ignored and denied the emotional support he desperately sought.

Upon returning from school one afternoon, he went to his room. It wasn't a typical kid's space. The closet was organized and the shelves were dusted and clutter free with everything in perfect order. He changed clothes, made sure things were picked up and put away, then headed off to the kitchen for a snack. That's when he saw a note from his mother on the counter.

> *I can't stay here anymore.*
> *Just not happy. Sorry.*

Later when his father came home, Barry was lying in bed with a pillow pulled over his head. The man never acknowledged her unexpected departure. There were no comforting hugs, no explanation, nothing.

To make things worse, Jack blamed his younger brother. "She probably couldn't stand being around you."

From that day forward Barry Johnston decided he couldn't count on anyone. He'd succeed on his own, make something of himself, prove his worth and earn everyone's respect.

And he had.

The gifted neurologist scrutinized the lobby looking directly into the faces of those lingering about. Most didn't notice his probing stare. Others ignored him and turned away, continuing with their affairs.

Johnston ran a hand over his head and pushed back the strands of thinning hair. Off to the right was the concierge's desk and registration. Positioned in the rear of the spacious atrium was a stone fireplace with an array of leather-bound couches and chairs tactically placed nearby. The doctor walked across the room to sit down.

Patience wasn't one of Barry Johnston's virtues but he waited, becoming more and more agitated with each passing minute. He glanced at his Cartier watch and muttered, "Where the hell is Jones? What kind of game is this bastard playing? He'd better show...."

Eventually a dark-skinned man in his early twenties approached. He wore a New York Yankees baseball cap with a backpack slung over his shoulder. The phrase 'Island Man' was tattooed on his right forearm. A scraggly black goatee attempted to cover the tip of his chin. "Doc Johnston?" he asked in a strong Latino accent.

"Yes that's right, I'm Dr. Barry Johnston." He stood to address the younger man. "Are you Mr. Jones?"

"Nope, de name's Manny. How you doin' Doc?"

Johnson asked suspiciously, "What's going on? I was supposed to meet with Jones."

"De plan change."

"I don't like changes. What if I don't want to talk to you?"

"Look Amigo, Jones ain't comin'. Deal with dis Latino or else."

"Don't threaten me, you…."

"No threat Doc. Fact. I take dis friggin' backpack home to de City."

"Jones's the one I've been speaking with on the phone. He didn't say anything about sending someone else."

"Can't help, it's me you workin' with." Manny added menacingly, "Is dat a friggin' problem?"

"How do I know you're legitimate?"

The Latino glanced around and then pulled the backpack off his shoulder. He unzipped the bag and held it out for the skeptical physician to peek inside. "Satisfied?"

It was stuffed with cash.

Johnston took a deep breath. "All right, you've got my attention."

"Now we talk."

"So Manny, do you have a last name?"

"Yeah."

A long pause ensued.

"Well, what is it?"

"Ain't nothin' you need worry 'bout. Just call me Manny."

"And you can call me *Dr.* Johnston."

"I stick with Doc."

The physician's jaw tightened, choosing not to argue.

The two moved away from the main lobby.

Johnston asked, "Have you ever been here before?"

"Georgia?"

"I was referring to Stone Mountain."

"Nope, ain't had de pleasure, Doc."

"Very well, come with me. I'll show you around and we can speak privately."

Stone Mountain State Park was located twenty miles east of Atlanta. The public sanctuary was officially sanctioned in 1958 and boasted amenities to accommodate camping, golfing, and fishing. The site also offered a variety of museums and shops, all catering to a multitude of tourists. The centerpiece of the state park was an enormous granite outcrop with a large monolith of three Civil War heroes carved on its north face.

A group of tourists stood in line awaiting the cable car to the top of the granite mountain. Looking toward the geological mass, Manny commented, "Big friggin' rock ain't it?"

"The circumference around its base is over five miles," Barry Johnston replied.

They climbed aboard with the others. Suspended from a bundle of tightly woven iron strands the red cable car ascended the enormous stone protrusion. Everyone stood in front while Dr. Johnston and Manny sat alone in the back.

"By the way, you might want to take off that Yankees cap. You're in the South now."

"You got problem with my boys?"

"A lot of the locals have a problem with Yankees, baseball and otherwise. Some haven't bought into the fact the war's over."

Manny adjusted the backpack on his shoulder. "What's dis war?"

Like most immigrants he wasn't familiar with American history. At age thirteen the family had moved from Puerto Rico to Newark. His father disappeared shortly afterwards. His mother surrendered to a drug addiction that was supported by turning tricks. Manny was left to fend for himself and hadn't seen either parent for years.

He was intelligent but never had a decent opportunity or a proper environment to develop it. Seldom attending school, his "teacher" had been the gang-infested streets of the inner city where cunning, immorality and adaptability were taught. He eventually left the gangs behind but continued advancing to a more sophisticated and profitable level of lawlessness.

"The Civil War between the states. Down here it's called the war of northern aggression. People still hate admitting the South lost." Although well-traveled the neurologist was born in Georgia and remained proud of his southern roots.

"History Doc. Need to move on."

"Yes, I suppose so. There're more important things to worry about."

"Damn straight. Half million in dis friggin' backpack."

Johnston turned to stare at the largest relief sculpture in the world.

"Who dose muchachos?" Manny nodded the tip of his baseball cap toward the side of the mountain as the cable car continued its slow but steady journey. Three Confederate soldiers sat atop their steeds riding dutiful and proud with their hats held over their hearts. The entire carving covered an area larger than a football field.

"A lot of people revere those men as part of their southern heritage. The one in front is Jefferson Davis. He was the first and only President of the Confederacy. Robert E. Lee's in the middle. He led the Confederate Army. The other is Stonewall Jackson. Interesting story about Jackson. He was General Lee's most trusted subordinate. After being accidentally shot by his men, they had to amputate his arm. General Lee later remarked that Stonewall Jackson had lost his left arm, and he'd just lost his right."

"His main man, huh? Maybe one day, I be yours, Doc."

Johnston continued. "They were all well-educated. Each attended the United States Military Academy at West Point yet remained loyal to the South during the war."

"Loyalty good, but what dese muchachos fightin' for?"

"The Civil War was fought over states' rights. We didn't want the northern bureaucrats telling us what we could and couldn't do. Surely an 'Island Man' can understand that," Dr. Johnston stated while referencing the Latino's tattoo.

"What de hell does my island got to do with dis?"

"Puerto Rico drafted a constitution and became a commonwealth of the United States. On several occasions the citizens voted to remain independent and rejected statehood. So you see Puerto Ricans are very loyal to their heritage too. They've chosen to remain sovereign, similar to what these men wanted to do with the Confederacy."

The proud Latino nodded agreement.

"Too much government gets in the way of progress. Take my planned experiments for example. That research should've been sanctioned a long time ago, but our idiotic regulators wouldn't allow it. So I'm willing to conduct the tests without their approval. Ignoring this incredible opportunity makes no sense."

"And if you make some cash along de way?"

"Let's get one thing straight. I'm not the one getting filthy rich here. That'd be the folks you're working for in New York, whoever *they* are."

"Folks we workin' for, Doc. De folks *we* workin' for," Manny firmly repeated.

"The money's important, but it's not my main motivation. The clinical outcome's critical. Knowing that I can contribute to such a novel medical breakthrough and be recognized for it, well that's what really drives me."

"I see. You doin' dis for mankind...and maybe ego too," the Puerto Rican astutely noted.

"Yes, I've got some things to prove."

"To who?"

"It's a long list."

"Your name on dat list, Doc?"

The narcissistic physician stared straight ahead. "Of course I'd like to be recognized for my contributions, leave a mark on the world and be remembered for my work."

Manny leaned forward. "No second thoughts 'bout de experiments? Conscience not bother you?"

"Sometimes a man has to pursue his convictions, right or wrong, moral or immoral. What I'm doing may have a tremendous benefit to mankind. Where there's great risk, there's also great reward. Those who take that risk will be acknowledged."

"So, is good to sacrifice one life for 'nother?"

"Absolutely, when the sacrifice means benefiting countless others. Sometimes an injured or diseased limb must be forfeited in order to save the patient."

"Not work out so friggin' good for Stonewall."

Johnston ignored the jab as the cable car finally approached the receiving station at the top of the granite mountain. The riders exited onto the precipice and quickly disbursed to look out over the surrounding countryside. The morning sky was perfectly clear as the sun bore down. Perspiration formed on the brows of the two men.

Manny removed the Yankees baseball cap and wiped sweat from his forehead. "Friggin' oven up here."

"What's wrong? Can't stand a little heat?" Johnston pointed toward the west. "Look over there, that's downtown Atlanta." The skyline of the city, which lay about twenty miles away, sprouted upward toward the blue sky. "Heart of the South," Johnston added proudly.

"Dat where you from?"

"I grew up in a suburb not far away. After medical school I left and practiced in California for a while. Eventually came back to work at the C.D.C."

"C.D.C.?"

"The Center for Disease Control and Prevention. It's headquartered in Atlanta. I'm in mental health."

"So don't work with normal muchachos?"

"Who's to say what's normal?"

"You and me normal, ain't we?"

Barry Johnston reflected for a moment. "You wouldn't consider the specimens I'll be working with normal?"

"Dey loco, not normal."

"A lot of people would say that, but I see it quite differently. I believe they're as normal as you and me."

"Maybe you loco too, Doc. How dey be normal?"

"Let's take a little walk and I'll explain."

Manny peered out across the barren rock summit. "Where de hell we go?"

"There's a trail that leads back to the base. We can talk on the way down."

Visitors to the top of Stone Mountain could return to the bottom either of two ways. One was to ride the cable car and the other was to walk. A path slightly over a mile long led able-bodied tourists down a slight decline to the foot of the mammoth piece of granite. As one would expect, not many chose to hike up.

"Know what you doin'?" Manny asked. "Long ways off dis rock."

"If I can make it, surely a younger man of your stature can too."

The men started their descent to the bottom of Stone Mountain. At first nothing was said as they navigated the hard, lumpy contours of the granite pathway. Finally Manny spoke up. "So Doc, you goin' tell me how de locos normal?"

"We're all alike in that we're all different."

"What dis crap? Sun done burn through dat bald head."

"I'll try and dumb it down for you." Johnston fired back, angry at the reference to his thinning hair.

"You not think dis simple Latino understand big important doctor?" Manny's voice was laced with sarcasm.

Johnston took a deep breath and calmly continued, "Everyone has these unbelievable mental abilities, a real hidden potential. We're all normal in that sense. But not everyone applies them equally. Only a rare few come close to using their entire mental capacity."

"So locos ain't usin' dey brains."

"No Manny, that's not what I'm saying. On the contrary these individuals may be utilizing more than the average person. In that sense we're the ones disabled or challenged, not them."

"You sayin' dey smarter?"

"Not necessarily smarter but certainly more opportunistic."

"Thought you was goin' dumb dis shit down."

The men stopped to rest as Barry Johnston struggled to find the right words. "When the brain is damaged by disease, injury or in some cases birth defects, it'll compensate for the loss."

"Other parts kickin' in to help out?"

"In some cases, yes. For instance, stroke victims are impacted by the disruption of blood to the brain. With therapy other sections of the brain may be developed to compensate for the loss."

"You say some?"

"That's right, there're other more complex situations that also occur. One is Savant Syndrome."

"What's dat?" Manny asked, surprisingly curious.

For the first time the two men were at ease and actually enjoying their conversation. The young Latino was attentive and interested in the clinical explanations, while the egotistical doctor reveled in providing them.

"It's a rare and complex neurological condition that's tough to understand and tougher to explain. A Savant processes information much differently than you or I. Although our left brain is dominant, we use both hemispheres to some extent. This gives us a range of basic skills. On the other hand a Savant's left brain is inferior while the right half is dominant. He may not be able to reason or think but has great depth in certain, specific areas."

"Not understand dis depth shit."

"For example, the individual may not be able to dress in the morning but has the intellectual depth to sit at a piano and play a sonata note for note after hearing it only once. He might not have the ability to write his name but can paint a beautiful portrait. Many Savants possess uncanny recall for meaningless detail or have the ability to perform complex mathematics, much more than the average person."

"Dey geniuses."

"In some ways they are. I've read about a woman who's completely blind but gets around by making clicking sounds. The experts believe it serves as sonar."

"Like on submarine?"

"Exactly. Then there's this woman who can hardly communicate but can tell you the exact time without looking at a clock."

The young Puerto Rican stared intently, mesmerized by the information.

"Another autistic child draws city landscapes after seeing them only once. He drew an extremely detailed replica of Tokyo after taking a short helicopter ride over it."

"How dey do it?"

The accomplished physician was eager to demonstrate his intellectual superiority. "As I said before, most people rely on the left hemisphere of their brain. That's the part that generally controls logical thinking. The right side is used for procedural routines like memory. Because of its usefulness, the higher functioning left half is usually dominant."

"Dat ain't so with Savants?"

"For whatever reason they aren't fully using the left hemisphere. Instead their right side has become dominant. That section is more fully utilized and enhances memory and other artistic behaviors."

"Why can't de rest of us do it?" Manny asked, scratching his goatee.

"That's the billion dollar question…and the goal of my experiments. I want to determine if humankind can trigger all of its unused mental capability. Maybe someday it'll be possible for us to maximize both the left and right hemispheres of our brain. Have them work more effectively together as one."

As the men continued their hike down to the base of the granite outcrop, Manny shifted the backpack on his shoulder. "Don't know 'bout dis left and right brain shit, Doc. But we got other business to talk 'bout."

"Yes, I suppose we do."

"You got specimens yet?"

"I've identified some possibilities."

"Identifyin' easy," Manny firmly stated.

"Don't worry, I'll handle it."

"'Nother thing, de work needs to be tight, no friggin' leaks. Make sure your ass only one tied to dis shit. Nobody else. You got dat… *Dr.* Johnston?"

The neurologist reached out to catch the backpack tossed at his chest. "Got it."

"Hope no turds left in de toilet."

"There won't be. My experience trumps your hope," Barry Johnston confidently replied. "I'm risking my professional career on this experiment. I've got a lot to lose if it's exposed."

"You bein' paid half million dollars to make sure is not. De rest come when job done."

"There's something else." Barry Johnston asked, "When's the compound going to be delivered? Nothing happens until I get that drug."

"Take care of when back in de City." Manny added with a smile, "Count on me, Amigo. I be your main man. Just like Stonewall."

CHAPTER 4

Dr. Barry Johnston circled upward in the parking deck toward the second level and his reserved space. The Mercedes' convertible top slowly closed as the physician straightened his windblown hair. He took out a handkerchief and wiped the dash free of dust then got out of the car. With an Italian leather briefcase in hand, Johnston headed toward the employee entrance of the Center for Disease Control, his expensive Berluti shoes clicking across the concrete.

He flashed a photo I.D. to the guard.

"Mornin' Dr. Johnston," the uniformed officer politely stated. The man had worked security at the C.D.C. for years and knew many of the employees. Acknowledging the government-issued I.D. he added, "Gonna be a hot 'un today."

Johnson set his briefcase on the platform and opened it.

The guard performed a cursory check. "Still ain't no rain in sight neither." Closing the case, he placed it on the conveyor and watched it slowly disappear into the square, metal x-ray machine.

The man persisted. "No Siree, not a drop 'spected this week. Everybody's so dang worried 'bout the price of gas. Ask me, we better start worryin' 'bout runnin' out'ta water." He grinned through a set of uneven, tobacco-stained teeth.

Johnston tossed his keys into a basket and walked through the metal detector.

"Have a good 'un." The guard turned his attention to the next employee in line.

Barry Johnston ignored the cheery farewell and hurried down the hallway. With each step he grew more and more irritated. The Atlanta Journal Constitution, the local newspaper, was conducting a story on the C.D.C. and he'd been asked to give an interview. Johnston remembered the prior week's confrontation with his boss, Director David Lantz.

"I'm too busy for this nonsense. Can't somebody else do it?"

The Director had dealt with his harsh personality before and knew how to stroke his ego. "Sorry Barry, but you're one of our most qualified staff. I really need your help on this."

"What's the purpose of the interview anyway? More sensationalism from that biased, left-wing tabloid? Are they going to print another story about how the C.D.C.'s a prime target for a terrorist attack with all the dangerous pathogens we house? Big surprise! I've got news for them, the word's already out. There's no scoop."

"This is different. We want to show the C.D.C.'s kinder, gentler side."

"Excuse me?" Johnston asked skeptically.

"We'd like to turn the focus, remind the public we do more than just study deadly viruses. The brass wants to spin how we impact everyday life. You know, monitoring the quality of healthcare, providing children's vaccines, that sort of thing."

"Look, I guess what you're trying to do makes sense, but...."

Lantz interrupted, "As head of our Public Health Research Group it only follows that you'd give the interview."

"Think about it. Even though I'm the obvious choice for this, being kind and gentle isn't exactly my strong suit."

The Director chuckled. "Well, I can't argue with that, but you're a professional. You can handle it. Just give these reporters an hour or two, that's all I'm asking."

Johnston finally relented. "Fine."

By the time he reached his office, Barry Johnston was fuming. He stopped to speak with an attractive young woman sitting in a nearby cubicle. "Any calls?"

"No Sir."

"There're some newspaper reporters coming in for an interview at nine o'clock this morning." Johnston lowered his voice. "Give them a little time and then buzz in, tell me I have an emergency."

"What should…?"

"I don't care. Just make something up. Oh, and if Gwen Shealy calls, put her through immediately."

Johnston proceeded into his office. Although the walls proudly displayed his credentials, there weren't any other personal effects. A credenza and massive wooden desk dominated the room.

The physician glanced at his expensive Cartier watch. *Eight forty-five. Still fifteen minutes before the reporters show up. Time to make a call,* he concluded.

It would be his second attempt to contact the woman. Several days earlier he was greeted by voice mail. "You've reached Gwen Shealy. I can't take your call right now but if you'll leave your name and number, I'll get back to you as soon as possible. Wait for the beep and have a blessed day. Thanks."

I'll try again, maybe I'll catch her, he thought while dialing. One ring. Two. Three. Four. Once again, a recording intercepted the call. "Damn it," the doctor cursed. He waited then spoke in a controlled tone. "Mrs. Shealy, this is Dr. Barry Johnston from the C.D.C. I called last week and left a message. We met at a mental health seminar not long ago." Johnston had begun frequenting events which drew families dealing with brain-related ailments. "You may not remember, but we discussed your...well your unfortunate family situation. I'd like to talk with you about an opportunity which might benefit us both. Please give me a call as soon as you get a chance. My phone number is...."

Meanwhile, Director Lantz escorted an A.J.C. reporter down the hallway. The man was tall and lanky with sandy brown hair. It was cut short, partially concealing a natural wave.

"The gentleman I'm interviewing...uh, this Dr. Johnston fellow, can you spell his name?"

"J-o-h-n-s-t-o-n. Barry Johnston's responsible for our Public Health Research Group. He's well-respected within the scientific community. Been with us for several years, but I'll let him fill you in on his background."

"Great, I look forward to it."

"And this is Dr. Johnston's assistant."

The young woman looked up and smiled. Her perfume wafted up to greet them.

"Emma, this is Roger Hall from the Atlanta Journal Constitution."

"Yes Sir, he's expecting you," she stated. "Would you like some coffee, Mr. Hall?"

"Black, thanks."

As they entered the office, Director Lantz introduced the reporter.

Johnston looked past them into the hallway. "I thought they were sending two of you guys."

"There was a little mix-up," Roger Hall answered.

Director Lantz interjected, "I'm afraid that's my fault. The Journal sent a photographer too, but I failed to remind them there aren't any pictures permitted inside the facility."

"It's no problem. My colleague's waiting outside in the van. He'll get a snapshot of the building or something when we're through in here."

"I'd like to finish as quickly as possible. Can we get started?" Johnston stated bluntly.

"Of course. I appreciate you taking time from your busy schedule."

"I'm sure."

Director Lantz turned to the reporter. "I'll be back in my office if you have any other questions."

"Thanks, I'll get you an advance copy of the article before it's released."

Lantz nodded. "Gentlemen, please excuse me." He left the reporter in Barry Johnston's competent but unpredictable hands. *Hopefully he can get through this without pissing off the guy too much,* the Director thought while walking away.

Emma entered the office carrying two cups of coffee. "Will there be anything else?"

"No thank you," Johnston responded placing his mug on a coaster. "Please remember I'm expecting an important call from Mrs. Shealy. If she phones, put her through immediately. I really need to speak with her."

The physician then turned his attention to the reporter. "Well, have a seat."

Hall placed his coffee cup on the corner of the desk and sat down. Johnston immediately opened a drawer and retrieved another coaster, sliding it under the mug.

"Sorry," Roger apologized as he sat with his pen poised over a pad of paper.

Barry Johnston stared at the man, silently conveying his displeasure.

The reporter cleared his throat. "I understand you've been with the C.D.C. for a while."

"Almost eight years now."

"That's a long time. What's your background?"

In his typical brusque manner, Johnston asked, "What difference does that make? I thought the story was about the organization and how it contributes to society."

"It is, it is. I'm just trying to establish your qualifications for our readers."

"I believe my current status at the C.D.C. accomplishes that but if it's necessary. I'm a neurologist. Attended the University of Georgia and later graduated from Emory Medical School." Johnston nodded toward the framed certificates on the wall. "Does that suffice?" he asked sarcastically.

"Again, I'm only trying to let the readers know the information in the article comes from a reliable source." He glanced up at the diplomas.

Johnston continued. "When I first came to the C.D.C. they offered me a management position in the Center for Health Promotion. I was interested in research and eventually transferred into my current role."

"I see. What exactly do you research?"

"Disabilities for one thing. Are you familiar with the Metropolitan Atlanta Developmental Disabilities Study?"

"No, afraid not." Hall began writing, then erased and brushed the remnants of his error to the floor. "Can you repeat that?"

"The Metropolitan...Atlanta...Developmental...Disabilities... Study," Johnston said slowly. "M.A.D.D.S. was conducted from 1984 to 1990."

"And what was its objective?"

"To determine the rate at which certain disabilities occurred in children." The doctor waited until Hall stopped writing. "Then in 1991 an offshoot of that study, the M.A.D.D.S. Surveillance Program was started."

The reporter scribbled furiously. "Okay, let's talk about the Surveillance Program."

"As I said before, the goal of the initial study was to simply track the occurrence of disabilities in children. Then the C.D.C. received a grant allowing us to conduct research on them."

Hall stopped writing and glanced up. "Research on disabled children?"

"That's right."

The reporter hesitated before stating, "That might sound a little cold to some people."

"It shouldn't."

"But...."

The doctor shook his head. "How old are you, Mr. Hall?"

"What? I'm...I'm in my forties. Why?"

"Would you like to find a cure for, say Alzheimer's before you get older?"

"Of course I would."

"For that to occur, scientists must understand more about the disease. We have to study those affected in order to learn. It's that simple."

"No one's questioning the necessity of research, Dr. Johnston."

"Oh no, as long as it doesn't step on any moral toes. Look, the C.D.C. was accumulating all this data but wasn't using it. Knowing how often a disability or disease occurs doesn't necessarily help the scientific community. So what if Autism occurs four times more often in males than females? Big deal! That's just a statistic. We need to prevent and treat the disorder. That only happens through scientific study."

Johnston paused to take a sip of coffee. The observant reporter noted his perfectly manicured fingernails as he lifted the mug and replaced it on the wooden coaster.

"Along the way, researchers may uncover valuable information that can be harnessed for other purposes. For instance, did you know that humans only utilize a small percentage of their intellectual capacity?"

"I've heard that before."

"Finding ways to develop the other unused abilities is pretty exciting, don't you agree?"

"I suppose, but if you don't mind I'd like to get back to that children's surveillance program. You mentioned Autism. Is that the only disability studied?"

"It's one of five."

"What're the others?"

"Mental retardation, Cerebral Palsy, hearing loss and vision impairment."

Hall asked, "How are children with these disabilities identified? How do you find them?"

"The C.D.C. searches common sources, places where these youngsters receive treatment and training."

"You mean like hospitals?"

"Yes, they report cases detected at birth. Clinics and pediatricians also report those diagnosed later in life. Surprisingly, the most useful source is public schools."

"Really?"

"That's right, Mr. Hall. Since some parents are unaware or ignore the signs, many children aren't identified until after they enter school. Most states offer special programs for those with learning and physical disabilities. The names enrolled in these programs also help establish our database."

"I assume you keep their identity confidential."

"From the general public, yes."

"The individuals aren't identified by name, are they?"

Johnston let out a disgusted sigh. "Of course they are. How else could we track them?"

"I don't know, maybe by number or something?"

"The names of our subjects are highly restricted. Rest assured the C.D.C. is in full compliance with HIPAA"

"What's that?"

"The Health Insurance Portability and Accountability Act. Federal law requires an individual's medical information be protected. Because of concerns about confidentiality, we oversee and screen any request for information."

"Can you elaborate on how that process works?" the reporter asked.

"The researcher must fill out an extremely detailed application. He has to be very specific about the data desired, what's being tested and how the information will be used. It's a long and drawn-out process with lots of bureaucratic red tape."

"Regardless, some might think it's a little 'big brother-ish' to have a government agency maintaining such personal information in a database."

"Some people probably do. However, they'd also be narrow-minded idiots," Johnston replied sharply.

The reporter stared at the pompous man.

"Don't be so naïve. The government has personal information on all of us." Johnston leaned back in his chair. "Do you pay taxes?"

"Of course I do."

"Don't you fill out a federal tax return every year and send it to the Internal Revenue Service?"

"But that's not the…."

"There's some very private information on that form isn't there? If I'm not mistaken the I.R.S. is a government agency. Guaranteed, you and I are both in their database."

"That's hardly the same thing. I voluntarily put the information on that form." Taking a conciliatory tone the reporter smiled, "Well, maybe 'voluntarily' is the wrong word."

The doctor glared, refusing to be pacified.

"Information on a tax return isn't the same as an individual's medical history," Hall continued.

"There's a big difference."

A loud buzzer sounded before Emma's voice came over the intercom. "Excuse me, but Gwen Shealy is on the phone."

"Put her through." Dr. Johnston turned to the reporter. "I have to take this call."

He picked up the handset and whirled around in his chair ignoring the reporter. "Hello, Mrs. Shealy. Thanks for returning my call."…
"Don't worry about it."…"Was it your cell?"…"Oh, I understand."…
"Would you prefer I call your home phone?"…"Certainly. One minute, I'll write it down." He grabbed a pencil. "All right, go ahead."…"Let me repeat that number. 4-0-4-6-8-4-3-1-5-0."

Roger Hall paged through his notes, all the while listening to the one-sided conversation. Subtly he jotted down the name, Gwen Shealy, and her telephone number.

"Frankly Mrs. Shealy, I didn't know if you'd remember meeting at the mental health seminar."…"How's your father doing? Any change in his condition?"…"Yes, that's a hard decision to make."…"It's difficult to accept when a loved one is faced with such an illness. The situation certainly takes a toll on the entire family, emotionally and financially."

The reporter was surprised by Johnston's sudden compassion.

"I seem to recall you mentioning that."..."And your son's Autism, any new developments there?"..."Yes, he probably will."..."I sympathize with your situation, Mrs. Shealy. That's one of the reasons for my call."..."I'd certainly like to meet and discuss it."..."Anytime that's convenient for you."

Johnston scribbled some notes and stuck the paper in his shirt pocket.

"I've got it."..."Fine. I'll come by Golden Years. See you then." He hung up and turned his attention back to Roger Hall, "Now what were we discussing?"

"Uh...the ethics of tracking children afflicted with disabilities."

"I'll assure you the C.D.C. is very ethical, even to a fault. The organization enforces some very strict standards of conduct."

"Then all parents are informed their disabled children are being studied?"

"What are you implying?"

Roger Hall elaborated. "I'm sure some of the first subjects involved in this surveillance program are adults by now. Are they aware their medical information is stored in some government data base?"

Johnston leaned forward and stared at the reporter. "Let me ask you a question. Do you believe a woman with an autistic son is more concerned about ethics or finding a cure for her child's condition?"

"Maybe you should ask the woman."

"I just spoke with one. The answer's obvious." Johnston's anger was building. "For science to advance, society must be willing to make certain sacrifices!"

"You're talking about human beings not some lab animals. Do they know they're being tracked?" the reporter pushed further.

Johnston's face turned red. "Self-righteous jack-asses like you annoy me. While the most intelligent researchers in the world strive to cure cancer and other maladies, you sit there with your pen and paper trying to conjure up some story to entertain the masses. Quite typical of the press."

"I'm just doing my job."

"Yes, well don't worry. The Birth Defects Prevention Act of 1998 authorized the surveillance. I'm confident the proper protocols were followed with all the 'I's dotted and 'T's crossed. No one's rights have been violated."

"Are you sure about that, Dr. Johnston?" the reporter fired back. "How about that telephone conversation you just had? Does discussing someone's medical condition in front of me comply with your ethical conduct and that...that HIPAA law?"

Emma's soft knock on the door interrupted their argument. "I'm sorry to bother you again Dr. Johnston, but the lab just called and you're needed. It's a bit of an emergency."

"Finally!" Johnston declared aloud. Rising from the chair he curtly added, "This interview is over, Mr. Hall."

* * * * * *

The A.J.C. reporter left the building and returned to the van. "Let's go," Roger Hall ordered, slamming the passenger door.

"Ain't we getting a picture?" the waiting newspaper photographer asked.

"No pictures today."

"Then why in hell did I come along?" He wiped his brow and started the engine. "I've been sitting out here sweating my balls off for nothing."

"Just drive."

Back at the office Roger Hall hurried to his cubicle, throwing his notebook on the desk. The reporter pressed his temples as he rocked back and forth in a squeaky chair.

The assistant editor approached. "How'd the interview go?"

"Not so good. Didn't get the story we were after."

"Why not, what happened?"

"The asshole doctor wasn't real cooperative."

"Want me to get involved? Make a phone call?"

"Nah, his boss seemed like a decent guy. I'll buzz him later on, try and reschedule."

"Okay, but remember we have a deadline."

Hall rehashed the altercation and thought about his next steps to complete the article. *Wonder if there's another angle. Maybe I should contact that woman he spoke with and get her side of the story.* Hall flipped through his notepad to where he'd jotted her name and telephone number. The reporter then Googled "Find Address" and went to "The Official White Pages". He typed in...Gwen Shealy, Atlanta, GA.

The woman's address immediately popped up on the screen.

* * * * * *

Barry Johnston went to Director Lantz's office and informed him of the confrontation. At first he was upset, but when Johnston offered his resignation, Lantz's frustration turned to surprise.

"What are you talking about, Barry?"

"I'm resigning."

"Why? Just because of this? If so, you're making a mistake."

"I'm tired of all the bureaucratic red tape."

"Don't be ridiculous. We're talking about your career," the Director reasoned.

"That's why I'm quitting."

"What are you going to do?"

"I've got other options. Plan to conduct some private research, try and make a real difference in the world."

"Barry, you're doing that here. Your contributions at the C.D.C. are making a difference."

"Not enough." Johnston repeated, "Not enough."

At home that night Barry Johnston poured a drink. The Dewars slid smoothly down leaving his throat warm and tingly. Sitting alone in his secluded lake house, the doctor was engulfed by a new excitement. *No more idiotic constraints to deal with. I'm better off on my own not having to answer to anyone. Finally I can do something worthwhile for the world. Live up to my potential...and be recognized for it,* he rationalized.

Johnston drained the cocktail glass and placed it on the granite counter top in the kitchen before walking downstairs to his office. He took a small silver key and unlocked a metal filing cabinet next to his desk. Inside were several folders. Dozens of possible specimens had been considered but ultimately rejected. Only one particular candidate was perfect. Not only were the medical and physical characteristics ideal, but his personal situation was conducive for the plan.

Johnson pulled out the folder marked…TYLER SHEALY.

CHAPTER 5

There weren't any second thoughts or regrets for leaving his job at the Center for Disease Control. Instead, an invigorating freedom consumed Barry Johnston.

Traffic was light as he steered his Mercedes down the highway toward Cumming, a small bedroom community north of Atlanta. The once rural landscape had partially disappeared as a plethora of cookie-cutter strip malls and convenience stores dotted the roadside. The sultry southern countryside once filled with hundred-year-old oaks was slowly vanishing as humanity crept from the city toward the less-congested suburb.

Johnston turned into a Jiffy Mart where a patron filled his tank at the gas pump. A late model Ford and a red pick-up truck were parked in front of the store. Off to the right was a pay telephone booth. With the influx of cell phones, the structure was nothing more than a technological dinosaur. Standing around the booth were several Mexican day workers wearing ragged blue jeans and T-shirts.

Barry Johnston maneuvered through the parking lot and approached the illegal immigrants. He opened the window and peered at the group. Addressing the sole female, he asked, "Where's Hector?"

The shapely twenty-year-old had a pretty face with long, shiny black hair. She responded in broken English. "Hector go to Reynosa."

"He returned to Mexico? Why?"

"For younger brother."

"Angelina, I didn't know you had another sibling."

"*Se,* Dr. Johnston."

"Why didn't he come to the States with you before?"

"Young, not want to leave home. Not afraid no more, wants to come."

"When are they returning?" Johnston asked sharply. "Hector needs to finish the cabinets in my basement."

"Not know." Nodding toward the other men, Angelina asked, "Would like somebody else? Jose hard worker. Not speak good English but can do job."

Eyeing the man distastefully Dr. Johnston responded, "I'll wait for Hector. See if he gets back anytime soon." He then asked, "You're still coming to clean my house aren't you?"

"*Se,* Dr. Johnson. Every Saturday, that was deal, is right?" She brushed several errant strands of hair off her forehead. A hopeful smile crept across her face.

"Yes, that's the agreement. Get in."

The Mexican woman hurried over and slid into the automobile for the ride back to the physician's home at Lake Lanier.

Along the way Johnston glanced at the young Hispanic. "When did Hector leave?"

"Two days, Thursday."

"You aren't frightened being left alone?"

The woman shook her head. "Not afraid."

"Those other men, you're not worried about them?"

Angelina waved off the suggestion. "They not bother."

"Well, you still need to exercise caution. There're a lot of unscrupulous people out there these days."

"I take care of self," the woman confidently stated. "God watch over me."

They soon reached Eagles Point, a prestigious residential area on Lake Lanier. In recent years, the wealthy had moved there, building luxurious homes and bringing their expensive tastes with them.

Johnston turned off the highway onto a narrow driveway lined with trees. A few yards ahead stood a wrought iron fence blocking the entrance. To the left of the barrier was a metal post with a keypad. Johnston stopped and reached out the window to punch in a series of numbers, prompting the gate to automatically swing open. The driveway led to his secluded lake home which was nestled on a two acre lot sloping toward the water. At first glance the house appeared reasonably modest with rustic wood siding covering its exterior. While not visible, a full daylight basement doubled the size of the structure. A large deck overlooked the reservoir where Johnston's pontoon boat was securely anchored to a private dock.

They entered the house. The interior was spacious, due in part to the sparse but adequate furnishings. There were no decorative ornaments or pictures hanging on the white walls, creating an impersonal and somewhat sterile feel.

"Angelina, I've got some matters to take care of down in the basement. Why don't you start up here first?"

"*Se*, Dr. Johnston. Kitchen, bathroom, wash dirty clothes. Will clean all."

"There's probably some Chinese food left in the refrigerator. You'll need to throw it away along with anything else that's old, all right?"

The woman smiled and nodded.

"Let me know when you're finished." He turned and walked down the staircase into a divided basement. On one side was his bedroom with a private bath, and on the other a laboratory and office.

Johnston entered the laboratory. Plantation shutters covered a large window facing the water. They were open, allowing light to flood the room. An adjacent doorway led to a flagstone path and the lake beyond. An examination table sat in the center of the room. A long counter with numerous drawers was constructed against the opposite wall. A backpack lay on the counter top along with a U.P.S package postmarked from New York.

Several partially completed cabinets hung directly above. "I hope Hector returns soon. Really need to get those storage cabinets finished," he mumbled. The man was compulsively neat and always organized. Loose ends annoyed him.

Next to the counter was a stainless steel wash basin with spigots protruding over the drain. Glancing at a mirror hanging on the wall above it, Dr. Johnston raked a hand through his hair. A few strands came free and joined several others in the sink waiting to be washed away.

He opened a nearby refrigerator, grabbed one of two bottles of water and took a drink.

Johnston slung the backpack over his shoulder before picking up the U.P.S. package. He stepped into the office at the rear of the lab where a desk and filing cabinet sat side by side. A bookshelf perfectly organized with volumes of medical manuals filled another wall.

He checked his email, filed some documents then returned upstairs.

"Angelina, where are you?"

"Here," she called out. The housekeeper was busy cleaning an already spotless bathroom. Barry Johnston insisted on a sanitary environment. His bathrooms were pristine, but he was still adamant about getting them thoroughly scrubbed and disinfected routinely.

"I need to run an errand. I'll be back in a minute."

"*Se.* Have much to do," the woman replied, leaning over and wiping the inside of the commode with a brillo pad. A can of Lysol was sitting on the back of the toilet.

After cleaning the bathroom the young Mexican entered the laundry for her next chore. A flimsy plastic basket packed with wadded garments rested on the floor next to a set of Maytags. She began separating clothes, putting whites into one pile and colored items in another. Then she noticed a piece of paper tucked inside a shirt pocket.

> *Golden Years Nursing Home*
>
> *G. Shealy   404.684.3150*
>
> *T. Shealy   Specimen / Savant*

Worried the message might be important, she decided to take it downstairs for Dr Johnston.

The well-intended woman entered the office and stepped toward the desk. She tucked a corner of the note under Johnston's laptop computer. Turning to leave she noticed a partially unzipped backpack on the floor. Walking past she glanced down to see bundles of money stuffed inside. "Holy Mary, sweet Mother of Jesus!" Angelina exclaimed stopping in her tracks.

"That's a lot of money isn't it?" a somber voice stated. Barry Johnston was standing in the doorway holding a pack of Evian.

Startled, she replied in a shaky voice, *"El doctor Johnston, me asustaste. No sabía que eras casero. Perdonarme por favor para venir adentro aquí."*

"Speak English," he ordered in a cold, hard tone.

"Very sorry, Dr. Johnston. Come to leave paper found in shirt." She pointed to the note underneath the laptop. "Not want to lose."

"I see." He stepped toward the desk and picked up the paper. "Angelina, I thought you were told never to come here without me. Only Hector was given permission to work in the basement alone."

"Did not take dollars, Dr. Johnston. Would not steal. Is all there, see." She pointed.

He reached down to close the backpack. "That's not my concern." Johnston's anger grew. Not only had Angelina invaded his privacy, she'd disobeyed a direct order. The controlling physician had little tolerance for subordinates, especially those who didn't follow the rules.

But Angelina had been a good employee. She was dependable, never complaining and always grateful for the job. His anger softened.

He knew that some took advantage of day laborers. Mexican workers illegally entering the United States without the proper paperwork were hired for laborious, difficult jobs that no one else wanted. They were often disrespected and worked extreme hours for a paltry sum of money. *What a life, to be poor and uneducated, never genuinely contributing to society,* he thought.

Then in an instant Johnston's diabolical mind began churning. What if something good could come from this unfortunate situation? Angelina could do more for humanity than just clean houses.

I can use her now, Johnston reasoned. After all, there was no guarantee he'd be able to get the Savant, Tyler Shealy, for his experiments.

Although Angelina didn't meet any of the selection criteria, with her as a specimen he could start the experiments sooner, even today. And what an ideal situation! Hector, her only connection was gone. No one would miss her for a while. But what about when he returned? Hector probably wouldn't take kindly to his sister being the subject of a medical experiment.

Johnston's impatience overcame caution and he rationalized, *They're Illegals. It's not like they could go to the police.*

"Will go upstairs, finish cleaning, okay?" the young woman nervously stated.

"Wait just a minute." He moved toward her. "We have a slight problem."

"No, no problem, Dr. Johnston." Angelina wrung her hands together.

As she turned to leave, the man grabbed her arm. "We need to talk."

"Talk?" she asked, stiffening at his touch.

"It's all right." Johnston smiled and loosened his grip. "Come into the laboratory and sit for a minute."

"I not in trouble?"

"No, not at all. Everything's fine."

They left the small office for the examination room. "Sorry there aren't any chairs in here. Have a seat on the table and I'll get you a drink." He walked over to the refrigerator, pulled out the last cold bottle of water and handed it to her. "I'm sorry for getting upset. I know you'd never do anything inappropriate."

"Would not steal."

"Of course not. Now please relax. Sit." Johnston calmly motioned toward the examination table.

Angelina obeyed, hopping onto it.

"You're doing a wonderful job. Couldn't ask for anyone more conscientious." The man stepped to the counter and opened a drawer keeping his back toward Angelina. He reached in and grasped a syringe. "When did you say Hector's returning from Mexico? I really want to get these cabinets finished."

"Uh…not sure." She took a drink from the bottle. "Go work now?"

"Take a break." As she relaxed, Johnston probed. "Those other men you were with this morning at the gas station, who are they?"

"From Mexico. Not know well. Come and go quickly, try to find work. Go where jobs." She took another sip of water, then wiped her mouth.

The physician closed the drawer and walked back to Angelina. His arms were positioned down by his side. A cold, determined stare bore into the Mexican woman.

"What is it? Something wrong?" She noted his unusually hard expression.

Johnston suddenly lunged forward pinning her on the table.

"Wh…what you do? Please, Dr. Johnston. Please stop!" She struggled to get up, but the weight of the middle-aged man kept her secure.

He rammed a syringe through her tight blue jeans, injecting a sedative into her leg.

"Ahh!" she cried out as the needle penetrated her flesh.

Angelina kicked and flailed in vain but his size and strength were too much for her petite frame. Johnson continued to hold the struggling woman down. Her brown eyes finally closed and she drifted off into a dizzy, nightmarish haze.

Johnston lay on the beautiful young Mexican until her breathing steadied. The slight rise and fall of her chest was comforting as he lingered for a few moments. Staring down at her soft olive-tinted skin, he whispered a name from years past. "Tina."

They'd met shortly after moving to California. Johnston had just graduated medical school and was beginning an internship near Los Angeles. The hours were long but he didn't care. As a matter of fact he welcomed the physical and mental demands of practicing medicine. It was his personal paradise.

Tina was short and thin with long, flowing hair. Johnston fell in love the minute he looked into her blue-green eyes. It took Tina a little longer. However her feelings became much stronger upon discovering he was a doctor.

Their whirlwind courtship consisted mostly of phone calls and an occasional lunch, as that's all Johnston could fit into his busy schedule. When he proposed, Tina immediately accepted and the two were married within months.

Medical internships are grueling and the newlyweds quickly found that married life came second to his career. Their time together was limited. But Tina didn't seem to mind. She was content to simply spend his money. Unfortunately interns didn't make a lot.

Johnston enjoyed the work and reveled in the respect received from his colleagues. The gratitude showered by his patients was intoxicating. A feeling of superiority settled over the new physician and for the first time he truly felt valued.

Tina felt differently and their marriage began to crumble. Nothing made her happy and they fought constantly. She eventually moved out after confessing to being in love with a rich and powerful businessman. No amount of pleading could change her mind and divorce papers were soon served. Following the required six-month waiting period the divorce became final.

Johnston was devastated at losing the love of his life. Someone else he desperately wanted to please had shunned him again.

Determined to succeed, Johnston persevered and completed his internship. Unwilling to face the humiliation of the marital failure, Barry returned to Georgia leaving behind all the sympathetic looks and accusatory glares....

He climbed off the young Mexican woman lying on the table. Johnston picked up the plastic bottle and meticulously mopped the spilled water from the floor.

"I didn't plan it this way," he muttered softly while smoothing her hair. "But researchers must learn to improvise." He began unbuttoning the young woman's blouse.

Angelina awoke some time later, naked and secured to the examination table. The shutters were closed and darkness blanketed the room. The young woman's arms and legs ached from the tight leather straps. The fog refused to lift. Where was she? How'd she get here?

She tried desperately to free herself from the restraints, but it was useless.

"Help! Please help me!" She repeated in Spanish, *"Por favor el dios, me ayuda, por favor!"* The words echoed off the walls before dying in the room. Tears began streaming from the woman's desperate, brown eyes.

The thud of footsteps vibrated down the staircase. Dr. Johnston entered the laboratory and flipped the light switch.

"Hello Angelina," he stated calmly. "I'm glad you're finally awake."

The groggy day laborer became frantic, looking at the man in disbelief. "What...why you do this?"

Johnston moved to the sink and washed his hands. Reaching into a drawer he pulled out a stethoscope and stepped to her naked body. His stare migrated up her shapely legs to her breasts, finally meeting Angelina's terrified eyes. "I'm sorry, but you shouldn't have come down here."

"Please let go," she begged, struggling to free her arms from the straps.

"I can't do that." Johnston placed the stethoscope against her chest and listened. "You must try to calm down. Your heart is beating much too fast."

"I...I not understand," she sobbed.

Again, the man eyed her naked body. "You're so young and beautiful." He reached down and pushed the long black strands of hair from her forehead.

Cold chills ran down the woman's spine as Johnston began to slowly drag his hand over the contours of her body. First her face, then downward across two small but developed breasts. His touch was deliberate yet soft as he absorbed the warmth of her trembling body. Angelina recoiled, closing her eyes.

"I need you," he finally confessed.

"No, please no! I not...not worth it."

The doctor shook his head. "It's not your flesh I want."

She fought, jerking and pulling at the restraints.

"Stop that!" Barry Johnston barked, slapping her face. "You're making things worse."

She blinked, stunned by the blow.

"There now," he said. "Sorry I hit you. It's not something I enjoy."

Angelina then noticed the bag of fluid hanging from an IV pole next to the examination table. A tube connected the bag to a large needle inserted into the back of her hand.

"What...what is that?"

"It's a midline catheter," Johnston replied, carefully checking to make sure the needle was still secure. "This way, I won't have to find a vein each time. It'll be much easier and more comfortable for you."

He went to the office and carefully pulled a vial of clear liquid from the opened U.P.S. box. After retrieving a syringe from the drawer, he returned to his subject.

"Please," the woozy victim begged, watching him stick the needle inside the bottle to withdraw some fluid. Pointing the needle toward the ceiling, Johnston tapped the syringe twice. Tiny bubbles rose to the top of the solution. The physician pushed the plunger slightly, forcing the air and a small stream of serum to shoot out. He then injected the drug into the IV port.

Tears trickled down the woman's cheeks. She muttered, "Home... family."

Johnston leaned down to whisper in her ear. "Yes, your family's back in Mexico."

"*Se…Mexico.* Come to America."

"Why'd you come to the United States, Angelina?"

"Better life…for family."

He stroked the wetness from her cheeks. "I understand. That's what I'm doing, trying to make a better life for mankind. But I can't do it alone. I need you. You're going to make a significant contribution to society."

Drifting in and out of consciousness, Angelina's fading thoughts were of home. She'd grown up in Reynosa, a small Mexican town just across the border from Hidalgo, Texas. Born into a family of poor farmers, she'd spent her life working their fields of corn and sugarcane. Young and adventuresome, Angelina wanted more. So she and Hector came to the United States.

"*Madre. Padre. Deseo venir a casa,*" she uttered. "Mama. Papa. I want to go home."

* * * * * *

Over the next few days all of Barry Johnston's waking moments were spent in the laboratory analyzing results and adjusting the dosage. He documented reactions, changes in speech and behavior.

Angelina lapsed into respiratory distress one afternoon and her heart stopped. Johnston attempted to revive her but failed. He made the appropriate notes detailing the outcome, then loosened the straps restraining the deceased Hispanic.

That night, the sky was pitch black as a blanket of clouds shielded the stars and crescent moon. The air was cool and fresh, having been cleansed by a late evening thunderstorm.

The puttering of the pontoon boat carried across the lake. Eventually the engine was cut and the vessel glided to a stop, rocking slightly as it floated atop the choppy lake waters. A lumpy, rolled-up piece of blue canvas tied together with nylon rope lay on the deck. Barry Johnston bent down and hoisted the bulky bundle overboard. With a soft splash the woman's body hit the water, bobbing like a fishing cork at first. As the air slowly escaped the tarp it began sinking to the bottom of Lake Lanier.

Later Johnston sat in his office with his laptop computer. The neurologist opened the file *CT-POTENTIAL* and scrolled down to a field labeled *SPECIMAN*. He began typing....

The physician leaned back in his chair and raised his arms to stretch. Frustrated by the outcome of his experiment, he rationalized the human toll as a necessary cost of progress. While saddened by Angelina's demise, he soothed his conscience with a salve of knowledge that had been gained, convinced her death wasn't in vain.

It has to be the dosage. I've got to get it calibrated.

He finally rose from the desk. Passing through the laboratory, he glanced over and mumbled, "I'll need to call somebody tomorrow and get those cabinets completed."

Johnston then went to bed having little trouble falling into a peaceful sleep.

CHAPTER 6

Perceptions are that people go to hospitals to live…and nursing homes to die.

Taking care of the elderly during the twilight and most vulnerable time of their life is hard. It'd been a long day at Golden Years nursing home. For hours Gwen looked after patients in the final stages of life. She tended to their needs, passed medications and responded to call lights. While the work was noble it was also very demanding. The nursing duties were hard enough but interacting with family members was even tougher, especially when it meant explaining why their loved one had passed away. Sometimes nothing she did or said was good enough. When the end finally came, Gwen could see the pain in their grieving eyes. Even if the words weren't spoken she sensed their accusations. *Oh my God, no!...It can't be!... You should've done more.*

She sympathized but knew the blame was unfounded. The sad truth was that people eventually die. Some simmer slowly in a pot of bleak reality as their families pray for an improbable miracle.

The strain wore on her. Gwen stared blankly ahead into the evening traffic, wondering if she'd missed her chance. No husband to share her world. No money for the nicer things. No time for herself as it was all spent on others. Sometimes she just wanted to run away but instead pushed forward, taking life as it came, one day at a time hoping for a better tomorrow.

Gwen pulled into the driveway of their small rented house. The neighborhood was constructed some years back in order to accommodate the workers of a nearby textile mill. Although the factory and its blue-collar jobs were now gone, there still remained a decent market for inexpensive rental property.

A huge magnolia tree stood off to the side separating the tiny paint-peeled dwelling from a similar structure next door. The tree's beautiful white flowers emitted a heavenly scent while tiny pineapple-shaped cones were scattered on the ground underneath its mature, ragged branches.

The front door was open. As she entered, comedic banter from a sitcom bounced around the room. Canned laughter hooted from the nineteen inch set signaling the misfortune of the program's main character.

"Daddy, where are you?" Gwen called with a hint of concern.

Budgie squawked, "Daddy. Daddy."

On the table in the kitchen was an empty bowl. Next to it sat a plastic jug of milk and a box of Cheerios.

Gwen hurried to her father's bedroom. She knocked gently before looking inside, finding only an unmade bed.

She stepped down the hallway. "Tyler, are you in there?"

"In here…in here." He opened the door.

"Where's Granddaddy?"

"Gone. Granddaddy gone. Gone," he repeated without making eye contact. He ran a finger under his runny nose to wipe away the persistent slime. The sleeve of his T-shirt was stained with dried yellow mucus.

"What do you mean, gone? Where is he?"

"Get corn flakes. Wanted corn flakes. Not Cheerios. Wanted corn flakes."

"Not again! He left the house alone?" Gwen yelled rushing away.

"Corn Flakes. Made from rolled corn dough. Toasted. William Keith Kellogg. 1906. Offered <u>Jungleland Moving Pictures Book</u> to people who bought cereal. Rooster. Cornelius Rooster. Cornelius Rooster," Tyler repeated over and over after she'd left the room.

* * * * * *

The car inched along the unfamiliar street as Roger Hall leaned forward and tried to read the addresses. A horn blasted from a tailgaiting vehicle.

"Go around," Hall mumbled. He pulled to the curb and stuck his left hand out to motion the impatient motorist around. The car sped by as its driver made an obscene gesture. Ignoring it, he pulled back onto the road and continued toward the next intersection.

The reporter was hoping to interview Gwen Shealy for an article about the C.D.C.'s involvement with disabled children. He'd learned to be assertive, even aggressive in researching a good story, but wondered what kind of reception he'd receive this time. Would he ask the right questions and garner any information from the woman?

His grip on the steering wheel tightened knowing she'd undoubtedly have some questions of her own.

* * * * * *

The summer sun was dropping below the urban horizon creating a peaceful orange backdrop. The scent of freshly cut grass filled the air.

A black couple sat in rickety, wooden rocking chairs on their front porch trying to capture the cooling effects of an evening breeze. As they spoke, both gazed at their tired, decaying surroundings rather than each other.

"When the hell ya gonna get the air conditioner fixed?" the woman disgustedly asked. The armpits of her blouse were stained with dark, damp patches of perspiration.

"Whenever we gets some extra money, that's when," he answered, rubbing a hand over his sweaty bald head.

She waved a folded magazine back and forth, creating a draft while keeping the squadron of pesky evening mosquitoes at bay. "Well, it's hard livin' like this. That blasted window fan don't do no more than push hot air around. It's plum useless."

"It'll cool off now the sun's goin' down."

"I reckon," she answered.

"Hell, you way too mean and crusty to melt. A little heat ain't gonna hurt you none."

The woman shook her head, used to his gruff words after thirty-plus years of marriage.

He nodded toward the sidewalk where an elderly man shuffled by. "Who's that old codger out yonder?"

Ernest Shealy wandered aimlessly along as evening shadows began to creep over the worn day. He paused to stare at the couple relaxing on the porch.

The black woman waved.

He immediately looked away and kept walking. Surrounded by dusk, he became more confused with each wayward step. His mind struggled for answers. Nothing made sense. Where was he? Where was he going? What was he looking for? Then the questions disappeared as other thoughts stormed through to blow them away. Random memories swirled about, some landing for a few brief moments before drifting off.

Ernest began babbling. "Daddy's gonna beat me if I don't get back to the fields. There's cotton needin' to be picked. Where's my sack? I'm comin' Daddy. I'm comin'." He bent over and reached out a hand, slowly opening and closing his fingers as if pulling the white puffy fibers from their thorny burrs.

Memories of his childhood vanished and were soon replaced by those as a parent. "Listen to me, Gwenny. Now go off to school and make somethin' of yourself. There's plenty time for marryin'," he spoke into the dark, steamy night. "Your mama and me want you to do good."

The moment vanished as the loud hum of a low-flying jet approaching Hartsfield Jackson Airport distracted him. The lights of the aircraft glided slowly by on its way to the nearby airfield. "Those God-damn M.I.G.'s," the Korean War Veteran cursed. "Where's our F-86 Sabres? They'll take care of those sons-a-bitches. Blow the Red bastards out of the damn sky. Blow'em out of the sky," he ranted.

A corner streetlight flickered before casting its light into the night. A cadre of gnats, moths and other flying insects immediately began congregating around the beacon. Ernest Shealy slowly lowered his aging body to the curb.

Two young boys in frayed cut-off blue jeans whizzed down the sidewalk on their bicycles. "Hey, old man," one yelled, his dirty bare feet pumping furiously on the bike pedals. "Wha'chor name? Wha'cha doing?"

"Why don't you go on home?" the other hollered, cycling close behind. "It's suppertime."

Ernest sat quietly, staring out into the street as the youngsters peddled away. Lost, he didn't know his name or where home was. The frustration was now intensified by an increasing dose of fear.

He shielded his eyes from the headlights of an approaching car. The vehicle stopped briefly then slowly pulled away. A short distance down the street its red brake lights flashed and the car began backing up, stopping just a few feet away.

The door opened and a tall, lanky figure with sandy-colored hair got out and walked toward him. He was wearing jeans and a blue sport coat. "Sir, you all right?"

Ernest Shealy looked away initially avoiding eye contact with the Good Samaritan.

"My name's Roger Hall. You need some help?"

The elderly man peeked up, then reached out silently asking for assistance.

Hall grasped the weathered hand and helped him stand. "There you go."

"Thanks young fella."

"Are you okay?"

He nodded.

Roger Hall saw a different answer etched on his wrinkled brow. "You certain?" he asked, looking into a pair of unsure eyes.

Ernest softly responded, "Can you help me?"

"Yes Sir, whatever I can do. Just tell me what you need."

"Can you take me home?"

"Sure. Where do you live? What's the address?"

The old man paused before responding. "I...I...don't know. Can't remember right off."

"No problem, we'll figure it out." Roger thought for a moment. "Let's see now. What's your name?"

Embarrassed, the elderly man shook his head. "Can't seem to remember that neither."

Hall now realized the man's demented condition. "How about a billfold? Do you have a wallet with some identification?"

Ernest reached around and patted his empty pants pocket.

"That's okay. Tell you what, I've got a cell phone in the car. Why don't you come with me and I'll call the police. They'll help us figure things out. We'll have you back home in no time. I promise."

Cell phone! A spark ignited in the old man's memory, "Call Gwenny's cell phone. Gwenny Shealy. That's my girl. She'll come fetch me."

Roger couldn't believe it. What were the chances? "She won't have to. I'm on my way to see her right now. Got the address in the car."

The old man's eyes softened.

"Don't you worry, everything's fine. I'll take you home…is it Mr. Shealy?"

"That's right young fella. My name's Ernest Shealy." He finally remembered.

* * * * * *

Roger Hall waited patiently while Gwen tended to her tired but safe father in the bedroom.

The observant reporter looked around at the modest setting. On the wall were a series of framed photographs showing an infant growing into a teenage boy. Hanging from a hook in the corner was a cage with a green and yellow parakeet sitting on its perch.

Gwen walked in wearing scrubs that clung softly to her feminine curves. She ran a hand through her short brown hair exposing a face free of makeup.

Roger immediately noticed her shapely figure and wholesome beauty.

"Thanks again for bringing Daddy home. I was worried sick."

"Glad I could help. He okay?"

"Yeah, this time anyway. Thank the Lord."

"Does this happen often?"

"It's happening more and more. Don't know what I'm going to do. Daddy's got Alzheimer's. It's moderate right now but will get worse." Her voice cracked. "I...I watch him go downhill a little more each day."

"I'm sorry Mrs. Shealy, can't imagine what it's like."

"Bless his heart. He gets so confused. He watches and if I'm upset it scares him even more. Lord knows I try to be positive but...." Her green eyes began shimmering with a tearful mist.

Roger Hall looked into a lovely but tortured face.

"Lord knows. Lord knows," the parakeet squawked from its cage.

"Hush up Budgie," Gwen scolded. "That's my son's parakeet. Silly bird talks all the time." She walked over and draped a towel over its cage. "There. That should keep you quiet for a while."

"How old's your son?"

"Nineteen."

"Good looking young man," he glanced toward the pictures on the wall. "Must really like baseball."

"He sure does. How'd you know?"

"He's wearing Atlanta Braves gear in most of those photographs."

"Yeah, Tyler's obsessed with the team. He can tell you anything...." She paused. "Will you just listen to me bending your ear about my family? I'm sorry, Mr. Hall."

"Don't worry about it. And please call me Roger."

"Can I get you some sweet tea?"

"No thanks, I'm fine."

"Sure odd finding Daddy on your way here." After a short pause she asked, "Anyway, why did you want to see me?"

He nervously cleared his throat. "I'm a...I'm a reporter for the Journal Constitution."

"A reporter? Lord have mercy."

"The newspaper's running an article about the C.D.C. and its impact on public healthcare. That sort of thing."

"Sounds real interesting, but I don't get the paper any more. One less expense to worry about."

"Tell you what, I'll send you a copy when my story's published."

"I don't want you to go to any bother."

"No trouble at all."

"So what's this article got to do with me?" she asked.

"One of the angles I'm researching involves the C.D.C. files on disabled children. I believe your son's in the database."

"You're here to talk about Tyler?"

"If you've got some time and want to contribute."

"How'd you get his name?"

"Well, you see…."

"Surely the C.D.C. didn't give you that information?"

"Not exactly."

"What exactly then?" Gwen asked, bristling a bit.

Deciding to come clean, the reporter began. "I uh…I was conducting an interview with one of their physicians, a Dr. Barry Johnston."

"Dr. Johnston gave you my name?"

"No, no." Roger Hall sighed. "The truth of the matter is…well…I was in his office and overheard your telephone conversation with him."

"Good Lord."

"I know it was a private conversation and wrong to eavesdrop."

"It sure was. There're laws against that." As a Licensed Practical Nurse, Gwen was fully aware of the federal privacy regulations.

"But…."

Gwen interrupted. "Anything connected to a person's medical condition is protected. It's illegal for Dr. Johnston to disclose that kind of information or for anybody to use it."

"I'm real sorry."

Gwen warned, "I could sue you both."

A tense silence fell over the room.

Finally the reporter offered, "I realize my behavior was inappropriate. But my intentions were good. The article will reach a lot of readers. It could heighten public awareness about Autism and the struggles families go through."

On one hand, Gwen was appalled at the audacity of the reporter. He'd gotten sensitive medical information about her son from a government agency.

On the other, the man didn't seem like a bad person. Maybe a little over-zealous about his job but not malicious. After all he'd taken the time to help a stranger get home safely. Most people wouldn't have bothered to get involved. They'd have driven past hoping someone else would make the effort. She was grateful for that kind act.

"So what do you think, Mrs. Shealy? Should I find myself a good lawyer or will you talk to me?" he joked trying to lighten the moment.

"I'll need some time to think about it."

"I understand. Probably shouldn't have barged in unannounced like this anyway."

Acquiescing a bit, Gwen replied, "Guess it was good you did. Otherwise, I might still be out looking for Daddy."

"Let me know if you're interested. I'd love to get your perspective." The reporter passed her a business card with his contact information. "Both my office and personal numbers are listed. Call anytime."

"I wouldn't want to disturb your family at home," she stated politely.

"Don't have a family. Just me. Please call whenever it's convenient for you. I know your work schedule is probably hectic."

Although she was uncertain about the request, his motives seemed sincere and honest.

"I'd better get going. Thanks for your time."

Gwen watched him walk to the car. She couldn't help notice the lean frame beneath his jeans and sport coat. The man's sandy hair was neatly combed and complimented the chiseled, rugged features of his face. He moved with a sure-footed, confident air that was quite attractive.

She sat down on a worn sofa to relax for a few minutes before starting her evening chores. Every precious moment, every hour of the day seemed to always be focused on others. There just wasn't any time for her. Gwen loved her family more than anything in the world and felt lucky to have them. At the same time she wondered if there should be more in life. What would it be like to live in a big house, take vacations to exotic places and do it all with someone to share her innermost secrets and passions.

But those were only wistful dreams, not reality.

Gwen took a deep breath, rose from the couch and headed toward the kitchen to fix supper. That was reality.

CHAPTER 7

arry Johnston awoke after a good night's sleep. The failure of the experiment and loss of his specimen was more troublesome than the untimely death of the beautiful young Angelina.

He spooned freshly ground coffee into the espresso machine and waited for it to brew, then stepped into the living room and turned on the television. *Good Morning America* was teasing the audience with their programming. Along with news about some child star's latest escapades and a sneak preview of the "Summer Concert Series", they would also cover a story on prescription drugs.

Johnston scanned the channels, eventually returning to A.B.C. where a pretty young woman now appeared on the screen. The female host was reporting on the high cost of drugs and how senior citizens were struggling with the decision to either buy food or medicine. According to the gorgeous blonde, the greedy pharmaceutical companies were getting rich while the most vulnerable members of society were paying the price.

"Ignorant Bitch," Johnston spouted at the television. "Another bleeding heart liberal distorting the truth. We need the pharmaceuticals to make money. If they don't, guess what? Investment in research stops and new cures will never be discovered. Why don't you talk about that?"

The reporter finished the story, failing to make his point.

"Ignorant Bitch," he repeated, tossing the remote aside.

Savoring the strong aroma and flavor of the espresso, he thought about his upcoming meeting with Gwen Shealy.

She'd called and cancelled, incensed that he'd disclosed some private medical information to a newspaper reporter. Johnston apologized and admitted that it was an unintended mistake. After allowing her some time to calm down, he explained the importance of their meeting and how it could potentially change her life. She finally relented, agreeing to see him at Golden Years Nursing home.

There the persuasive physician would present his proposal. In his view, it'd be an offer impossible to refuse.

* * * * * *

As Barry Johnston entered Golden Years Nursing Home, his nose crinkled at the smell. Heavily scented cleaning agents mixed with the odor of incontinent old people formed a unique stench.

Several residents in wheelchairs were positioned in front of a big screen T.V. in the lobby. Some slumped forward with their eyes closed, oblivious to their surroundings. Restraints held their limp bodies securely in place, preventing them from falling onto the floor.

Johnston took a seat on a nearby sofa and waited.

All morning Gwen's stomach churned. Having Dr. Johnston come to the nursing home might be a mistake. What if the Administrator found out? She couldn't afford to lose her job but didn't want to miss a chance to help her family. Meeting him was probably useless, but the opportunity sounded so enticing.

"What'd ya bring to eat, Baby Girl?" Latrisse asked, hurrying down the hallway to catch up.

"Nothing today. I'm…uh…meeting somebody."

"Well now, ain't holdin' out on me are ya?" She winked.

"Oh Lord no, nothing like that." Hesitating, she added, "Just talking to somebody about Daddy, checking out some options."

"Good luck. See ya later."

Although it had been some time since their first encounter at the mental health seminar, Gwen immediately recognized the man. He stood out like a sore thumb in his brown Armanti suit and gold tie.

"Dr. Johnston?"

"Mrs. Shealy, it's so nice to see you again." He stood to greet her.

"Hope I'm not late. Got busy with a patient."

"Not at all. You're right on time. I appreciate the opportunity to meet."

Gwen smiled nervously.

"Can I take you out for a bite of lunch?"

"Oh no thanks. I've only got a half-hour so maybe we should just talk here. There's a bench outside."

"Certainly." Johnston followed her to a wrought iron bench beneath a crepe myrtle. Its branches spread out, providing a blanket of shade from the noon sun.

"I'll get right to the point, Mrs. Shealy. Do you enjoy your job here?"

"I like what I do. Always wanted to become a Registered Nurse. Don't know if that'll ever happen though."

"More specifically do you like working at Golden Years?"

"It's a decent job. The folks here are good to me. They're aware of my family situation and let me take off whenever I need to. There're days when my daddy...well, things come up."

"I understand. That's very accommodating of management. You deal with issues most people don't even think about. With Alzheimer's whittling away at your father's life and leaving him alone at home with your son, it must be quite difficult." He glanced at the facility. "Frankly working in this environment has to be taxing. Caring for people sent here to die. Seeing them suffer day after day, knowing there's nothing to be done. I suspect it wears on you too."

"It does, especially with my situation at home."

"What if I could offer you something better? Something that could make your life a lot easier. Might even allow time to pursue that R.N. license you mentioned."

Gwen listened intently.

"If I may be so bold, money must be a concern for you."

She shrugged her shoulders.

"Frankly Mrs. Shealy, if it's not an issue now it will become one sooner or later. Your father's illness will only worsen. The medications and the eventual care he'll need won't be cheap. And who knows what your son's expenses might be?"

"With God's help, we'll manage."

"Forgive my candor, but it can't be easy to leave them alone every day."

"I worry about them all the time. Especially with Daddy wandering off the way he does," she confessed.

"I certainly understand." After a short pause he added. "Maybe I can help."

"How's that, Dr. Johnston?"

"Come to work for me. I can pay much more than you're making here."

"Excuse me for asking, but why would you offer me a job? You don't know me from Adam."

"I don't blame you for being skeptical. This must seem odd."

"A little."

"Frankly, I need someone rather quickly." Johnston leaned back on the bench and crossed his arms. "I consider myself a pretty good judge of character. I bet you're conscientious and good at what you do. Just as important, you need the work which increases the chance you'll make a loyal, dependable assistant. And finally, Mrs. Shealy, I'm also sympathetic to your circumstances. A woman alone and facing the trials you'll have down the road...this may help you."

The two were quiet as several visitors entered the facility.

"Tell me about the job," Gwen continued.

"First of all I no longer work for the C.D.C."

"What happened?"

"I resigned for professional reasons. I was there for several years but finally decided to pursue something new. Plan to go out on my own, delve into private research. I'm tired of doing things other people's way, following their rules and regulations. Don't want to ask anyone else's opinion or permission. If I want to take a day off, I'll do it."

"That's wonderful. Not many get that chance."

"Although I won't have any associates I'll still need someone with a nursing background. That's where you come in. I'd like to offer you the position."

"Like I said, I'm just an L.P.N."

"I realize that."

"What would I be doing?"

"I need someone to help with my administrative tasks. Things like maintaining clinical documentation, completing grant requests and some reporting."

"I don't have experience in some of those areas. Quite frankly, don't know if I'm qualified."

"Believe me, I wouldn't offer the job if I had any concerns. Now for the first few months you'll stay very busy but once things settle down, I might be willing to subsidize some additional training."

"I have to say that's real exciting. Just wish I was as sure…."

"Look Mrs. Shealy, you've got the proper nursing background and you'll pick up on the administrative duties quickly. What you don't know, you'll learn. Wouldn't it be nice to get away from the bedpans and suffering you see around here? Compared to the stress of your current position, this will be a walk in the park."

"Where's your office located?"

"Lake Lanier, I have a place right on the water. It's a two story house with several rooms in the basement. I've turned a couple of them into an office and lab."

"Lake Lanier? I'm sorry Dr. Johnston, but that just won't work. There's no way I could be that far from my family."

"You won't have to. There's more to my offer. Something I believe may help your situation immensely."

"My situation?"

"Yes, your family situation. You see, my house is very spacious. I'll be living downstairs and spending the majority of my time there. The upstairs has three extra bedrooms, completely furnished. It's very private and would be perfect for your family. The best part is you wouldn't have to leave them alone anymore." Dr. Johnston added, "It's a nice place, I'm sure you'd like it."

"I don't doubt that. It'd be far better than where we live now but I can't afford the rent."

"Don't worry about it. You can live rent free."

"I couldn't do that."

"Why not?"

"I just couldn't. It's a very generous offer, but I wouldn't feel right."

Johnston expected the sanctimonious response. "Mrs. Shealy, I'm not offering you the house just because of your family. This isn't charity." The doctor smiled attempting to ease her mind. "My motives aren't that noble. Living on the property will be a requirement for whoever's hired for the position. You see, I don't work normal hours. I'll be conducting my research at all times of the day. It just depends on when I'm engaged and productive. The hours will be long and the demands great. I need someone who'll be available at the drop of a hat. You might even have to give up some weekends."

"But free rent? I just don't know if…."

"Consider it part of your compensation package."

Gwen thought for a few moments. "I have health insurance here. It's real important for my family."

"Of course you'll need medical and dental benefits. That goes without saying. I'll take care of it." Then Johnston added, "Oh yes, then there's your salary. The position pays $65,000 a year. That's probably considerably more than what you're making here. With a free place to live and your insurance, I think it's a pretty attractive package."

"It's real generous," she agreed.

The foundation had been laid. All he needed was to back off and let the woman make the decision. "So, Mrs. Shealy, I believe we've covered everything. Can I assume you're interested?"

"Yes, of course I'm interested. You've given me a lot to consider."

"Good. Take some time and mull it over." He stood. "I really believe it'd be a good opportunity for you and your family. I know you'd be a great resource for me."

"Thanks. I appreciate your offer. If it's all right, I'd like to think about it and give you a call tomorrow."

"You've got my number."

Gwen watched as the doctor straightened his tie and walked away.

At home that evening, all Gwen thought about was the incredible offer. Opportunities like this didn't happen every day. A sizeable pay increase, a free place to live and insurance which meant everything for someone facing enormous medical expenses in the future. But most importantly she wouldn't have to leave her father and son alone. What other job would allow her to be home with them? Everything inside urged her to call and accept. What was she waiting for? "This should be an easy decision," she mumbled.

However a trace of uncertainty continued to gnaw within. Like an annoying fly, doubt kept flitting back. Barry Johnston was a well-respected, intelligent physician who'd worked at the C.D.C. for years. Other than that, what did she really know about him?

How would her family take the move? Would it be hard for them to adjust to a new home? Tyler would be taken from his comfort zone. He struggled enough with minor changes in his routine. How would this affect him? Would he...could he adapt?

Lord, help me. What should I do? she struggled.

Was this a chance to get out of their deteriorating neighborhood? Gwen remembered her father wandering away and the guilt for leaving him, testing fate when she knew the dangers. In the end, that was the deciding factor.

She dialed Johnston's number. "This is Gwen Shealy. Hope I'm not calling too late. I almost waited until tomorrow but …."

"It's quite all right, Mrs. Shealy," he assured her. "I'm a late night person. Must admit though, I didn't expect to hear from you so soon."

"Well, I've been thinking about your offer and wanted to get back with you."

Johnston sat smugly in his chair sipping a Dewars and water. "So what have you decided?"

"I'd like to accept."

"That's wonderful. I'm excited to hear it."

"At this point in my life, with my family situation, I think the opportunity's too great to pass up."

"I'm glad you feel that way. Why don't I call you back tomorrow and we'll finalize everything? How does that sound?"

"That sounds fine."

"Great, I'll talk to you then." He hung up and raked a hand through his thinning hair.

Barry Johnston walked to the liquor cabinet to freshen his drink. He sipped the scotch and reveled in this latest victory. Things were going just as planned. He had another specimen.

The easy part was done. Now he had to figure out how to conduct his experiments on the Savant without raising suspicions. The devious physician was confident he'd find a way to conceal his work, just like his ever-expanding bald spot.

CHAPTER 8

Tap...tap...tap. Roger Hall drummed a pencil on his desk. "Damn, what a long day," he mumbled staring at his computer monitor's screensaver where a beautiful white sand beach and azure water beckoned him to relax in a hammock strung between two palm trees.

Hall propped his feet on the desk and leaned back. The chair squeaked in protest. He was supposed to be researching a new assignment on the local drought but couldn't get motivated. His thoughts kept drifting back to Gwen Shealy and another unfinished story about the C.D.C.'s Surveillance Program on disabled children. For some reason he couldn't get the woman out of his mind.

A colleague from the Sales Department interrupted. "I see you're hard at work."

"Hey man, what's going on?"

"Up for lunch later?" the chubby salesman asked.

"Sorry, can't today. Too much to do," Hall replied through a wide-mouthed yawn, tossing his pencil onto the desk.

"Yeah, I can see that."

"Hey, I'm having a tough time concentrating. Supposed to be researching this drought piece but can't get into it."

"Maybe you need a break," he persisted. "I'm going to Fat Mac's Barbeque Shack. How about an early lunch?"

"See you're still eating healthy. How's that lifestyle change working for you?"

"Lasted about a week."

"About a week longer than I figured." Roger chuckled.

The salesman pulled out a tattered, worn cowhide wallet. "By the way, I got four tickets for tonight's Braves game. You want 'em?"

"Why aren't you going?"

"Mother-in-law's in town and the wife informed me we were going out for dinner."

"Take her to the game. Eat there."

"Don't think so. Baseball ain't her thing."

"Guess I see who wears the pants in the family."

"Yeah, I know my place. You know what they say—happy wife, happy life." He handed over the tickets.

"Man, these are great seats!" Roger exclaimed.

"Yup, first base side right behind the home dugout."

"Where'd you get them?"

"You know us sales weasels, always falling into this kind of stuff." Walking away he added, "Let me know if you change your mind about lunch."

Roger thought, *Wasn't Gwen Shealy's son a baseball fan?* He remembered the pictures hanging on the woman's living room wall. *Maybe they'd like to go.*

She hadn't responded about his article. He could follow-up and see if she'd decided to contribute, then offer the tickets. He dialed her home telephone.

"Hello," a male voice answered.

"May I please speak with Mrs. Shealy?"

"Not here. Not here."

"Is this Tyler?"

"Yes. Tyler. Tyler Shealy. Yes."

"This is Roger Hall. I was at your house a few days ago."

"Roger Hall. Brought Granddaddy home. Roger Hall."

"That's right. Listen, I need to speak with your mother. Is she available?"

"Not home. Not home."

"Do you know how I can get in touch with her?"

"770-679-9133. 770-679-9133."

"Great." The reporter quickly scribbled it on a pad. "Thanks."

The telephone went dead as the teenager abruptly hung up.

Roger dialed the number. "Gwen, this is Roger Hall from the A.J.C. We met the other evening when your father...."

"I remember you, Mr. Hall." A few awkward seconds passed before she asked, "How'd you get my cell number?"

"Called your house and Tyler gave it to me. Hope that's all right."

"I guess so," she stated guardedly.

"I'm sorry for bothering you again. Do you have a few minutes?"

"I'm at work, but I suppose."

"How's your father doing?"

"Daddy's fine. Thanks again for bringing him home."

"Glad I could help."

"What can I do for you, Mr. Hall?" she stated impatiently, needing to get back to her nursing rounds.

"You're supposed to call me Roger, remember?"

"Sorry." Her tone became frosty. "Hope you aren't calling about that piece for your paper because I'm really not interested. Just don't have the time and frankly I'm not real comfortable with it."

"I can't blame you. We didn't exactly start off on the best footing. You know, about the way I got your address and all."

"Yeah, I was a little upset about that."

Hoping to interject some humor, Roger asked, "Have you made up your mind on that legal matter?"

"Not sure what you're talking about."

"You were considering a lawsuit. Just wondering if I need to contact an attorney."

"No, you're both off the hook." She paused then added, "Wouldn't make much sense to sue my new employer."

"New employer? What are you talking about?"

"I'll be leaving Golden Years next week. Dr. Johnston offered me a job."

"He what?"

"He called and asked if I'd go to work for him."

"At the C.D.C.?"

"No, he resigned, going out on his own to do research."

"You're going to work for him?" Roger's suspicions were raised as he recalled his heated interview with the physician regarding the surveillance of disabled children.

"I am. So you don't have to worry about getting sued anymore," she joked. Her tone continued to soften.

"Thanks, that's a load off my mind."

They both chuckled politely.

"Well…guess I'd better get back to work," Gwen said. "Sorry about your story."

"Actually the story isn't the reason I called. I…uh…I was thinking…hope you don't take it the wrong way but…well, a buddy of mine gave me four tickets to the Braves game tonight. I remembered your son's a baseball fan and was wondering if you guys might be interested in going. Call it a peace offering."

"A peace offering or a bribe? I'm not going to change my mind about the article."

"Don't expect you to. Promise to leave my notepad at home. This is strictly social. I know it's short notice. If you've got other plans, I certainly understand."

"Well, Tyler would be thrilled. He really does like baseball."

"So you'll join me?"

"Sure, why not? Getting out of the house will be good for us."

"It'll be a late night. Game doesn't start until eight," Roger warned.

"We'll be fine." She added, "It's sure nice of you to ask."

"I'll pick you up around seven."

"That's good, we'll be ready."

The rejuvenated reporter jiggled the desktop mouse and the beach scene disappeared from the screen. Just as he began typing, a loud voice interrupted his thoughts. "Hall, get down here right now."

"Damn, what's the hurry?" Roger mumbled, grabbing a notepad before stepping down the aisle to the editor's office.

"I'm sending you and a photographer out to Lake Lanier."

"I haven't even started my article on the drought. We got plenty of time to get pictures of the lake levels."

"This ain't about that."

"What's going on?"

"They just dragged a woman's body out of the water," the editor quickly explained.

* * * * * *

A small media group had gathered where the body was pulled from the lake. Yellow tape stretched around a swath of shoreline. Police officers were stationed nearby to prevent curious onlookers from crossing. About thirty feet inside was a mound draped by a white sheet shielding it from discerning eyes.

While the cameraman jockeyed for a better vantage point, Roger spotted an acquaintance from Fox News. "Hi Celia, what'd I miss? Have they told you anything?"

"Hey Roger. Not much. Got to make us barracudas good and hungry before they throw us a little fishie. You know how it works."

"Figured out who it is?"

"Heard it was some Hispanic woman."

"Hispanic? In this area? How'd that happen? Didn't she know this part of Lake Lanier is only open to rich white folks?"

Celia laughed. "Bet the people over at The Point love having all this going on right around the corner."

Eagles Point was a huge inlet shaped like a balloon. Access to the cove was controlled through a narrow gap that only spanned a hundred yards before opening up to several miles of shoreline. The property had previously been owned by an individual but was eventually sold off to wealthy developers. Now all along the banks of the inlet were multi-acre lots with some of the most exclusive homes on Lake Lanier. Their well-furnished balconies overlooked the water where expensive boats bobbed up and down alongside private docks.

"Authorities know how long the body's been in the water?" Roger asked.

"Haven't heard. Rumor has it she was naked though, not a stitch of clothes. I'm guessing she was skinny dipping and drowned."

"Completely naked, huh? Now it's getting interesting."

"So a dead woman isn't intriguing unless she's stripped?"

"Sex sells," the tall, lanky reporter joked.

"Hold on, here comes a cop," Celia stated. "Maybe they're going to tell us something."

A representative from the sheriff's office walked forward, stopping in front of the journalists. The man turned his head and spit a nasty brown wad of tobacco juice. The chatter ceased as he addressed the group in a slow southern drawl. "I'll answer a few questions then ya'll gonna have to clear out so we can get the gurney in here for the body."

Hands shot into the air as the aggressive media shouted away.

"Folks, I can't understand if everybody's talkin' at once." He pointed at a woman representing a suburban newspaper.

"What time was the body discovered?" she asked.

"Long 'bout nine-twenty this mornin'."

"Is the victim a male or female?" someone else yelled.

"Female. Think she's Mexican or Hispanic anyways, don't know that for a fact."

"Anyone filed a missing person's report fitting that description?"

"None I know of." The man spit to the side then wiped the remnants of tobacco juice from his lips.

"Sir, we've heard rumors that the woman was naked. Can you confirm that?"

"Uh, yeah. That's right."

"Any signs of sexual abuse?"

The officer squirmed, slightly embarrassed at the question. Uncomfortable with the line of questioning, he said, "Okay, that's it. Ya'll gonna have to hold your questions 'til…."

A man from W.S.B. Television interrupted. "Were there any signs of foul play?"

The policeman looked over his shoulder and spit again, splattering tobacco juice on the ground.

The reporter persisted. "I was told there were ligature marks on her ankles and wrists. Can you confirm or deny that?"

"Sorry, I can't tell ya'll nothin' more. We're gonna have to wait for the coroner's report."

A chaotic burst of questions shot from the crowd. Holding up both hands to quiet the group, the officer said, "Folks, that's it. Our office'll let ya'll know when we have more. C'mon now, clear out'a here."

Several insistent reporters shouted again, but he was finished. "Clear the area! Now!"

Begrudgingly, the group moved away toward their vehicles.

Roger hopped in the van.

"Didn't give us much did he?" the A.J.C. photographer said as they pulled away.

"Not much to give," Roger answered. "Kind of interesting though. Hispanic woman, no missing person's report, buck-naked, in this part of Lake Lanier. Strange."

"Crazy ass world we live in. Nothing surprises me no more."

"Me either."

"You want to drive through somewhere and grab something to eat?"

"Sure."

"Where you want to go?"

"Doesn't matter to me, just make it quick. Need to get back and crank this story out. I'm going to a baseball game tonight."

* * * * * *

Gwen Shealy left work promptly at five o'clock. She turned the radio on catching the end of a news report on a drowning in Lake Lanier. At the same time another vehicle changed lanes cutting her off. "Sweet Jesus!" Gwen slammed on the brake narrowly avoiding the car's bumper. "Good Lord, what are you doing?" she shouted through the open window. The temperature seemed to rise as adrenaline pumped through her body.

Maybe she'd get lucky and traffic would be light. That hope quickly vanished as every vehicle within eyesight came to a complete stop. Eventually cars started inching forward until the congestion broke open. Finally she made it home.

Grabbing her purse, she crawled out while daintily tugging the sweaty scrubs from her butt cheeks.

"Yoo-hoo," shouted the seventy-two-year-old lady living next door.

"Hi, Mrs. Clayton. How's your day?"

"Fine Sweetie, just fine. Hot enough for you?"

"Yes, Ma'am."

"Hotter than blue blazes today." The old lady wore a big, floppy straw hat, shielding her face from the sun. "I was out this morning and saw your Daddy sittin' in that chair over yonder. I worried 'bout him. Thought he might stay out in the sun too long so I kept an eye on him."

Mrs. Clayton was the quintessential nosy neighbor, but Gwen was thankful. "I appreciate you watching after him."

"You're welcome, Sweetie. You wanna come see my new flower bed. Just planted my chrysanthemums today."

"I'd love to Mrs. Clayton, but I'm kind of in a rush. We're going to a baseball game tonight and I need to get ready. Maybe some other time?"

"Baseball game? My goodness, don't know how you young folks stay up so late."

"Well, I should go. See you later."

"Sure thing, Sweetie. You run along now and have a big time."

When Roger Hall arrived, the family was waiting patiently.

Tyler was wearing a Braves baseball cap and a white T-shirt. Despite the heat, he'd insisted on bringing a Braves jacket. Gwen talked to him, but when the Savant set his mind to something it was nearly impossible to dissuade him. So she'd compromised. "We'll take the jacket, but you can't wear it." Gwen stuffed it into a large canvas bag along with some bottled water, several packs of crackers and Juicy Fruit gum. Tyler's Albuterol inhaler was also carefully packed.

"Sorry I'm late," Roger apologized.

"Don't worry about it," Gwen said. "We just finished getting ready."

"Hi, Mr. Shealy. How're you doing?"

"Daddy, you remember Roger Hall. He brought you back home the other night."

The old man nodded.

Roger turned to Tyler and asked, "Are you ready to watch some baseball?"

Through a wad of gum, he answered, "Yes. Baseball. Braves baseball. Yes."

"That's right. High five." Roger raised his hand in the air.

Tyler ignored it, climbing into the back seat beside his grandfather. "High five. Bad number. Five," he repeated. The teen wiped his nose and began thumbing through a handful of baseball cards, announcing the statistics of each player.

"He doesn't like odd numbers," Gwen explained.

"I'll try and remember that." Roger then asked, "What's in the bag?"

"Just a few snacks."

"You didn't have to do that. They sell food at the park."

"I know but it's so expensive."

"Everything's on me tonight." He looked at the size of the bag. "You guys must be real hungry."

"Tyler's jacket is in there too."

"Don't think he'll be needing a coat tonight. It's over eighty degrees."

"I know but it's the only way I could keep him from wearing it."

"Okay…well…guess that makes sense."

Exchanging glances they smiled. "Not really," she admitted.

Once everyone was settled in, Roger headed toward the interstate. Taking the exit to Turner Stadium, he then turned onto Hank Aaron Drive and pulled into a parking lot five blocks from the stadium.

As the foursome walked past hordes of tailgaters, the distinctive smell of grilled hamburgers and hotdogs circulated through the evening air. Street vendors selling everything from giant sponge fingers to overpriced drinks yelled out, all trying to entice fans into purchasing their goods before entering the stadium. "T-shirts! Get your Braves jersey's here! Boiled peanuts! Hot boiled peanuts only a dollar!"

"Bald peanuts?" Tyler asked. "No hair. No hair. Peanuts don't have hair."

"No Hon, their boiled…not bald peanuts," Gwen explained.

They fought through the throngs of people toward the gate. Attendants ripped their tickets in half before allowing them through the turnstile and inside the beautiful confines of The Ted.

The group reached the entrance to the field as the National Anthem began playing. At the end of the tunnel a vast manicured green lawn lay before them. To the left was the baseball diamond, its corners marked by three white bags and a pentagonal home plate. The first and third base sides were outlined by perfect white lines. Uniformed umpires stood at attention, their hats removed while paying homage to the flag gently flapping from a breeze blowing in from right field.

The anthem came to a close and a roar erupted from the crowd as players burst from the dugout to take their positions on the field.

Tyler's usually impassive face radiated as he turned side to side drinking in the surroundings. Gwen embraced his special moment hoping it wouldn't end.

Noticing her expression, Roger asked "You all right?"

"Perfect. He's having a great time."

They made their way to four seats located directly behind the Braves' dugout. "Anybody for a dog?" Roger asked.

"Dogs not allowed," Tyler stated matter-of-factly. "No dogs. No dogs. Not allowed."

"You're right, I meant hotdog. Anybody hungry?"

"Yes. Hotdog. Meat by-products and fat flavorings with salt, garlic and paprika. Erythorbate and nitrate preservatives. Served on sliced bun." The boy never took his eyes from the diamond.

"Wish he hadn't told me that, but I'll get us one anyway."

Gwen laughed. "You need any help?"

"Nope. Stay here. I'll be right back."

She watched his lanky frame trot up the steps.

The game began and the first three Dodger batters were shut down by the Braves pitcher. In the bottom of the inning Atlanta had a runner on base before Roger returned with his arms full.

"How'd you carry all that?" Gwen reached out to grab a cardboard carrier with four Cokes.

"Talent," he responded while balancing another box filled with hotdogs and peanuts. The Braves coat was draped across Tyler's lap. "See you had to break out the jacket."

"Lord knows I choose my battles carefully. Learned a long time ago not to make a big deal out of little things."

"Sounds like a good philosophy. A lot of us could follow it."

"We can't thank you enough for all this."

"Don't be silly. I'm enjoying it as much as anyone."

"I doubt it, look at him." She nodded toward Tyler chewing on a hotdog while watching the game.

"Yeah, he looks pretty content." Roger took a sip of Coke then set the plastic cup underneath his seat. "You know I never asked the other night. And uh...please tell me if it's none of my business but did Tyler...? I mean was he born...?" he stuttered, searching for the right words.

"You're not gathering information for your article are you?"

"Absolutely not, I wouldn't do that."

She took a deep breath. "Tyler was born with Autism. Not sure how much you know, but it's a brain disorder. Autistic people can't function normally. They're constrained and have a tough time interacting with others. Autistics do the same thing over and over, sometimes to the point of being irrational."

"Kind of like Obsessive Compulsive Disorder?"

"In a way. They cling to strict routines and panic at any little change."

"That must make your life interesting."

"Just a might. Once his mind's made up there's no changing it. Take that jacket. As hot as it is, he insisted on bringing it and no amount of arguing was going to change his mind. Like a bulldog latched on to a bone."

Tyler excitedly spoke up. "Watch! Watch! Watch now!" He pointed toward the batter and sneezed several times. "Score. Score runs. Braves score now!"

The pitcher went into his wind-up and on the very next pitch, Chipper Jones smacked a homerun over the center field fence.

"Did he just predict that?" Roger looked toward Gwen.

She smiled, unable to respond over the roar of the crowd.

Tyler jumped up and began reciting statistics for the baseball player. "Larry Wayne Jones. Born April 24, 1972. Deland Florida. Drafted by Atlanta Braves in 1990, first round pick. First round pick. Life time batting average .310. Batting average .310. Career runs batted in 1375, 1375."

"Brain disorder or not, he's sharp as a tack," Roger yelled, competing with the home fan's cheers of enthusiasm.

Once the noise subsided Gwen continued. "His intelligence level's high but only about certain things. Tyler's got a condition called Savant Syndrome which rarely affects people with Autism."

"Don't Savants have some special abilities?"

"He's blessed with several. For instance a remarkable memory. Can tell you the batting average of any player in Major League Baseball. On the other hand he can't tie his shoes."

Roger glanced down at Tyler's untied tennis shoes. "Any others?"

Gwen hesitated before responding. "Yeah, sometimes it seems he has this ability to predict things like that homerun."

"You know that could've been a coincidence or just wishful thinking."

"Maybe. But it's not the first time." Gwen smiled and added, "It can be handy." Then she grew serious. "But it can be scary too. He spouts information all the time and is very insistent about most of it. I never really know when to take him seriously or when he's just being Tyler."

Roger thought about the responsibility of raising an autistic son while caring for a parent with Alzheimer's. The challenges Gwen faced every day were overwhelming. "Boy, you've got your hands full. How do you handle everything so easily?"

"Easily? Are you kidding me? I'm a mess most of the time."

"Not from what I've seen."

"We get by, but I worry what'll happen with Daddy."

"That's a tough predicament all right."

"And it's getting tougher. If you hadn't come along the other day, Lord knows what could've happened."

"At some point won't you have to put him into a nursing facility or something?"

"Probably. Thank God this new job with Dr. Johnston came along and bought me a little time."

"How's that?"

"I'll be able to work from home, won't have to leave them alone anymore. It's the main reason I took the position."

"That's great!"

"Course I'll have to move the family but it'll be worth the hassle."

"You're moving? Where to?"

"Lake Lanier."

"Nice area. Matter of fact, I was just up there around noon covering a story." Roger lowered his voice. "Some woman drowned."

"I heard about it on the radio. How terrible!"

A controversial play at first base caused the partisan fans to boo. A deep, dull roar smothered the stadium. The Braves' manager raced from the dugout and planted himself in front of the umpire pointing his finger and yelling. He was promptly ejected and play eventually resumed on the field.

"Anyway, sounds like a great opportunity. Must've gotten a big raise. Housing around the lake's expensive."

"Oh, I couldn't afford a place of my own. We'll be living with Dr. Johnston." Gwen took a sip of Coke. "It's part of my compensation."

"You're living in the same house with Johnston?"

"It bothered me a little at first, but he claims we'll have our privacy. His office and bedroom are in the basement. We'll be upstairs."

"What do you know about this guy?"

"He's a physician and held an executive position at the C.D.C."

"Just be careful." Roger remained silent about the confrontation he'd had with Johnston.

Tyler's monotone voice suddenly broke into their conversation. "Pee. Bathroom. Pee."

"I've got to go too," Roger stated. "C'mon, we'll stop and get some nachos on the way back."

"Nachos. Chips, cheese, Jalapeno peppers. Jalapeno pepper from the species Capsicum Annuum originating in Mexico. Named after Xalapa, Veracruz. Chili pepper has warm, burning sensation when eaten. Hot. Nachos hot. No Nachos." Tyler stood to make his way toward the aisle.

"Okay, we'll get whatever you want." They headed up the steps to find the closest restroom.

By the seventh inning stretch the Dodgers were pounding the Braves. Many fans had taken their enthusiasm and left. However Tyler wouldn't hear of it. Gwen tried to persuade him to go, but he refused.

"Game not over," he insisted every time she mentioned it. "Game not over."

"I'm sorry Roger, but do you mind staying?"

"Not at all. We'll stay until they roll the tarp on the field if he wants."

"Don't say that too loud. He might take you up on it."

Roger settled back and stretched his long legs over the back of the empty seat in front of him.

When the game finally ended they made their way out of the ball park and down the dimly-lit street toward the parking lot. It only took a few minutes to get away from the stadium traffic as many had left early.

"Tomorrow morning's going to come awful early," Roger said, passing a slow-moving minivan.

"Afraid so, but it was worth it. This was such a neat experience for him," she said, glancing over a shoulder toward Tyler and Ernest, both already asleep in the back. Roger's strong jaw was illuminated by oncoming headlights. "You were very sweet to invite us."

Without taking his eyes from the road, he smiled.

He has a nice profile, Gwen thought as she leaned back in her seat. *And a good heart.*

Roger parked in front of the house.

"Wake up you guys, we're home." Gwen stated softly as she turned toward the backseat.

"Wh...what? Where...where in hell are we?"

"We're home, Daddy, from the baseball game."

The old man fumbled to find the door handle. "God damn it, where's the blasted knob!"

Roger stepped around the car and opened the door for him.

Ernest pushed the glasses up the bridge of his nose then struggled to get out. His inflexible body wasn't able to maneuver within the cramped Honda. "God damn these Jap cars. Ain't nothin' but tin cans with wheels."

Tyler was still asleep, oblivious to the commotion. "Wake up Hon, let's go inside and get to bed." Gwen tapped his knee which was crunched against the back of the driver's seat. His body was awkwardly slumped on the door with his head against the window.

"I'll help get everyone inside," Roger offered.

"That's all right, we can manage from here." Gwen responded. "It's late and you probably need to get going."

Roger ignored her and helped Ernest. His hand firmly held the elderly man's forearm as he shuffled toward the front door. Gwen and Tyler followed closely behind.

Once inside, Tyler grabbed his Braves jacket and went to his bedroom. Gwen led Ernest to his, while Roger waited on the sofa.

She soon returned, tired but content.

"Everybody get settled in okay?"

"Yeah, I think so. They were both worn out."

"How about you?"

"I stay that way around here."

"Guess I should go, let you get some sleep." He stood to leave.

"Would you like a cup of coffee? May help you stay awake on the drive home. It's the least I can do after taking us to the game."

"That's awfully nice, but it's late and I don't want to put you out."

"No trouble at all. I'd like one myself. Be nice to just sit and relax a little before bed."

The two locked eyes for a few brief seconds.

"Are you sure?"

"Why don't you sit down and I'll be back in a jiffy." She stepped away to the kitchen.

A few minutes later Gwen returned with two steaming mugs. "It's just instant, hope that's okay."

"Perfect. Thanks." He took one of the cups.

They sat next to each other on the couch.

"Tonight was a real treat for Tyler. He doesn't get out much."

"How about you?"

"What about me?" she asked.

"Did you have a good time, or was it just another chore for your family?"

"When they have a good time...well, then I do too."

"Do you ever take any time for yourself, do what you enjoy?"

"Oh heavens, I don't know. It's hard enough just to keep up with Daddy and Tyler." She paused before adding, "That's what I enjoy, taking care of them."

"Can I ask you a personal question?"

"Sure, why not."

"Tyler's dad. Is he still around, still...?"

"No. He left when Tyler was little. Not part of our lives anymore," Gwen replied sharply and quickly.

"I'm sorry."

"Nothing to be sorry for. It's over."

"Shouldn't have brought it up. None of my business anyway."

"What about you, Roger? Have there been any special women in your life?" she boldly asked.

"Had a serious relationship in college. Jenny and I planned to get married, but after graduation we got jobs and grew apart. Both too worried about our careers I guess."

"Do you ever see her anymore?"

"We've talked on a few occasions but never could find time to get together. Just wasn't meant to be. Anyway, all of a sudden I look in the mirror and I'm in my forties." He sighed. "Truth is, never found anyone that'd have me." He lifted his mug to take a sip of coffee.

"That can't be. I think Jenny missed out. You're a very handsome man with a lot to offer."

He blushed. "I've been called a lot in my days but never handsome."

"Well you are. Jenny or any other woman would be lucky to have someone like you."

"Bet you say that to all your gentlemen friends."

"You've got to be kidding me. What gentlemen friends?"

"Are…are you seeing anyone?"

"Heavens no. Don't get me wrong, I'd like to meet somebody one day but don't know if it'll happen. My family has to come first right now."

"Aren't we a pair? Look at us, letting our lives just drift by."

"Lord knows time sure does slip away," she agreed.

"Well, you know, maybe it's not too late, Gwen."

"What do…?"

Roger interrupted by leaning over and gently kissing her.

CHAPTER 9

After years of living in the same low income rental, the family packed and moved to Dr. Barry Johnston's spacious house on Lake Lanier. The physician arranged every aspect of the move including having most of their modest belongings stored.

The new accommodations offered a vast improvement over their living conditions in the city. The change also gave Gwen an opportunity to work at home, close to her family.

A dinette sat in a nook where a huge bay window overlooked the lake. The mid-morning sky was crystal clear and blue. Not a cloud in sight. Over a late breakfast Gwen asked, "How you doing this morning, Daddy?"

The old man seemed reasonably alert. But in the throes of Alzheimer's, his capacities tended to fade in and out like waves washing ashore before retreating out to sea.

"Fair to midland," he responded without looking up from a plate of scrambled eggs and grits.

"Sleep all right last night?"

"Woke up and be damned if I could get back to sleep. Lay there wide awake."

"Maybe you'll do better once you get used to this place."

"Where in hell are we anyways?" The man raised his head and looked around.

"Daddy, this is where we're living now. We're staying with Dr. Johnston on Lake Lanier. I'm working for him."

Tyler spoke up, parroting information he'd read on the internet. "Lake Lanier. Chattahoochee River dammed by United States Corps of Engineers. 1957. Created Lake Lanier. Northwest Georgia. Thirty-eight thousand acres. Six hundred ninety-two miles of shoreline."

"Who's this Johnston fella?" a confused Ernest asked.

"Dr. Johnston owns this house. He lives downstairs," Gwen patiently repeated.

In a rare moment of humor, Ernest cracked, "Shoot, that's right. I'm gettin' so damn old even my memories got whiskers, least the ones I can still conjure up."

"This place will start feeling like home before long. Just think, I won't have to leave you and Tyler anymore."

The elderly man's brow wrinkled as he slowly pushed away from the table and leaned back. The flash of normalcy passed and his eyes projected uncertainty. The hollow stare didn't go unnoticed. Gwen knew he'd drifted away once again.

* * * * * *

Johnston sat in the basement office planning the next phase of his experiment when the cell phone rang. "Hello."

"Hey Doc. Dis is Manny. Open de friggin' gate and let me in, Amigo."

"Do you have my money?"

"We talk inside."

"I need more than talk. What about that additional compound you were supposed to send? It's late. I need those chemicals!" Johnston demanded.

"You let in or not? Friggin' hot out here."

"The code's 2-2-6-2. Punch the keypad, the gate will open."

"*Muchas gracias.*" Manny pushed the buttons and was rewarded with a high-pitched beep followed by a mechanical hum as the iron barrier swung open.

Johnston hurried upstairs to wait at the front door.

Moments later the Latino entered the house. "Nice crib. You do good, Doc."

"Come with me and keep your mouth shut." Johnston led him to the family having breakfast. "Gwen, this is Manny, a business associate of mine from New Jersey. He helps negotiate prices with my chemical suppliers."

"Pleasure to meet you, Manny. We'll probably be working together."

"*Bueno.*" Manny eyed the woman's shapely figure which was exposed in a pair of shorts. He reached up to scratch his scraggly goatee.

"Gwen's my new assistant. She'll be helping with my research." Pointing toward the old man, the doctor continued. "This is Mr. Shealy, Gwen's father and over there's Tyler, her son. They're staying with me."

The Latino nodded.

"Don't let us interrupt you. Please finish your breakfast. Manny and I have some business to resolve downstairs."

Gwen eagerly offered, "Can I help?"

"I appreciate it but not right now. It's probably best if we discuss it privately. You know how these vendor arrangements can be."

She smiled politely but was confused. Wasn't she supposed to be involved in this part of his practice?

Johnston attempted to appease her. "Maybe Tyler would like to take a swim. After breakfast, why don't you go down to the dock and enjoy the lake for a while. I guarantee things will get busy soon and you won't have a lot of free time. Better take advantage of it now."

"If you're sure I can't help."

"No swim. No swim," Tyler said anxiously. "Drown. Drown. Death caused by suffocation when liquid interrupts body's absorption of oxygen. Hypoxia, acidosis leading to cardiac arrest."

"It's okay," Gwen assured the teen. "You can just wade in. Now go put on a pair of shorts. All you do is sit around. A little exercise will be good for you." She winked at the men. "We'll be out of your way in a jiffy."

"No. No swim!" Tyler repeated in an elevated, agitated tone. "Internet. Internet after breakfast. Not swim." The teenager stood and began frantically pacing the floor. "Want to go home. Go home. This not home. Go home. Internet always after breakfast, not swim." His arms and legs flailed randomly. He was struggling with the change in routine

"Calm down, Hon. We'll hook up your computer this afternoon," Gwen promised.

Johnston turned and headed down the staircase into the basement as the teen continued ranting.

"What his story?" Manny asked as they entered the laboratory.

"You just witnessed a potential candidate for my experiments. The boy's a Savant."

"You tell 'bout Savant last time we meet, right?"

"Yes. He has a unique way of thinking."

"What de hell he talkin' 'bout? Friggin' drownin'?" Manny chuckled at the odd behavior.

"What you witnessed was an example of the boy's incredible memory. Tyler's intellectually handicapped but has some amazing mental abilities. The boy can read and remember anything. He may not understand but can spout facts back word for word. He doesn't possess normal reasoning but can recall the most trivial details. It's truly a remarkable trait."

"So good specimen for de project?"

"That's right and the old man's another," Johnston added.

"He Savant too?"

"Of course not. Savants are rare. He's got Alzheimer's and is losing his ability to remember."

"Two for price of one."

"A perfect pair. One can remember anything while the other forgets everything."

"And de woman?"

"What about her?"

"You got plan?" Manny smirked.

"Exactly what are you implying?"

"Not bad-lookin' bitch. Know what I do, my Amigo, if I was you."

"You're not me."

"You like women don't you, Doc? Rope not swing other way?"

Johnston leveled a glare at the Latino silently conveying his disgust at the insinuation.

"Not questionin' manhood, only messin' with you. What de script for bitch? She not stand by while experiment on family."

"Let me worry about the woman."

"I like to experiment on her." Manny rubbed his unkept beard again.

"You're a swine. And by the way, when are you going to shave that horrid thing off?"

"You jealous I got more hair on chin dan you got on bald head."

While Johnston fumed, Manny leaned forward and continued taunting, "C'mon, what de plan? You goin' waste her? Maybe she have accident...like woman dey find in lake."

"What?"

"Is shame. Was Latino girl."

"Smart-ass punk. You don't know what you're talking about."

"Know 'nough."

"You need to keep your mouth shut."

"Hope you not threaten me. Be big friggin' mistake," Manny said menacingly.

The arrogant physician wasn't about to let some young hoodlum get the better of him. "Listen, I don't give a damn about you. All I care about is this project."

"Police roaming 'round like fleas on dog ass. Can't afford no friggin' screw up so boss pull plug."

"He what?"

"Word come down. You hold off on de experiments."

"You're telling me how to run my project?"

"Not how, when. For now you chill."

Johnston deplored complications and unexpected obstacles. But more than that he hated being told what to do. "For how long?"

"Will let know."

"What do you propose I do in the meantime?"

"You smart Amigo. Figure out."

"What about my money, that additional compound?" the physician asked.

"Doc, you not listenin'. De friggin' experiment on hold. No money, no chemicals. Nothin'."

Johnston shook his head. "You can't be serious."

"As friggin' heart attack. Need to get through dat bald head you not in charge."

Desperate, Johnston asked, "Who is? I need to speak with them directly."

"Sorry. Not part of deal."

"Give me their God-damn name and phone number."

"No can do."

"But it doesn't make sense. I'm assuming we all want this project to succeed. There's so much to be gained. If you could only arrange…."

"Sorry, not happenin'. I be in touch." Manny walked away.

An angry Barry Johnston followed him upstairs. "When? When will you know something?"

The Puerto Rican moved to the bay window overlooking the lake. Gwen and Ernest sat on the dock gazing out at the reservoir while Tyler splashed around in knee-deep water. "When boss man say so. I talk to him when get back."

"Talk's cheap. We need action now! I'm tired of waiting!"

Manny smirked. "Look on bright side, Doc. Got good scenery while waitin'. Bitch not bad lookin', nice ass." He turned and left the lake house.

Angry and disheartened, Barry Johnston stood at the bay window gazing out toward the lake.

That damn Angelina ruined everything, he thought, wishing the Mexican woman had minded her own business. With the police nosing around, those supporting the project had cold feet and wanted to suspend the experiment.

What am I going to do? Should I proceed? I've got to make a decision. After careful thought, Johnston concluded he'd come too far to abandon the plan. There were two perfect subjects living under his roof. He would move ahead with the research regardless of what Manny or anyone else dictated. So what if the chemicals had been cut off? He still had enough to start on Tyler. But how could the drug be administered without raising suspicion?

And the woman? What am I going to do with Gwen Shealy? He was prepared to dispose of her, but he had to be careful. It could be disastrous if more suspicions were raised.

Despite his misgivings, the confident physician still felt he could outwit them all…his benefactor and the local authorities. Determined to clear every hurdle, he would go forward.

His attention soon focused on the pier.

There hadn't been much rain and the lake level was considerably lower than normal. It had dropped several feet leaving a dry, rocky border around the shoreline, separating it from the wooded banks.

Ernest lounged quietly in a chair, staring blankly out over the reservoir.

Tyler waded further out into the water. "That's far enough," Gwen warned. He'd never learned to swim. Childhood experiences like summer camp, sleepovers and sports just weren't feasible with his disabilities. Although not at fault, she still harbored guilt about what he'd missed.

In up to his chest, the teenager turned and began moving back toward shore. "Rocks. Hurt feet. Hurt feet."

A few boats sped across the lake's rippled surface. Others sat anchored while people fished or swam in the cool, soothing water.

Gwen reached into her pocket and pulled out a vibrating cell phone. "Hello."

"Hey, this is Roger. Hope I'm not interrupting anything."

"Not at all. How are you?"

"Fine thanks. Just wanted to call and see if you guys got settled okay."

"Yeah, we made it. Everything's unpacked or stored."

"Good, glad to hear it. How's your Dad and Tyler?"

"It's early but I think they'll be fine once everybody gets used to the new place. They're still adjusting, but I'm around and that should make it easier."

"How's the job with Johnston going?"

"To tell the truth I haven't done much yet. Dr. Johnston says he's trying to get things set up and will let me know when he needs help. Between you and me, feel kind of guilty not doing anything."

"Sounds like a sweet deal. Wouldn't complain too much," Hall joked.

"Guess you're right."

"So what're you doing with all your spare time?"

"Just sitting out on the pier, enjoying the lake. How about you? What are you up to?"

"I'm watching some pretty woman sunbathe."

"Oh really?"

"Yeah." Then he added, "She looks a lot like you."

"What?"

"Look straight ahead. See the red boat headed your way?"

"Is that you?" The sun glistened off the water as she squinted to see.

"Okay if we dock and join you guys for a few minutes?"

"Sure, permission to come ashore," Gwen playfully responded.

An open bow Stingray with two men aboard soon glided up to the pier. Roger yelled from the passenger seat, "How's everybody?"

"Hey there."

"This is Gene. He owns the boat. The newspaper's paying him to chauffer me around while I report on that woman who drowned. Guess there was some suspicious bruises around her legs and arms like she'd been tied up or something. From what I'm hearing they've got some other evidence too but been real quiet about it."

"That's scary."

"You know the body surfaced not far from here." Roger turned and pointed out toward the lake.

She glanced toward Tyler and Ernest. "Can we talk about something else?"

The reporter understood and nodded agreement.

107

In an effort to change the subject Gwen stated, "Tyler sure had a great time the other night at the baseball game. It was awfully nice of you to take us."

"I'm glad he enjoyed it."

"We all did," she replied while pushing her windblown hair behind her ears.

"Yeah, me too."

Tyler mumbled under his breath, "Not nice. Bad."

"What'd you say, Hon?"

"Roger Hall. Bad," he repeated.

"Tyler, that's rude!"

"Hey Buddy, what's wrong? I thought we were friends. Maybe we'll have to go to another Braves game sometime. What do you think?"

The teen jerked and looked away.

"I'm really sorry, Roger," Gwen apologized.

"Don't worry about it." Then he added, "Wish I could stay longer but got to get back to work. The paper's only renting the boat for a couple hours."

On cue the driver turned the key prompting a low rumble from the engine.

"Sure good to see you again," Gwen offered, disappointed to see him go.

"Hope I didn't interrupt your morning."

"Not at all, I'm glad you happened by."

The reporter winked. "Got to be honest, I really didn't."

A smile spread across her face.

The Evinrude revved and the boat sped away, skimming through the cove.

Gwen waved and then turned back to Tyler who was slapping the lake's surface and yelling, "Roger Hall bad man. Bad man."

"Hon, why would you say such a thing? Don't you remember, he helped Granddaddy get home that night and took us to a Braves game?"

"Bad. Roger Hall bad," the Savant repeated before letting out an ugly cough.

"He's not a bad man, so quit saying that," she admonished wondering what had prompted the outburst.

"Hey Gwenny," Ernest called out, demanding her attention.

"Yes Daddy, you need something?"

"When we goin' home?"

"You mean back inside the house?" She pointed to the doctor's estate.

"We're stayin' there?"

"This is home now, Daddy. We talked about it a little while ago."

"Damn, that's right. Now I recollect."

Gwen knew that Alzheimer's was caused by deposits of plaque in the brain, not changes in the environment. However her heart broke thinking she might have aggravated his situation by uprooting the family. Maybe the move had been too much and caused him to withdraw even more.

"It'll be okay, just think of all the time we'll spend together. You're going to love it here…."

Suddenly, Tyler began hacking and gasping. Every expulsion of irritating air was followed by a desperate attempt for more.

"Daddy, get up. We've got to go inside now!" Wading into the water, she put a supporting arm around his shoulders and began leading him toward the house.

Dr. Johnston, who'd been observing from the bay window saw them coming. As they got closer he detected the teen's struggling cough and hurried to open the door.

"He needs help!" Gwen blurted out.

"What happened?"

"He's having a bad asthma attack!"

The doctor helped him into a chair while Gwen ran to the medicine cabinet for an inhaler. Several years earlier when Tyler started having the attacks, the pediatrician had prescribed Albuterol.

Dr. Johnston knelt down and spoke in a soothing tone. "Listen to me. You need to slow down your breathing."

Panting, the teenager responded, "Can't…can't…breathe."

Gwen shoved the inhaler into his mouth and pushed down. "Take a breath," she ordered.

Tyler's gasping slowed and his color gradually improved, but a high-pitched wheezing persisted.

"His symptoms have gotten worse since we moved. I'm taking him to the emergency room," she stated.

"No…hospital," Tyler uttered. "No…hospital."

"No use taking any chances," Johnston agreed, ignoring the Savant's plea. More worried about his project than the teenager, he watched as they left. His mind raced. If something was seriously wrong with the boy, he had an alternative. Ernest could just as easily become his specimen.

On the way to the E.R., Gwen appeared in control. But hidden below her cool facade was complete turmoil.

"No…hospital. No…hospital," Tyler repeated. "Over 200,000… people die annually…hospital errors. People…die. People…die. Super bug…infections killed 10,000…in hospitals last year. Hospital… infections. No…hospital. No…hospital."

Tyler's continued ranting didn't help his breathing…or Gwen's nerves.

* * * * * *

They sat anxiously in the waiting room. A young woman tried to comfort a colicky infant who cried relentlessly. Two Mexican men spoke loudly in Spanish. One had a blood stained rag wrapped around his hand. Others sat quietly while a few dozed, an ominous indication of how long they'd been waiting.

"Any better, Tyler?"

"Hard…to…breathe. Hard…to…breathe." The wheezing persisted.

A nurse periodically peeked in and called out a name. Each time a ripple of hope washed across the remaining patients wondering if they'd be next.

Gwen approached the front desk. "How much longer will it be? My son needs to see a doctor. He's having trouble breathing."

"Name please."

"Shealy. Tyler Shealy."

The nurse looked at the patient roster. "It shouldn't be much longer, Ma'am."

Tyler was eventually admitted. The emergency room doctor took his vitals and immediately ordered a breathing treatment. A clear plastic mask was placed over his mouth and nose while a vat pumped medicated steam through an attached tube. After the treatment, the teen began breathing normally. Tired from the traumatic afternoon he relaxed and lay back on the examination table.

The doctor motioned for Gwen to step aside. "I believe he should be kept overnight. We need to determine if he's developed any new sensitivities."

"What are you going to do?"

"I've ordered some tests for tomorrow morning. We'll scratch some different allergens into his skin and watch the sites. If any redness or swelling occurs we'll know he's allergic to it."

"What if something else shows up?" Gwen asked.

"Let's wait and see how the tests turn out then we'll talk about it. I wouldn't worry too much."

"I need to stay with him. I'll also need a cot for my father. He can't be left alone," she insisted.

Ernest sat in the corner, unaware and lost in his own world.

"We'll take care of it. I'll have someone assist you," the physician replied.

Tyler was soon resting comfortably in a hospital bed.

Gwen called Barry Johnston to update him on their situation. "Tyler's breathing is better now. They've admitted him and will run some tests tomorrow morning. We'll be staying the night."

"Tests for what?"

"New allergies."

"I see. Well, let me know if there's anything I can do."

"Budgie needs to be fed and watered. I hate to bother you, but can...?"

"Don't give it another thought. I'll take care of the bird."

"Thanks, I appreciate it."

"Call tomorrow and let me know how the boy's doing."

* * * * * *

The next morning, a nurse came to take Tyler for tests. "Go home," he argued as Gwen tried to get him into the wheelchair.

The Savant refused to sit down. He flung his arms wildly and defiantly screamed, "No. No. Go home."

"Please Hon, they won't hurt you, I promise. Calm down."

Tyler ignored her pleading and stormed wildly toward the door. They finally caught him in the hallway, each grabbing an arm and leading him back into the hospital room.

"Go home. Go home," he continued to shout, still flailing away.

"Stay with him. I'll be back in a minute," the nurse instructed. She returned with a burley male orderly.

"What are you going to do?" Gwen asked.

"We need to give him a mild sedative. It'll calm him and allow us to complete the procedure."

The man grabbed and held the teen tightly while the shot was quickly administered. Tyler soon relaxed and was wheeled away, the orderly still by his side.

As Gwen waited anxiously in the hospital room, a familiar face appeared at the door. "Dr. Johnston? What are you doing here?"

"Hope I'm not intruding." He handed her a bag of bagels. "Brought you folks something to eat. Hospital food isn't the best."

"How thoughtful."

"I don't suspect you know anything yet."

"No, they just took him for testing. Said it would probably be a while."

Not willing to wait, Johnston glanced at his Cartier watch, "Sorry to rush off but I've got an errand. Give the lad my best."

"Thanks for coming by...and the bagels." She put the bag on a stand next to the bed.

"Please let me know as soon as you hear anything." Johnston turned and left.

Later, the doctor spoke with Gwen about Tyler's skin tests. They'd revealed a new reaction to mold. "I'm sure the drought and extreme heat haven't helped matters," he elaborated.

"What can we do about it?"

"We'd like to start your son on immunotherapy."

As a L.P.N., Gwen was familiar with the long-term treatment for allergies. A series of injections containing a small amount of the offending allergen is administered. Over time the dosage is increased to help desensitize the body. "How often will he have to take the shots?"

"He'll be on a strict schedule, probably once a day at first. The frequency usually decreases after a few weeks. But there's a possibility he may have to continue the treatment for several months. At first the injections need to be provided in a setting capable of treating anaphylaxis, so you'll have to schedule them with your primary physician. Once it's determined he's not at risk, we can look at giving the shots at home."

The thought of dragging Tyler to a doctor's office every day wasn't appealing, but she didn't have a choice.

The doctor continued. "His symptoms certainly won't disappear overnight. Some people don't see improvement for a while. Of course there are those who must continue the injections indefinitely. It just depends on the individual."

How was Gwen going to fit another obligation into her stressful life? More importantly how was Tyler going to react to this change in his daily routine?

* * * * * *

That evening at home, she discussed the diagnosis and treatment with Barry Johnston. "They'll have to give Tyler the injections at the doctor's office so they can monitor him for adverse reactions. I know it will really upset him but it needs to be done." Then she nervously added, "I hope this won't impact my availability. I'm going to be running him back and forth for a while."

As Johnston listened, a plan formulated. "Maybe I can help."

"What do you mean?"

"You know I could give the shots here. That way you won't have to take him to a strange place where he's traumatized."

"I guess it's an option, but are you willing to do that?"

"Certainly. I'm sure the injections could be safely administered and monitored. Between the two of us we could handle any emergency." He added nonchalantly, "Just a suggestion."

"That'd be wonderful if you don't mind. It sure would be a lot easier on Tyler."

"Glad to help."

"Thanks so much, Dr. Johnston. I really appreciate it."

Barry Johnston nodded and walked downstairs to his laboratory. *What a convenient inconvenience*, he thought. The perfect solution just presented itself. Allergy shots! With the remaining compound on hand, he could easily substitute it into the Savant's injections and begin his tests immediately. No one would ever suspect.

CHAPTER 10

Early the next day, Manny left Atlanta Hartsfield Jackson Airport on a flight to Newark. After landing he hailed a taxi for Midtown. During the ride over the Hudson River, the street-smart Latino sat quietly in the back thinking about his conversation with Barry Johnston. The message of a change in plans had been delivered, yet for some reason he doubted the headstrong neurologist would comply. And that could be a problem.

The cabbie navigated through the late morning traffic, eventually arriving at a tall office building on East 55th Street. Manny entered the complex and walked directly to a bank of elevators where a crowd of professionals waited. His jeans and sneakers were out of place in a sea of expensive business suits, all perfectly fitted to some not so perfect bodies.

A subtle bell announced the arrival of the elevator. The door opened and the crowd quickly stepped inside. Those closest to the front began pushing buttons as passengers announced their destinations. "Twelve please…fourth floor…hit nine please." Manny reached through the group and pushed sixteen. The doors closed and the elevator began its journey upward. After several brief stops it finally reached the sixteenth floor.

The Latino stepped out and turned toward two large wooden doors at the end of the corridor. Short of the entrance he stopped and pulled a cell phone from his pocket.

"Yes," a deep, solemn voice answered.

"Is Manny. Need to talk."

"Why are you calling me on this number? I thought we agreed to limit our communication, especially on my cell."

"Is important."

"It better be."

"Got friggin' problem down south."

The man squirmed in his chair. "Where are you?"

"Outside de office at elevators."

"You're here! What part of no contact don't you understand?"

"Understand 'nough, 'specially 'bout shit not goin' down like you want. Only doin' job."

A long pause ensued. "We can't meet here. I can't afford to be associated with you...or with Georgia."

"Want to talk or not?"

Again the connection fell silent. Finally the executive reluctantly responded, "All right. There's a small establishment called Mia's Pizzeria on the 400 block of East 64th. Puerto Ricans eat pizza don't they?"

"Bet friggin' ass. Eat cat turd if 'nough cheese on it."

"Meet me there at two o'clock, after the lunch crowd."

"Dis a classy joint?"

"No. They may even allow you in," the executive jabbed.

"Don't worry 'bout me. If you buyin' I get in."

The call went dead.

"Son a' bitch," Manny muttered under his breath, heading back to the elevators.

That afternoon the Latino sat in a secluded booth at Mia's Pizzeria. A short, plump waitress with a pretty face hurried over. "Hi there, I'm Luci." She handed him a menu. "Something to drink?"

"You got Corona?"

"I'm sorry but we don't carry Mexican beer here. We're an Italian restaurant. Is there another brand you'd like?"

"Just bring Miller."

"Sure thing. I'll be right back." The young woman hurried away.

The enticing smell of freshly baked dough filled the air.

The waitress soon returned carrying a frosty mug and a longneck bottle. "Have you decided what you want yet?" she asked, pouring the beer into the mug.

"Waitin' on Amigo."

"Sure thing. I'll check back in a bit."

He lifted the beer to take a drink…and waited.

Several minutes later, the waitress returned noting a nearly empty mug. "Can I bring you another cold one?"

Frustrated, Manny said, "Yeah and number two, extra cheese and mushrooms."

"What size?"

"Make large in case my Amigo shows."

"Tired of waiting?" The young woman sympathetically smiled, sensing his impatience.

"Is all good, more pie for me."

"If your friend doesn't make it, maybe I'll sit and have a piece with you." She winked before leaving the table.

Finally a man in his fifties approached the booth. "All right, I'm here. Now what's so important?"

"You late," Manny grumbled.

"I got detained at the office. You understand I'm sure."

"Yeah, my time not important. Not like big business man."

"I'm not here to quarrel. That would waste our time, now wouldn't it? You said there was a problem in Georgia. We both have a vested interest in what happens with our physician colleague."

"What dis 'we' shit? I just go between. You got lot more to lose dan me."

"That's not entirely true, Manny. I'm paying you quite handsomely for your assistance. You're very involved. As a matter of fact you play a very important role."

The waitress returned with a longneck beer in one hand and a large pizza in the other. "Here you go." She set them on the table, pushing the bottle toward Manny. "I see your friend's finally arrived." The young woman looked toward the newcomer. "Can I get you something to drink, Sir?"

Noticing the name tag, he replied. "Yes Luci, thank you. Could I get a large salad with Italian dressing on the side and a bottle of water?"

"Sure thing. Coming right up."

"You not eat pizza, drink beer with me?"

"That sort of thing would negate the effects of my exercise routine, defeat the purpose," the health-conscious executive responded. He turned to look at the other patrons scattered about the restaurant, ensuring none were close enough to overhear. "All right, let's get to the point. What's going on in Georgia?"

"Johnston off de reservation."

"You conveyed my message?"

"Word for friggin' word. Told him no chemicals comin' and need to circle for while, let heat cool."

"Did he understand?"

"He heard, don't think bought in."

The normally cool and collected businessman became irritated as his face reddened with anger. "He doesn't have a choice in the matter."

Manny pulled a piece of pizza to his plate stringing cheese across the table. "Somethin' else you not be happy 'bout."

The man paused to think. "He was involved with that Hispanic woman's death, wasn't he?"

"Bet my brown Puerto Rican ass."

The man slammed a fist down on the table, sloshing beer out of the mug. "What was he thinking? He does something totally unnecessary that could jeopardize our entire project. Now both the authorities and the local community have their antennas up. For such a supposedly intelligent man he certainly does some ignorant things."

Manny sat quietly listening to the rant. Although knowing his anger was justified, the young Latino enjoyed seeing the normally stoic businessman lose control.

The waitress appeared with a salad and a bottle of Aquafina. "Here you go," she placed them on the table. "Can I get you gentlemen anything else?"

"How 'bout phone number," Manny stated while leering at her.

The woman smiled and moved on to other customers.

"Beginnin' to like her," the Latino mumbled through a mouthful of pizza. He reached up to wipe some sauce off his lower lip and stared after the waitress as she walked away. "Big ass but nice face cards. I do her."

"I'm sure you would," the older man stated disgustedly. "I suspect you'd fornicate with a snake if someone held its head."

"You no friggin' saint either," Manny fired back. "We both screw people, just in different way."

The executive removed the top from the bottled water and took a drink, quenching both his thirst and temper.

"Now what we do?" Manny asked.

The man sat back. "What do you think Johnston's planning? You spoke with him, what's your assessment?"

"He keep workin' no matter what you say. Already got first payment so money not problem."

"And we've already delivered enough compound to get him started with the experiments." The executive added, "You made sure that initial shipment couldn't be traced, right?"

"I take care of everythin'. Nobody connect you."

"We can't afford any mistakes." He reached up to tighten the knot of his burgundy tie.

"What you worry 'bout? Got 'nough friggin' money to buy way out of prison."

"It's your responsibility to make sure that scenario doesn't occur."

Licking his fingers with a loud smack, Manny asked, "Speakin' of money when I get paid?"

The man pulled a thick, white envelope from his pocket and slowly slid it across the table to the brash Latino. "Make sure you earn this."

"Long as you pay, I do job."

"I'm still concerned about Johnston's intentions. I'm afraid he can't be trusted to make prudent decisions. May let that oversized ego get in the way of good judgment, get both of us in trouble."

"Could be problem." Manny ripped off another bite of pizza.

The man began cutting lettuce into smaller pieces using a knife and fork. "There are always alternatives."

"You got plan?"

The well-dressed executive speared some salad and chewed slowly before swallowing. He lifted a flimsy, paper napkin to his mouth and wiped gently. "There's too much at stake not to."

"What is it?"

"Our thoroughbred has demonstrated he can't be corralled. That's not acceptable."

"How we get back on de range?"

"We don't."

"You let do what he friggin' wants?"

"I didn't say that. Apparently there's no use trying to reason with him. He's already demonstrated that my authority doesn't matter. I'm afraid he'd risk the project again."

"So?"

"So we put him down, then tie up any loose ends. And by loose ends, I mean the specimen and his family," he responded coldly.

"Whoa Amigo!" Manny threw his hands up. "You not sayin'...."

The man stared ahead, his silence confirmed Manny's suspicion.

Suddenly the Puerto Rican wasn't hungry. He pushed the plate away. "I not bargain for dis shit. What you get me in?"

"Look, you're involved whether you like it or not. We've both got a lot at stake if something goes wrong and the project gets exposed."

"I not do nothin'!"

"Tell it to the judge when he sentences you for being an accomplice to the crime. Face it Manny, you knowingly and willingly helped me. You're as culpable as me in the eyes of the law."

"What de hell culpable mean?"

"It means you're going to jail too."

Manny's stomach began to churn. "I don't know, Amigo."

"No one has to...unless we're exposed." He coolly lifted another forkful of salad to his mouth.

The Puerto Rican thought for a while. "Dis cost you big time. Extra for family. Not worry 'bout old man and boy, both idiots. De bitch is problem."

"Trust me, you'll be handsomely rewarded for your efforts."

The waitress returned to the booth. "If there's nothing else I'll just leave this for you." She laid their tab in the middle of the table. "Hope everything was okay."

"Everythin' good," Manny replied.

The young woman smiled and discreetly handed him another piece of paper. "I think you asked for this earlier."

"What's that?" the executive asked as the waitress winked and walked away.

Manny opened the note, "Bitch's phone number."

* * * * * *

The businessman sat comfortably in a leather seat as the corporate aircraft cruised over the puffy white clouds below. The midsize Learjet 55 left New York destined for Miami, Florida. The lone passenger sat sipping a glass of orange juice as two pilots guided the aircraft southward.

The co-pilot emerged from the cockpit and stepped down the narrow aisle, stooping to maneuver the five foot, eight inch fuselage. "Sir, we'll be landing at Miami in about thirty minutes."

"Thank you, Jordan."

"We've called ahead and arranged a car to pick you up at the hangar."

The executive nodded approval. He stared out the tiny window, mesmerized by the patches of cushy clouds floating in the vast, open sky. Their hypnotic shapes magically created distinctive images in his mind. The puffy face of an old man with a long, scraggly beard dangling from his chin suddenly materialized. Then the image slowly melted and transformed into a white medieval castle.

Another cloud formation caught his attention. A horse's head and long, sleek neck angled downward. The image caused him to reflect upon his childhood in an affluent area outside of Boston. Like all the houses in the wealthy neighborhood, his family's sported a manicured lawn and a swimming pool. As a kid he'd unwillingly spent time at their horse farm where his younger sister became an accomplished equestrian. The recollection brought about a devastating memory, one of tragedy and suffering.

"Will you come on?" the twelve-year-old girl begged.

"What's the big hurry?" He turned the radio off, quieting a static-filled voice.

"Just wanna get to the barn. Now come on!"

"Didn't realize getting my driver's license made me a full-time taxi for you." Charles reluctantly grabbed a baseball cap from the coffee table. "How long's this gonna take, Courtney? The game's in the fourth inning."

"Don't know. But Mom says you can't just drop me off. Nobody's gonna be there so you have to stay until Dad comes."

"Damn it," the teenager muttered under his breath.

"I heard that, Chucky." She pranced victoriously out the door. His new Camero was parked in the three-car garage of their two-story home.

Passing through the rolling countryside the boy turned on the radio and searched for the baseball game. He finally gave up and settled on a station playing Rod Stewart's "Tonight's the Night".

Courtney reached over to find another station.

"Don't even think about it. My car, my tunes."

The vehicle slowed and turned onto a dirt road running between two rows of elm. Attached to one of the trees was a sign, "Chapel Farm".

Minutes later Courtney was inside the barn brushing her big thoroughbred mare. Stiff bristles worked through the horse's hair, loosening and extricating dirt from the animal's shiny coat.

"God, it reeks in here," the teenage boy stated.

"I kind'a like the smell."

"Horse crap stinks."

Courtney positioned a thick pad and Passier saddle onto the horse's back. She attached the girth and tightened it slowly. "Good girl, Belle," she said patting the huge animal's neck. Turning to Charles, she asked, "Wanna give her some sugar?"

"Are you kidding?"

"Scared, Chucky?"

"Just don't like horses. They're big and smelly. Now hurry up." He plopped down on a nearby trunk with a loud thud.

Belle jumped and looked around warily. The girl stroked the animal's neck. "Be quiet, you're spooking her."

Rolling his eyes he sarcastically replied, "Sorry."

Courtney led the animal to the ring then donned a black velvet helmet and mounted the horse.

She walked around the ring, first one direction then the other. On the third pass she directed the mare to trot by gently squeezing its belly with her lower legs. Belle responded by picking up the two-step gait.

Charles sat in a chair at the end of the ring fuming. Instead of listening to the game he was stuck baby-sitting his little sister.

She stopped. "Can you come and help me?"

He reluctantly rose from the chair and stepped carefully over a pile of manure.

"Hold the reigns so she stands still. I need to adjust my stirrups."

"Damn, Courtney! You're just doing this 'cause you know I don't like horses."

"She's not gonna to do nothing."

Charles held on as she adjusted the stirrup leathers. The horse stood perfectly still ignoring his quivering hand.

"There, was that so bad?" Courtney gathered the reigns again.

He walked across the ring and opened the gate. "I'll be right back," he shouted. "Gotta go to the bathroom."

"Did this little ol' horse scare it out of you?"

He started to the barn wondering about the score of the baseball game.

"Hey, Chucky, wait. You forgot to close…."

Suddenly, a loud animalistic snort traveled up the slight incline. Turning, the young man was horrified. Belle's front feet had left the ground with the animal's entire body resting on its hind legs. Twelve hundred pounds of horseflesh towered high in the air...with Courtney hanging on for dear life. Sunlight glistened off the animal's sweaty muscled body accentuating its strength and power.

Charles started running down the hill.

"No wait. Don't run. You'll scare...."

But it was too late. The horse bolted for the open gate. Throwing its head toward the ground and bucking wildly, the animal tried to heave the terrified rider. Courtney became more and more unseated with every stride. All proper riding skills were forgotten. Instead of wrapping her legs around the horse's barrel, the girl's knees began creeping up and digging into the animal's shoulders.

She yanked the reigns forcing the bit to clang inside the horse's mouth. Belle gripped the metal and pull ahead, bursting out of the ring. Courtney's right foot slid through the stirrup iron and became wedged against the animal. Her body flew out of the saddle and hit the ground with a sickening thud. Still tethered to the horse, the vulnerable young girl was dragged across the field toward the woods.

Charles watched helplessly as they disappeared into the forest behind the barn. The sound of an approaching car snapped him from the terrified stupor. Yelling at the top of his lungs he ran toward the vehicle. "Help! Courtney fell off the horse! They're in the woods over there!"

Their father jumped out and ordered, "Use the telephone in the barn and call for an ambulance." The man started running, his eyes searching the underbrush.

Belle was soon spotted with a black riding boot dangling from the right stirrup.

Courtney was lying nearby on the ground. Both legs were bent with a sharp jagged bone protruding through the skin of her ankle. Several cuts along her arms were covered with leaves and grass. Her shirt was ripped, exposing a dislocated shoulder. The girl's head was tilted at an odd angle, only partially covered by a lop-sided helmet. Bright red blood leaked from an ear.

The man pressed two fingers against her neck and tried to find a pulse as a siren wailed in the distance.

Days later, Charles sat in the hospital room while the doctor talked to his parents. Courtney lay motionless in bed. Needles and wires protruded from the small battered body as a ventilator forced her lungs to expand rhythmically. Thump-a-whoosh. Thump-a-whoosh. The girl's head was wrapped in white gauze starkly contrasting a blackish bruised face.

"We've done all we can," the doctor assured the family. "Your daughter's suffered extensive head trauma. The rest of her body can recover but I'm afraid there's evidence of a brain injury." He paused briefly as their mother began sobbing.

"What does that mean?" the father bravely asked.

"I'm sorry, but right now we just don't know how she'll respond. There's a chance she may never regain consciousness."

"Can we bring in another expert, get a second opinion? Money's no object. I'll pay whatever it takes."

"I can certainly provide the names of some other specialists." Turning to leave the doctor added, "If you have any questions, please contact me. Again, I'm very sorry."

For several minutes, the room was deathly quiet except for the continuous rhythm of the ventilator.

The woman mumbled, "Why? Why'd this happen? Why would God allow this to happen to our little girl?"

Charles knew God wasn't to blame. It was his fault. He was supposed to take care of her. He left the gate open.

His father turned toward him. "Come with me, Son."

"Where we going?"

"I said come with me!"

They drove to their sprawling home where the man disappeared inside to retrieve a .34 revolver from a solid oak gun cabinet. He returned to the vehicle and laid the gun on the seat before heading back to the farm.

Belle was grazing in the pasture. The giant chestnut thoroughbred looked up as the two approached, then continued munching on the tender grass.

A few yards away the man stopped, lifted the revolver toward the animal's head and pulled the trigger. A loud pop echoed across the field piercing the skull and dropping the mare to the ground. Handing the gun to Charles he ordered, "Finish it."

"No Dad, I don't want to! Please don't make me."

"Do it."

Swallowing hard, the sixteen-year-old obediently moved forward and stood directly above the downed animal. Belle's big eyes closed as a second and final bullet carved a tiny, bloody hole between them.

Charles spent the next several years in the room of a private care facility holding the flaccid hand of his younger, brain-dead sister. Courtney's fragile body withered from inactivity and became nothing more than a stagnant shell kept alive by machines and drugs—useless drugs that couldn't do anything to restore her scrambled brain.

Charles's thoughts returned to the present. The accident had changed his life in many ways. The terrible mishap was the catalyst prompting his career within the pharmaceutical industry and the hopes of discovering more innovative medicines. Something to help Courtney.

Shaking off the nightmarish memories, he went to the rear of the aircraft to retrieve a small piece of luggage. He pulled out a white golf shirt and a pair of khaki pants. At the bottom of the bag were a Florida Marlins baseball cap and a pair of sunglasses.

He waited as the Learjet sliced though a patch of light turbulence on its descent into Miami. The jet soon landed and taxied to a row of hangars used exclusively for private aircraft. The sides of the gray, framed buildings were lined with palm trees, gently blowing in the warm breeze. The thunderous sounds of passenger jets continually arriving and departing the nearby runways filled the tropical air.

The executive exited the plane and was immediately escorted to a waiting limousine. "Where would you like to go, Sir?" the driver politely asked while holding the back door open.

"Take me to the corner of 8th and Ocean Drive on South Beach."

"Yes, Sir."

The car headed east on Dolphin Expressway toward South Beach. The driver eventually pulled into a parking space, and then turned to the backseat. "Sir, we've arrived, 8th and Ocean."

The News Cafe sat on the corner. The lot was sprinkled with large, brightly colored umbrellas, each covering a small table underneath. The sidewalk café was partially filled with brunch patrons. Directly across the street was a small park with a white sandy beach bordering the Atlantic Ocean.

"Wait here," Charles ordered.

"Yes, Sir."

He got out and began strolling through the eatery. An elderly couple with matching gray hair occupied one table, enjoying coffee and bagels as they spoke in their thick New York accents. Two younger women dressed in halter tops and tight fitting shorts sat at another. Both were blonde, tanned and bosomy. A middle-aged man was reading a newspaper at a table next to the sidewalk. A slight ocean breeze flowed through the cafe making it difficult for him to steady the flapping tabloid.

Off in a secluded corner next to the kitchen sat a lone man also wearing a Marlins baseball cap. A small heart-shaped birthmark was located just below his right earlobe. He was staring at Charles.

Soon the two were facing each other.

"You a Marlins fan?" the seated man asked, noting the baseball cap.

"No. I'm from New York."

"Yankees?"

"Prefer the Red Sox," Charles replied.

"Me too. Anybody but the Yankees. Looking for somebody special?"

"Maybe."

"Well maybe I can help you."

"How's that?"

"I do hard jobs that nobody else can." He paused a few seconds before adding, "I understand that's what you're looking for."

"Mind if I sit down, Mr....?"

"Why don't you just call me Conti, and yes, have a seat. I understand there may be...uh, let's say...a hangnail that needs clipping."

"And you can discreetly deal with matters of this nature?"

"Absolutely, if the price is right. You know hangnails are very delicate issues. People think they're just annoying but can be much more," Mr. Conti replied.

"Yes, they can get very messy if not properly handled. Sometimes there may be an infection or residual scar left behind." Charles added, "I assume you won't let that happen?"

"I'm a professional. There won't be any problems. That's why I demand top dollar for my services."

Behind the dark shades the executive stared hard at Conti, noting the heart-shaped birthmark on his stern face. "Can you guarantee no mistakes will be made?"

"I know you've done your homework. That's why you contacted me. What did your sources tell you? That I'm the best," the man stated boldly. "Otherwise, you wouldn't be here. So let's get down to business. You want me to take care of this hangnail or not?"

Charles asked, "How much is this going to cost?"

"Five hundred thousand dollars."

"A quarter of a million and you've got a deal."

Conti shook his head. "Five hundred or find somebody else."

Charles paused for a few moments. "You've got some big balls my friend. I like that. All right, you've got a deal. Half up front and the rest when the job's finished."

"Done."

"Good." Charles added, "You're not a very good businessman. I would have paid seven-fifty if I had too."

"Yeah and I would have taken four hundred."

Both men smiled before reaching across the table to shake hands and consummate their deal.

"Now that our negotiations are over, who is this hangnail that needs clipping?" Conti asked.

"There's this Puerto Rican in New Jersey, named Manny...."

Charles couldn't afford to take any more chances. He was responsible and would be the one to suffer the consequences if the project was exposed.

Dr. Barry Johnson, the specimen and his family must first be eliminated. That would be Manny's job.

Then Manny would need to be subsequently erased from the trail. Mr. Conti would ensure that final hangnail was clipped.

* * * * * *

Upon returning to New York, Charles made his routine stop at the private care facility before heading to the office. The walls of the room were adorned with pictures of a young girl riding horses. Sitting next to his sister's bed, he stroked the nearly transparent skin covering her hands and whispered, "Hold on. We had a few minor setbacks, but I'm not giving up. We're still working on something that might help. I'll do whatever possible to bring you back."

CHAPTER 11

D r. Johnston began administering Tyler's allergy shots…or what Gwen thought were allergy shots.

The ability to forgo a daily trip to the doctor's office had made life much easier and less traumatic for the Savant. The physician's perceived kindness only increased Gwen's desire to fulfill her new job duties. However, every time she'd offer to help, he encouraged patience, promising to put her to work soon.

Meanwhile Gwen continued to orient the family into their new life at the lake. "I need to pick up a few things at the grocery store. Why don't you guys tag along?"

Neither responded.

"Hey, did you hear me? Want to go?"

"Hell no," Ernest stated bluntly. "I'm watchin' television."

Noticing the fingerprints and smudges on his glasses, she said, "How can you see anything through those dirty lenses?" Gwen cleaned them with her shirttail and handed them back to the old man. "Better?"

He slid them back on. "Purdy damn chipper."

Tyler was engrossed in a book.

"I won't be long. Hon, watch out for your granddaddy while I'm gone."

"Yes. Watch Granddaddy. Watch Granddaddy."

She leaned down to hug him. "What're you reading?" Neuropsychological Profiles was boldly imprinted on the cover.

"Where'd you get that?"

"Kitchen counter. On kitchen counter."

"That's Dr. Johnston's. I told you to leave his stuff alone. Give it to me, I'll take it downstairs."

Tyler handed her the book.

"What's it about anyway?" she asked, scanning the front and back covers.

The young man replied softly, "Me."

"What?"

"Book about Savants. I'm a Savant." He uncharacteristically looked directly at her.

Is it possible? Can he comprehend this? she wondered. Logic told her no, but the frightened look in his eyes conveyed otherwise.

"Hon, are you okay?"

"I've never been okay." He shamefully looked away.

Gwen reached out and placed a comforting hand on his shoulder.

The teen pulled away. "Give book back. Take back to Johnston."

"Alright. I'll…I'll be…back in a jiffy." She reluctantly left and went downstairs.

Barry Johnston was in his office. She tapped on the door frame. "I'm sorry to disturb you."

"What is it?"

"You left this in the kitchen. Tyler picked it up and was looking at it. Hope that's all right."

"It's fine." He reached for the book. "Must have left it there last night when I came up for coffee."

Still stunned by the Savant's earlier comments, she remained frozen.

"Is there something else?" Johnston asked.

"It's just Tyler. He…he seems different this morning."

Johnston sat up in his chair, immediately interested. "Different? In what way?"

"Oh never mind." She shook her head. "You really never know what he's going to say or do. Anyway, I need to run to the grocery store for a few things. Is it all right if I leave him and Daddy here? They're watching T.V."

"Certainly, I'll keep an eye on them. Don't think they can wander off too far with the lake and fence surrounding the property. Oh and don't forget, Tyler needs his shot later today. I'll give it to him when you get back."

Johnston placed the manual back on the bookshelf and continued working, excited that the drug might already be having an effect.

A loud buzz from the intercom system sounded. "What now!" He stepped to a wall panel next to the door. "Who is it?"

"Uh, h… m… n…." The voice faded in and out.

Johnston interrupted the indistinguishable garble. "You have to talk directly into the speaker, I can't understand."

Overcompensating, a stern voice blasted back, "Sorry. My name's Randall Padgett. I'm with the Forsyth County Sheriff's Department. Here to see a Dr. Barry Johnston."

"Why do you want to see him?"

"Sir, that's a private matter. I need to speak with him directly. Now, is Dr. Johnston available?"

"I'll meet you at the front door." Johnston remotely opened the gate allowing the vehicle onto the property. He hurried upstairs and through the living room where Ernest and Tyler sat glued to an afternoon soap.

A gray sedan crept down the narrow driveway, stopping in front of the lake house. A stocky black man wearing a short-sleeved shirt with a dark tie approached the porch where the physician waited. "Hello. You Dr. Johnston? Dr. Barry Johnston?"

"I am."

Hearing the strange voice, Tyler quietly wandered over to stand behind the partially opened door, hidden from the two men outside.

"As I mentioned, I'm Detective Randall Padgett from the Forsyth County Sheriff's Department." He flashed an identification badge.

Johnston nodded. "Detective Padgett."

"Nice place you got here. Great view." The black man looked around curiously, taking in the surroundings. "That your boat down yonder?"

"Yes it is." Johnston stated bluntly, "I'm a little busy, how can I help you?"

"I'll try not to take much of your time. I've been assigned to investigate the death of a young woman whose body washed up nearby."

"I heard about it. What a shame."

"They all are."

"You know it happens all the time. That lake's a dangerous place if one's not careful."

"Yes Sir, but we believe foul play may have been involved." He paused to watch for a reaction. "I'd like to ask a few questions if you don't mind. Mind if we go inside and talk?"

Johnston declined. "I have some house guests. Wouldn't want to alarm them. Can we speak out here?"

Padgett leaned forward and glanced through the crack in the doorway. "I suppose."

Tyler was still hidden behind the door, chewing gum at a frantic pace.

"So Detective, what makes you believe foul play was involved in this...uh...unfortunate situation?"

"Some unusual things were noted during the autopsy."

"Like what?"

"I'm sorry, but I'm not at liberty to discuss those details."

"Of course, I understand."

"Did you notice anything strange around the time of the victim's death? Suspicious persons or activity?"

"Nothing comes to mind."

"Nothing at all?"

"Not that I can think of," Johnston insisted. "But I'm a very private person. Generally keep to myself. Look around." He waved a hand, urging Padgett to observe the property. "This place is isolated for a reason. I enjoy my privacy."

"I can see that. Still, you must get out sometimes. Notice any Mexican immigrants in the area? Are you aware of anyone in the community, any neighbors employ day laborers?"

"Oh, that's right. I read the victim was Hispanic."

"Yes Sir, she was."

Johnston rubbed his chin, appearing to search his memory. "I'm sorry, can't think of any." He asked, "Do they know the poor girl's identity?"

"Not yet, but we're working on it," the detective answered. "So far it's been tough to come by any real leads. The immigrant population is very transient. Here today and gone tomorrow. Even if they know anything, many are afraid to come forward because of their status. Scared they'll be deported."

"Must make your job difficult."

Padgett nodded. "Are you a practicing physician?"

Caught off-guard, Johnston asked, "What do you mean?"

"You know, do you treat patients, write prescriptions? That sort of thing."

"I haven't been in private practice for some time. For the past few years I've worked at the C.D.C."

"You're employed at the Center?"

"Not anymore, I left recently."

"Still involved in the medical field?" the man probed further.

"Why do you ask?"

"I'm a detective, it's my job to ask questions."

"Presently I'm exploring the possibility of conducting some private research."

"Research, huh? What exactly does that involve?"

The egotistical physician replied. "It's very complicated. Suffice it to say clinical researchers conduct a wide-range of studies that make the world a better place to live. For people like you and your family."

The officer maintained a professional tone while injecting a hint of sarcasm. "And we surely do appreciate that, Dr. Johnston. But I wasn't asking about researchers in general. My question was more specific. What are you researching?"

"My studies will be geared toward neurology and the human brain," Johnston proudly explained.

"And where will your research take place?"

"I plan to conduct my work here, in my basement laboratory."

"You plan to undertake such a noble task at your residence? Seems an unlikely setting."

"Let me tell you a story, Detective Padgett. Have you ever heard of a drug called Zantac?"

"I'm not sure."

"Zantac was the world's largest selling prescription medication back in the early nineties. It was a marvelous drug prescribed to treat ulcers." Johnston paused before adding, "It put a lot of gastrointestinal surgeons out of business."

"Your point?" the detective asked.

"The active ingredient in Zantac is called ranitidine. That compound was developed in a modest fifteen-by-fifteen foot room, not some bureaucratic government laboratory. Independent research can occur anywhere and is critical in uncovering our next generation of life-changing medicines."

"All right Dr. Johnston, you've made your point. But what about the resources needed to support your work? It has to be expensive."

"I'm currently applying for some grants that'll help fund my efforts. Haven't received any yet, but I'm hopeful."

"So you haven't started anything, no research projects?"

"Not yet."

"No experiments or tests of any kind?" the detective repeated suspiciously.

"That's right." Anxious to end the probing questions, Barry Johnston abruptly stated, "Now if there's nothing else Detective Padgett, I'd like to get back to my guests."

"I appreciate your time." He reached into his pocket and pulled out a small, white card. "If you think of anything, please call me. Here's my contact information."

"I certainly will. Good luck with your investigation." Johnston started inside.

Tyler scurried to the couch and watched as the physician went to the kitchen and took a bottle of orange juice from the refrigerator. Johnston twisted off the cap and flipped it and the detective's card into a trash container underneath the counter. "Barney Fife. Next time you'd better bring Andy along," he chuckled, walking downstairs.

"Not Barney Fife," Tyler stated softly. "Detective Randall Padgett, Forsyth County Sheriff's Department. Not Barney Fife." He went to the trash can and retrieved the detective's business card.

Outside, Padgett lingered in his car gazing suspiciously at Johnston's front door. Years of experience and his gut told him something just wasn't right. He eventually drove away with more questions than answers.

CHAPTER 12

Gwen walked through the laboratory and tapped on the closed door.

"Yes," Barry Johnston responded from inside the office.

"It's me. You agreed to meet and discuss my job responsibilities."

"Just a minute." The muffled sound of closing file drawers filtered out.

Gwen looked across the laboratory at the examination table, still unsure what her duties were supposed to entail. Every time she asked, Johnston encouraged her to be patient and offered some vague explanation. "I'm still sorting through a couple of things, but I'll have something for you soon."

While happy to be with her family, Gwen wanted to earn her keep. Freeloading wasn't her style. Summer was transitioning to early autumn, and with each passing day she became more uneasy about the strange and so far non-working arrangement.

The office door finally opened. "Thanks for waiting. Come on in."

Gwen took a deep breath and stepped inside.

"I know you're anxious to get involved and I'm truly sorry there hasn't been more work to this point."

"You've been paying me for weeks now and I feel a little guilty. I haven't done anything. Just don't want to take advantage of the situation."

"If that's what you're worried about, then don't. Believe me, I'll get my money out of you once we get started," Johnston promised.

"Get started on what? I'm still unsure exactly what you're doing."

"Okay then, let's talk about it." The physician paused to collect his thoughts. "Maybe I should begin by explaining why I chose this path." He paused again. "As I've gotten older my perspective's changed. Sure I've made a lot of money as a practicing physician and then at the C.D.C. For many, that'd be enough. But for me something was missing. That wasn't my true passion, what I really enjoyed or wanted to do."

"Is that why you left the Center?"

He nodded. "What I want to do now…what we're going to do is make a difference in the world." Johnston looked away feigning humility. "That may sound pompous but it's my dream."

"You're a doctor. You made a difference healing people."

"I suppose, but there're many that can't be helped. At least not yet." Johnston pushed his thinning black hair over his head. "What intrigues me is the unknown. There are still incurable health problems that plague people. What causes these afflictions and how can they be avoided? When they occur, how can they be treated? The only way to answer these difficult questions is through research. That's what I want, the thrill and excitement of hopefully finding the next major breakthrough in medicine. It's an evolutionary process that never stops. I want to uncover the answers and lead the scientific community into the next paradigm," he stated boldly.

"Good Lord, that's ambitious."

"I think of myself as an explorer. Not like Columbus or Magellan who discovered new worlds but as a scientist who uncovers new medicines. While they expanded the world for mankind, I want to expand mankind's abilities within the world."

In reality, the neurologist had an insatiable need for recognition. The morality of his actions was secondary to his ego.

"There're theories I want to investigate, then maybe conduct experiments in those areas. Once my trials are complete I plan to publish the results. Hopefully that'll start a debate within the medical community. If I'm right and my work's accepted, I'll be credited."

"That's very noble, Dr. Johnston."

"There's a lot to be done before I...before we...can begin."

"Like what?"

"First of all, I've got to narrow my focus. Decide which targeted areas to explore."

"But I can help. Forgive me if I'm a little pushy, believe me that's not my intent."

The physician frowned while formulating a response. The supply of precious compound had been cut off, forcing him to ration the existing drug on Tyler. However it would soon run out, then what? And what was he to do with Gwen and the old man? He'd have to be careful about raising any more suspicions. At some point they'd have to be dealt with too. But when? Was now the time?

Johnston needed to keep the woman pacified while he secretly conducted his experiments. *The police will go away and I'll eventually get more compound,* he reasoned. *Once things settle down, I'll figure out what to do.*

"You're right. Delegating has never been one of my strong suits. I can't do it all and you can certainly help get things moving faster. I'll generate a task list for you."

"Thanks," she said, relieved that her persistence had finally paid off. "Now, when will you have it so I can get started?"

"I'll work on it this afternoon. And I'll get you a laptop too. You're going to need it."

* * * * * *

A glow radiated from the new computer as Gwen searched for potential grants. She diligently paged through the National Institute of Neurological Disorders and Strokes website looking for investigator awards which might align with Johnston's vision. A notebook listing several possibilities lay on the end table.

Ernest was stretched out on the sofa. His snoring caused a deep rhythmic vibration to gouge the air, but she continued working, oblivious to the noise.

Tyler sat on a chair watching the evening news. "And now an update on that mysterious death of a young Latino woman found in Lake Lanier last month."

A female reporter standing next to a black man appeared on the screen. "Thanks Lyle," the woman responded into her hand-held microphone. "I'm here with Detective Randall Padgett of the Forsyth County Sheriff's Department. Detective Padgett, can you give us an update on your month-long investigation? From previous reports we understand you've ruled out accidental drowning."

"Yes Ma'am, that's right. The young woman's death is now considered a homicide."

"What's brought the authorities to that conclusion? Can you tell us anything new?"

"The autopsy revealed evidence that foul play may have been involved."

"What kind of evidence?" the woman probed further.

The detective paused for a moment. "For one thing there wasn't any water in the victim's lungs. She was dead before being dumped into the lake."

"What else, Detective Padgett?"

"I'm sorry but this is still an ongoing investigation. I'm not at liberty to discuss any further details."

"Do you have any suspects?"

"We're following up on several leads. We'd also like anyone who may have information relating to this matter to please contact the Forsyth County Sheriff's Department."

"There you have it folks, the latest from Detective Randall Padgett on the Lake Lanier murder investigation. Now back to Atlanta."

Tyler murmured, "Detective Randall Padgett. 687-414-0776. Not Barney Fife."

Gwen momentarily peeked up from the laptop. She quickly dismissed the comments, accustomed to him spewing out random bits of information.

The popular local news anchor coaxed the audience to stay tuned and not flip channels during the upcoming break. "Up next we'll have tomorrow's forecast and find out whether we'll get any much-needed rain."

"Six inches below normal, no rain tomorrow," Tyler immediately responded to the man's comments, pre-empting his upcoming weather report.

A pharmaceutical commercial touting the potential benefits for its newest drug to combat erectile dysfunction captured the screen.

"Erectile dysfunction," Tyler repeated then chuckled.

Surprised at the nineteen-year-old's reaction, Gwen looked toward the T.V. noting a mature couple holding hands as they strolled romantically down a private beach. In the background a golden sun was gently resting over a dark blue ocean.

"What's so funny?" Gwen wasn't use to hearing him laugh, especially at such an adult matter. And one she didn't think he understood.

Tyler's cheeks turned crimson as he continued to stare at the television implying he knew much more. "Mom, will I ever have a girlfriend?" He spoke in a full, unbroken sentence.

"Maybe. Would you like to meet someone special one day?"

He ran a finger under his runny nose as a sheepish grin appeared on his face. "I guess not. Guess not."

"You could meet a nice young lady."

"No. Don't think so. No."

"Sure you could."

"Who'd want me?"

"What makes you say that? You're a good person, a good human being."

The teenager turned to face her and spoke in a coherent manner. "Mom, I know who and what I am."

Suddenly, Gwen was having a normal conversation with the Savant. *What's going on?* she wondered. *He's different. His words are meaningful and complete.*

Ernest's ragged snoring stopped. He sat up on the couch, stretched his arms and yawned exposing his toothless gums.

143

"Daddy, did you have a good nap?"

The man didn't respond but gazed blankly ahead.

Tyler answered instead, "He's gone."

"What?"

"Granddaddy's gone. It's not his fault." Tyler leaned forward and whispered, "Alzheimer's is bad. The amyloidal plaque around his nerve endings is preventing the transmission of chemical messages between his brain cells. It makes thinking and remembering real hard. Granddaddy's brain will eventually die. And so will…." His voice cracked and he was unable to finish the statement.

Again, Gwen was surprised at the full sentences and his heartfelt reaction. She stood and put both arms around the teen.

Ernest mumbled, "Sho a fine supper, Esther."

"He must've been dreaming about Grandma."

Gwen nodded.

"Real good eats. Ought'a hold me a while." His demented mind was still lost in the dream as the old man continued to ramble. "What's that young'un doin'? She gone to bed yet? Damn sho hope so. Maybe you and me can hit the sack early, work on gettin' that boy I been wantin'." A smile emerged on his wrinkled face.

"He always wanted a son," Gwen muttered softly.

The old man's smile vanished. Although back from the past, he was again lost in the present.

Barry Johnston appeared from his basement laboratory. "Hello everyone. How are you folks this evening?"

Gwen smiled. "We're doing fine."

"Don't mean to bother you but got a little hungry so decided to come up for a bite."

"There's plenty of left-over spaghetti in the frig. Please help yourself."

"Are you sure? I don't want to impose."

"Nonsense, we've already eaten."

"That's very kind of you." Dr. Johnston grabbed a plate from the cupboard and scooped a pile of cold pasta from a plastic container. He placed the plate into the microwave.

While waiting for it to warm, he returned to the living room and asked, "How're your allergies, Tyler?"

"Okay." The teen coughed and cleared his throat.

"It looks like you still have a few problems. Are you feeling differently otherwise?"

"No."

"Ready for your next injection?"

"No."

"I understand they're annoying and may sting a bit, but you need them if you're ever going to eliminate those nasty symptoms."

"I don't want another shot."

Johnston calmly turned to Gwen. "You know we need to do this."

"Hon, we have to try the shots for a while longer. Hopefully you'll get better soon and we can stop."

"Don't like needles. They hurt."

The doctor ignored his objection. "Just bring him down to my office before bed tonight," he instructed Gwen, determined to continue his experiments on the Savant.

Johnston retrieved the plate of hot spaghetti from the microwave and headed back downstairs.

* * * * * *

Gwen's eyes eased open. *What was that?* She cleared the cobwebs from her mind and looked at the alarm clock. *It's 3:30 in the morning.*

There it was again, that muffled sound!

Wearing a long nightshirt, she stumbled down the hallway to find Tyler standing next to the bird cage. "Tyler smart. Tyler is smart. Say it Budgie."

The bird sat on its perch, glaring back silently.

"Hon, what in God's name are you doing up at this hour?"

"Couldn't sleep so I got up."

"It's almost four o'clock. Is everything all right?"

"I'm okay."

"Are your allergies bothering you?"

"About the same, still a little stuffy."

"The shots...."

"I hate them," he interrupted. "They're worse than the allergies." Turning to the parakeet, Tyler stated, "Hate shots."

"Let that silly bird go. You're going to wake Granddaddy."

He turned and said, "Mom, I love you."

"I...I love you too."

"I'm sorry."

"Tyler, what do you mean? What are you sorry about, Hon?"

"I'm sorry for...for being me. Sorry that you've had to deal with me."

What's he saying? Is he referring to his Autism again? Does he... can he...really comprehend his condition? she wondered.

Tyler stared at her. His eyes were filled with uncertainty. Was it fear or hurt from finally understanding the truth? "I'm different."

"We're all different, that's how God made us. Everyone is special in their own way, including you."

"I'm special but not in a good way."

"That's not true! You're my angel." Now it was Gwen who projected uncertainty. "What's this about? Tell me what's going on."

"I'm beginning to feel strange. Things are becoming clear and more meaningful." He thought for a few moments. "Everything's opening up. At first I was curious. Didn't understand what was happening. Then I got scared, really scared about what was running through my head. After a while, that went away and I got angry."

"Angry at what?"

"At what I've missed. Why was I like that? Why'd it happen to me? I was cheated out of life."

Tyler no longer spoke in short phrases or simply repeated with little understanding. He was passionate. His sentences were structured, interactive and responsive.

"All those books I've read, they make sense now. They're not just words that I repeat like Budgie. I know what they mean and how they relate to each other. I'm not a parakeet. I'm a whole person, like you." A peaceful, relaxed expression appeared on his face.

Gwen was mesmerized, staring at the teen.

"What are you looking at?" he asked.

"Your smile. It's beautiful, so warm and real." Tears began forming in her eyes.

"Why are you sad? Is something wrong?"

"Heavens no."

"Then why are you crying?"

"Because I'm happy."

"I don't understand. Crying means you're happy?"

"They're tears of joy."

"What's it like, Mom?"

How could she explain something so wonderful?

Gwen looked into his watering eyes. She'd seen him cry as a child with a stomach ache or after a fall. But this was different. Now, for the first time, she saw emotion trickling down his cheeks.

She reached over to brush his tears away. "That's what joy feels like, Hon."

Miraculously the Savant seemed to have awakened.

CHAPTER 13

Day by day Tyler continued to blossom from his pod of Autism. Each morning brought new revelations for both him and Gwen.

A spear of light shot through the window, crossed the living room and rested on the wall. The sun rose forcing the beam downward toward the couch where Tyler had fallen asleep. The teen's long brown locks were tangled across his forehead.

Gwen tucked a fleece blanket around his shoulders and curled up in a chair next to the sofa. Was his recent transformation real or just a cruel fantasy to be snatched away?

In the past, talking with him had been like pulling teeth. She'd grown accustomed to the one-word sentences repeated over and over again, adjusted to his obsessive rituals and constant frustrations.

But now he spoke in complete sentences, looked directly into her eyes and smiled. New activities and changes to his daily routine no longer bothered him. How could it all be?

Tyler stirred.

"Good morning, Hon. I didn't mean to wake you."

"What are you doing?" He yawned and wiped the night from his eyes.

"Watching you sleep."

"Bet that's exciting," he chuckled kicking the blanket to the floor.

"Want some Cheerios?"

148

"How about oatmeal?"

"Oatmeal? Are you sure?" Gwen stepped into the kitchen and rummaged through the pantry.

Tyler followed closely behind.

"What flavor?"

"Let's try apple cinnamon." He grabbed a blue china bowl from the cupboard and stood quietly for a moment staring at it.

She noticed his fascination with the dish. "What's wrong?"

"Just wondering about our stuff. You know, things we had at our old house."

"I put most of it in storage when we moved."

"White bowls, we had white bowls. White bowls."

Occasionally Tyler reverted to short repetitive phrases. Each time Gwen worried he wouldn't return. "You're right, they were white." She nervously added, "I can get them if you want."

"These are all right. Kind of fancy but they'll do." He emptied the packet of oatmeal and added water.

"So what have you got going on today?" she asked.

"Nothing planned...other than my shot." The timer on the microwave sounded and Tyler carefully retrieved the bowl. "Looking forward to that," he sarcastically added while wiping his nose.

Gwen smiled, recognizing the uncharacteristic wit exhibited by the Savant. "I know you hate needles but having them administered here is a lot better than going to the clinic."

He began stirring the hot cereal.

"We're lucky Dr. Johnston's willing to do it," she added.

The teenager spooned oatmeal into his mouth, ignoring her comment.

"Tyler? You get along with him, don't you?"

"He's all right. It's just...."

"What?"

"I don't know." The teen paused while swallowing another spoonful of oatmeal. "He's a little strange. Always asks a bunch of questions, like he's interrogating me or something."

"You know he has to monitor your reaction."

"I understand, but it seems like he's watching me all the time." He scraped the remaining cereal from the bottom of the bowl then licked the spoon.

"I think you're a little sensitive. He's just taking an interest in how you're doing, that's all."

"I don't know. There's something about him I don't trust. I've got this feeling."

"Don't worry so much, just get better." ·

"Maybe I've got too much time on my hands."

"Well, maybe you should do something about that. Why not get out a little more? Go somewhere different. Have a new experience," she suggested.

"Like what?"

"I don't know. Look for a part-time job or something. You're nineteen years old. It'd be a perfect opportunity to spread your wings a little."

"Mom, I've been feeling better, but a job?"

"I'm not talking about running a business," she teased. "I heard Lanier Baptist Church needs someone to clean the sanctuary and mow the grass."

"How do you know that?"

"I checked out the area churches. Thought we'd attend services on Sunday morning. I visited Lanier Baptist one day last week and talked to the pastor. Mentioned you and he told me about the job. Oh, and I found out they have a young adult's group too."

"You really think I'm ready?"

"Won't know unless you try." The seed had been planted. Not wanting to force the issue, she'd let him think it over. It would be his decision to make.

But outside social interaction still frightened him. Would he be able to take the next step?

Gwen rinsed his empty bowl and placed it in the dishwasher.

Tyler conceded, "Guess I've got nothing else to do. Maybe we should go over and check things out at the church."

"That's wonderful, Hon. I'll call and arrange a meeting with the pastor. Why don't you go take a shower and change clothes while I finish picking up?"

Passing through the living room, Gwen stopped to fold the blanket lying on the floor. Protruding underneath the corner of the couch was an insert from the local newspaper. She pulled it out. "Oh my heavens!"

The advertisement promoted a lingerie sale. Several scantily clad young women posed seductively, displaying the skimpy undergarments. Tyler's interests were also evolving, another sign of the teenager's awakening.

* * * * * *

On the car ride over, Ernest stared blankly out the window.

Tyler sat quietly in front sporting a new blue shirt. His shoelaces were neatly tied.

"You nervous?" Gwen asked.

"Kind of." Entering an adult world, one he'd never dealt with before was scary. No longer could he retreat into his autistic cocoon when life got difficult. People would expect normalcy from someone who'd never been normal. Certain behaviors tolerated in the past wouldn't be deemed acceptable anymore.

"Hon, you don't have to do this."

"Everything's just changing so fast. It's a little overwhelming."

"If I'm pushing too hard we can go home."

"I'm fine. It feels good to express myself. Talking about a book instead of just reciting the words. I don't even panic anymore when I get two Cheerios on my spoon."

Gwen was also excited but nervous. She'd always been totally responsible for Tyler, accepting his Autism and embracing the tasks of nursemaid and protector. Would she finally be able to relinquish those roles and begin a new chapter in her life too?

The car slowed as they rounded a sharp curve.

Tyler continued. "It's hard. I've finally opened the door but can't see what's there. It's a little scary."

"That's the way life is, Hon."

"Just hope I can handle it."

"No one's forcing you to rush into anything."

The teen took a deep breath as they pulled into the church's gravel parking lot. "Like you said this morning, won't know unless I try."

Lanier Baptist Church sat about fifty yards off the main road. The building had been constructed in 1909 and was surrounded by pine trees. Located a few miles from million-dollar lake homes which had sprung up over recent years, it now seemed out of place.

Two squirrels jumped from underneath an azalea bush and dashed across the pine straw. The rodent-like animals leaped onto a tree and scampered up, circling the trunk while chattering angrily at the intruders.

A hefty man with a pot belly waved from the front door. He was dressed in dark trousers an inch too short and a short-sleeved shirt that was a size too small.

"Pastor Williamson, it's nice to see you again," Gwen acknowledged.

"Who we got here?"

"This is my father, Ernest Shealy."

The pastor reached to shake his hand. "Mr. Shealy, real nice to meet you."

At first Ernest looked cautiously at the stranger, then extended his hand.

Gwen continued, "And this is Tyler."

"Hello, young man."

"Hi," Tyler nervously replied.

"Your mama's told me a lot about you. Come on in." They entered the small sanctuary and walked down the aisle to the front. "Have a seat and let's visit."

The pastor informed them about Sunday services, a Bible study group that met on Wednesday evenings and the upcoming mission trip to the Gulf Coast. "Ladies here at the church are having a pancake breakfast next weekend to raise a little money and help cover expenses. You should come on by."

"You also mentioned there was a young adult's group," Gwen reminded him.

"That's right. Nice bunch of kids. All about Tyler's age and real active in our community. They visit old folks and collect toys for needy children around Christmas time. Things like that. Meet every other Sunday evening for fellowship. Once in a while the group'll take in a movie or go out to eat. Most the time they just bring a few snacks and hang around down in the basement."

Tyler listened attentively.

"My daughter belongs to the group. Matter of fact, she's downstairs in my office. I'll introduce you before you leave."

The teenager nodded shyly.

Ernest leaned over and whispered in Gwen's ear.

"Excuse me, Pastor Williamson. Where're the restrooms?" she asked.

He pointed to the front corner of the sanctuary. "Out that door and to the left. They're all the way at the end of the hall."

"Want me to take him, Mom?"

"No, it's okay. You stay and talk. We'll be right back"

The reverend turned his attention to Tyler. "Guess your mama told you about the job here at the church?"

"Yes Sir. She said you needed some help."

"That's right, couple days a week. Sound like something you'd be interested in?"

"Did she explain my...my situation?"

"Sure did. Praise the Lord! Way your mama talks, it's a miracle."

"I've never had a job or done much of anything on my own."

"Don't worry about it, Son. If you want, we can give it a try. With God's help I'm sure you'll do just fine."

They continued to chat until Gwen and Ernest returned, then the reverend showed everyone around. "Now this here is where the sweeper and all the cleaning supplies are stored," he said opening the door to the utility closet. "There's a small shed out back where the lawn mower's kept. Kind of old but works okay. Don't have much grass." He paused to think. "Guess that's it. If you're interested,

Tyler, you can get started next Monday. We can only pay minimum wage."

"That's all right, I'd like to try."

"I know you'll do a good job."

"Thanks so much," Gwen stated as they made their way out to the car.

"Hope to see you this Sunday for worship services." Snapping his fingers the reverend added, "Oh, wait a minute, almost forgot. Wanted to introduce my daughter. You got time?"

Tyler looked to his mother.

"Sure, go ahead."

"You and Mr. Shealy stay right here," Pastor Williamson offered. "I'll have your boy back in two shakes of a lamb's tail."

Tyler followed the man as he entered the church basement. "It's this way. Sorry about the mess. We had some water damage from a busted pipe. It's a blessing one of our parishioners is a plumber."

They approached an office at the end of the hallway. "Belinda, you here?"

"Yeah, Daddy."

A thin young woman sat in a beat-up office chair. She was dressed in a T-shirt that read FROG – FULLY RELYING ON GOD. Her threadbare blue jeans were ripped at both knees and she wore flip-flops exposing toenails partially covered in chipped red polish. Her black hair was pulled into a loose ponytail. A few strands fell free, brushing against her tan cheeks.

"Want you to meet somebody. This here's Tyler Shealy."

A huge smile spread across her face, exposing the girl's slightly crooked but white teeth. She tried securing a strand of loose hair behind her ears but it immediately fell back across her wide eyes. "Hey Tyler, I'm Belinda. Real nice to meet you."

He nodded.

"Tyler's family just moved to the lake."

Belinda's smile didn't waiver. "Welcome to the area. Where'd you come from?"

"We...uh...lived in Atlanta."

"Not that far away then. Do you like it up here?"

"It's fine."

"Tyler's going to help out around here. Cut the grass and clean the sanctuary for us. Take some of the load off me."

Belinda chuckled. "You mean me."

"His family might be joining us for Sunday services too."

"That'd be real nice."

Tyler's face flushed with color.

"I was telling him about our youth group and the things they help out with in the community."

"It's a great bunch of people. I don't know if Daddy told you, but we get together every couple weeks and just hang out. You know, go to dinner, stuff like that."

Dampness began forming in Tyler's armpits. "I think he mentioned it."

Pastor Williamson intervened. "Aren't ya'll meeting here this Sunday night?"

"We sure are. Everybody's bringing snacks and we're going to rent a movie. Why don't you join us, Tyler?"

"Umm, maybe."

"Oh come on," she urged. "We'd love to have you. It's real laid back. You'd have a good time," Belinda promised through her friendly smile.

"Okay, I guess so."

"Good, good," stated Pastor Williamson. "Well, hate to rush, but your mama and granddaddy are waiting. Told them I'd bring you right back so we better get going."

Before leaving he reminded Belinda to file some papers on his desk.

"I know, Daddy. I'll take care of it." As they turned to leave, she added, "It was real nice meeting you, Tyler. See you at Sunday services."

Outside, the two squirrels bravely descended the trunk of the tree. They eventually hopped to the ground and eyed the visitors leaning against the car. "Thought you guys got lost," Gwen joked as Tyler and Pastor Williamson returned.

"Sorry about that, it's my fault. Guess Belinda inherited my gift of gab. Hope I didn't make you wait too long."

"Not at all. We appreciate your time, Pastor Williamson."

"Glad you could come. And Tyler, I'll see you on Monday if not before."

The young man waved as the car pulled away.

"So you met the pastor's daughter?" Gwen asked.

"Uh-huh."

"What was she like?"

"Seemed nice."

"She pretty?"

"Yeah." He smiled and shyly looked away.

Gwen didn't press. As they rode along, she reminded him, "Don't forget you have to take a shot this afternoon."

"I know." Then he added, "I think we should go to church this Sunday."

"Okay," Gwen answered. "Let's do that…but you still have to take your shot.

CHAPTER 14

Gwen scanned the computer screen. She'd been working on the report for days and hoped to complete it before leaving for church. Clicking on the grant application, she pasted a section to her brief, then saved the document. "I'm almost finished," she stated out loud.

"Looks like you've been busy," Tyler announced.

Gwen jumped. "You scared me, didn't think you were up yet."

"Sorry. You work all night?"

"Just got up a little early."

"Can I talk to you for a minute?"

"Sure."

"I've been wondering about something." He hesitated. "My change. What do you think caused it?"

"I...I don't know."

"Well last night I was thinking. You remember when it first started?"

"Yeah, right after that bad asthma attack and you began taking those allergy shots."

"Do you think they might have something to do with it?"

"Honestly Hon, I don't know, but I'll talk to Dr. Johnston about it after church. Right now I need to finish this report."

"Hope he appreciates all your hard work."

"I believe he does." Barry Johnston unexpectedly entered the room.

"Morning," Gwen said.

"Don't mind me. Came up for a cup of coffee." He walked to the sink and filled the espresso machine.

"I've put together some information on a new grant you might be interested in."

"What? Oh good."

"I'll send it to the printer in your office."

"Hmm?"

"The grant information."

"That's fine."

Tyler sneezed and rubbed his eyes.

Johnston's attention immediately focused on him. "How're you this morning? Any different?" He wasn't concerned about the teen's allergies. The Savant's reaction to the experimental drug and continued transformation was all that mattered to him.

"A little itchy that's all."

Gwen asked, "Shouldn't the shots be working by now? He's still got the same symptoms. I haven't noticed any improvement."

"Let's not forget they won't be effective overnight. It'll take some time for his body to build up immunity to the allergens."

"I know. Just want him to start feeling better."

"All we can do is continue the therapy. We have to be persistent and stay on schedule."

"We're leaving for church in a bit, then we have plans for lunch with Roger Hall. We should be home around two or three."

"Let's administer the shot when you get back."

"Why does he have to come?" Tyler interjected. "Can't it just be us?

"I'm looking forward to seeing Roger again. It'll be fun," she offered.

Tyler still had reservations about the man but remained silent.

Their interaction with the reporter worried Johnston too. The family needed to be isolated. Close contact with outsiders complicated matters as the project could be exposed if others were involved in their lives.

Johnston took a sip of steaming espresso before turning back to Tyler. "Are you sleeping at night? Getting enough rest?"

"Sure, I guess so." Tyler glanced at his mother. "I'm...uh...going to get ready for church."

"Let me get out of your way too." Johnston turned to leave.

"I'll forward that grant information to you," Gwen reminded him. "Let me know if you have questions or need anything else."

"Excellent, thank you." Johnston returned to his basement office with his coffee. He closed the door as the printer sprang to life, spitting out Gwen's useless report.

The morning passed as Barry Johnston opened the CT-POTENTIAL file and entered test data into the computer spreadsheet. The soft clicking of key strokes filled the air as he diligently updated Tyler Shealy's clinical record.

EFFICACY:

- *Patient continues to exhibit positive outcomes.*
- *Mental and reasoning capacity expanded and steady.*

SAFETY:

- *No adverse side effects exhibited.*
- *No changes in physical functioning capabilities.*
- *No unusual or adverse behavior issues noted.*

PROGRESS NOTES:

- *Reduce dosage to 100 ml.*
- *Continue to calibrate dosages and monitor for maximum benefit with least risk.*
- *Trial is progressing with great success. Appears effective and safe.*

Johnston's thoughts were consumed with the project. New York had backed off and gone soft when things got complicated. *This breakthrough is due to my diligence. Those idiots didn't have the courage to proceed.* He vowed to push ahead no matter what. *I'll eventually get the recognition I deserve.*

The specimen was doing quite well, better than imagined. However the satisfaction was tempered as he needed additional data to confirm his findings. He also knew the compound was in short supply.

Johnston rose from his chair and began pacing back and forth in quick, deliberate steps. The obsessive physician's mind raced with alternatives. He turned to a bookshelf meticulously organized with volumes of medical manuals and other treasured readings, trying to decide if the answer was somehow hidden within their covers. Johnston bent to the bottom shelf where several hardbacks were neatly arranged. He grabbed <u>The Renaissance Man</u>.

Returning to his chair, Johnston leaned back and lifted his feet onto the desk. He flipped the book over and scanned the back summary.

> The true Renaissance Man, Leonardo da Vinci, was born in Florence, Italy in 1452. He was the illegitimate son of a local notary and a young peasant woman....

> Leonardo da Vinci was a universal genius and conceived ideas vastly ahead of his generation....

> The artist, who was also a scientist, mathematician, engineer, inventor and writer is widely considered the most diversely talented person to have ever lived....

> He greatly advanced the state of knowledge....

Johnston sat quietly for a few moments then laid the book on the desk.

"Renaissance Man," he uttered softly. The physician rose and stepped into the adjacent laboratory. His heart began to race.

The examination table where Angelina, the young Mexican woman succumbed to the physician's initial testing sat in the middle of the room. Johnston rationalized her unfortunate death as a critical learning experience.

Her demise wasn't in vain, he reasoned, staring coldly at the table.

Johnston walked over to the cabinets and opened a drawer, pulling out a syringe and a vial containing a clear liquid. He removed the plastic cap from the tip of the hypodermic needle and with a steady hand carefully inserted it through the rubber-tipped vial.

The man stared at the precious serum. In just a short time it had miraculously created an entirely new world for Tyler Shealy.

Johnston thought about the old man afflicted with Alzheimer's. *Can the compound cure him too? Just what are the boundaries of this drug? What are the possibilities? Can it create another Leonardo da Vinci?* he wondered. *But the risks! Is it safe? The Savant seems to tolerate the injections, but how will others fare? Is Tyler special or just lucky? More testing has to be done,* Johnston reasoned. *Proper scientific protocol dictates it.*

Unfortunately nothing he'd done was proper. Now the lack of additional compound had become a problem. How should the remainder of the precious drug be used?

Sometimes you have to crawl out on a limb, he thought. *That's where the fruit is.*

Dr. Barry Johnston took a long, deep breath and began rolling up his shirt's sleeve. Then he paused....

* * * * * *

The family arrived at Lanier Baptist Church. The grounds were already filled with people dressed in everything from suits to blue jeans. Parishioners shook hands and slapped each other on the back, exchanging pleasantries with friends and neighbors as they funneled toward the building.

Tyler got out of the car and smoothed his new khaki pants.

Ernest looked around suspiciously. "Where we at?"

"Granddaddy, we're going to church."

"Huh, what you talkin' 'bout? Where's Gwenny?"

"I'm right here, Daddy. Let's go inside."

They family found an open pew near the front. The sanctuary was filling as the pianist played an old upright Yamaha.

A choir of nine in black robes sat awaiting their chance to sing. Tyler searched the group, immediately spotting Belinda in the back row.

After a ritual of song, scripture and prayer, Pastor Williamson began his weekly sermon.

"This morning I'd like to speak to you about change. More specifically, impediments to change. Let me begin by saying I recently read a transcript of a sermon from the United Church of God. It was written by Mr. Gary Black. I found it to be a wonderful piece and decided to share it with you this morning. I'll start off as Mr. Black did, with a short story...

A police officer pulled over a speeding car. The officer said, 'I clocked you at eighty miles per hour in a fifty-five mile an hour zone, Sir.'

The driver said, 'Officer, I was on cruise control. It was just sixty. Maybe you should recalibrate your instruments.'

Without looking up from her knitting, the driver's wife said sweetly, 'Now don't be silly, dear. You know this car doesn't have cruise control.'

The officer wrote out the ticket as the driver looked at his wife. 'Can't you keep your mouth shut for once?'

The wife smiled. 'You should be thankful your radar detector went off when it did.'

As the officer made out the second ticket for an illegal radar detector, the man shook his head.

The officer frowned. 'I notice you're not wearing your seatbelt, Sir. That's an automatic seventy-five dollar fine.'

The driver said, 'Yeah, but you see, I had to take my wallet out of my pocket and I couldn't get to it without undoing my seatbelt.'

His wife said, 'Now dear, you know very well you never wear your seatbelt.'

And as the police officer wrote out the third ticket, the driver turned to his wife and barked, 'Why don't you shut up?'

The officer looked over at the woman. 'Ma'am, does your husband always speak to you in that tone?'

And she said, 'Oh, no officer, only when he's been drinking.'"

The congregation laughed wholeheartedly at the amusing tale. Pastor Williamson waited until they quieted.

"I don't want to even think about what might have happened later on. Obviously, this man had a few problems—lying, disrespect, drinking and driving. Some things needed to change.

Today's sermon is about impediments to change. What's in your life that needs to change? Hopefully your life's not like that, but when you think about it, the habits and attitudes you have, what would you do differently? What impedes positive change in your life? It isn't easy. What is it that holds back a transformation in our lives? What are the things that act as speed bumps in our lives and keeps change from occurring?"

Ernest had drifted away into his own confused world while Tyler focused intensely on the pulpit, listening closely to the sermon. Reverend Williamson continued.

"I'd like to narrow it down to three points, three things that hold us back. The first one I have for you is excuses. It's very easy to make excuses that keep us from changing.

Have you ever said or heard someone say, 'Well, I'm only human. Humans do bad things.' That's just an excuse, isn't it? We hear it a lot. We've probably said it, but it's one of those things that can hold us back. It's a speed bump on our path to spiritual progress."

A Lanier Baptist parishioner shouted, "Amen," from his pew. Others in the congregation silently nodded agreement.

"I have another story. Although it's not accurate in all its details, it generally gives the gist of what happened. It's called, *The Story of the Rail Width*.

The U.S. Standard Railway gauge, which is the distance between two railways, is four feet, eight and one-half inches. Why such an odd number? Because that's the way they built them in England, and American railroads were built by British expatriates using equipment from the U.K. Why did the English adopt such a peculiar gauge? Because the people who built the pre-railroad tramways used it. They in turn were locked into that gauge because people who built the tramways used the same standards and tools for building wagons, which were set at a gauge of four feet, eight and one-half inches.

Why were wagons built to that scale? Because with any other size the wheels didn't match the ruts on the roads. So who built these old, rutted roads? The first long-distance highways in Europe were built by Imperial Rome for the benefit of their Legions. The roads have been used ever since. The ruts were first made by Roman war chariots. Four feet, eight and one-half inches was the width the chariot needed to accommodate the rear ends of two war horses.

We really get into a rut in our life and say, 'Well, that's just the way I am.'

That's an excuse, isn't it?

Ken Blanchard, author of The One Minute Manager wrote, 'The chains of habit are too light to feel until they're too heavy to break.'

Now we can be overtaken by a bad habit before we know it. One study I read said that it takes seven times of repeating something to develop a habit. But it takes thirty times of not doing it to break one. It's easier to start a habit than it is to get out, so we tend to ride in those same ruts very easily.

Remember the old example of the circus elephants, how they're trained to stay where they are? They tie a chain to them when they're young and very small. The animals pull and try to break the chain but they can't do it. They try many times but learn that they can't break away. When they get older and a lot stronger, capable of breaking that chain, the trainers can put a little rope on them. The elephants already know they can't break it so they don't even try.

Sometimes sins can be like a ball and chain. We learn to live with it because we've tried to break away but it didn't work so we quit trying.

Well, we could ask ourselves, 'How much elephant effort have we really put into it?' I'm sure that praying about a problem is very important, but is that all there is in our arsenal? Is that all the strength and muscle we can put behind it? Oh, no. There's a whole lot more. There's practical things we can do in our lives. So it's important to ask ourselves, 'Do we have the little elephant mentality? Or are we really putting everything into it?'"

Tyler sneezed loudly and Gwen handed him a tissue from her bag.

"The second point I have is urgency. Sometimes we just don't see the urgency to change.

I want to tell you a story about urgency.

Picture a scene in the old west sometime in the 1870s. Weary cowboys in dusty Levis gather around a blazing campfire after a day on the open range. The lonely howl of a coyote counterpoints the notes of a guitar. The moon floats serenely overhead. Suddenly a billow of pain shatters the night. A cowpoke leaps away from the fire, dancing in agony. Hot rivet syndrome has claimed another victim.

You see, Levis had been made in those days with copper rivets at stress points to provide extra strength. On those original Levis, model 501, the crotch rivet was the critical one. When cowboys crouched too long beside the campfire the rivet grew uncomfortably hot. For years the brave men of the west suffered from this curious occupational hazard.

Then in 1933 Walter Haas Sr., the President of Levi Strauss, went camping in his Levi 501's. He crouched by a crackling campfire in the High Sierras drinking in the pure mountain air when he fell prey to hot rivet syndrome.

He consulted the professional wranglers in his party. Had they suffered the same mishap? An impassioned 'Yes' was the reply. Haas vowed that the offending rivet must go. At their next meeting of the Board of Directors they voted it to extinction."

Once again, a smattering of laughter rippled through the congregation. Many of the men squirmed in their seats, imagining the effect of the preacher's tale. Ernest reached down and rubbed his crotch.

"Some people change when they see the light. Other's change when they feel the heat. Which type of person are you? Do we change when we see the light? You know, I really need to change. I really need to work on that. Or do we put if off because it's really not urgent now? We wait until we feel the heat.

The man in the car with the police officer writing him ticket after ticket was beginning to feel some heat. Had he worked on some of those problems before, he might have saved himself a little bit. Are we the kind of people who change when we see the light or when we feel the heat?

Point number three. Sometimes we just don't have a real desire to change.

Vladimir Horowitz, a classical pianist was once told by a person who had heard his concert, 'I would do anything to play like you.'

He replied by saying, 'No you wouldn't, because if you did, you would.'

I would do anything? No, we just wish we could. It was wishful thinking. We have to look at a couple things if we really desire to change. Oftentimes it's easy to see things in our life that we'd like to change, wish would change but we don't want it bad enough.

In order to really desire change, we must look to the end and see the result. Let's go to Matthew 18."

Some parishioners scrambled to find the passage in their Bibles.

"Change brings reward. It's far greater than the pleasures of the sin today. We know that, but how much are we really focused on that reward? Have we really focused on what happens after this life as a result of being willing to change?

Matthew 18:8 says, 'If your hand or foot causes you to sin, cut if off and cast it from you.' Can you imagine cutting off your arm and tossing it away? Now I'm not recommending you do this, but think of the attitude. Look how far He's saying you have to be willing to go to change things.

How do we relate that verse to our lives? Do we want change badly enough that we're willing to do whatever it takes to achieve it?

Anybody know the name Aron Ralston? You probably heard of him several years ago. He was twenty-seven at the time, hiking a remote area near the Canyonlands National Park of southeast Utah. He was hiking through a rocky area and a big boulder came crashing down on his arm. He was trapped and there was no way for the rescuers to see him. He realized that he would die if he didn't break free, but he couldn't. He ended up having to take his pocketknife and cut off his right arm below the elbow."

A quiet mutter of horror spread throughout the congregation.

"Now, I can't even imagine what it would be like to do that. He proceeded to cut off his right arm below the elbow, applied a tourniquet, administered first aid, rigged some anchors and rappelled sixty feet to the canyon floor below. He was found by a couple of other hikers. The young man was able to walk into the hospital and get treatment. He wanted life so desperately he was willing to cut his arm off so he could walk off that mountain and find help.

You know, it takes less work to live with a problem than to change it. We get comfortable. It's so important that we don't have attitudes that discourage change in our life, attitudes that hold us back, ways of looking at change that are roadblocks or stumbling blocks for us. There are no shortcuts to salvation. We struggle but thankfully God is there to help us. Why doesn't He get rid of the struggle? Wouldn't it be a lot easier if we could just decide to change and it happened? It would be a lot easier if that were the case. Why doesn't He help us more and decrease the struggle?

I read a story once about a man who saw a cocoon. One day he noticed a little hole in the top of the cocoon and realized that a butterfly was about to come out. He watched that little butterfly struggle for hours to get out of that tiny hole but it didn't seem to be making any progress. In fact, after a while it seemed to just have given up. The man decided this was excruciating to watch so he took a pair of scissors and snipped the opening a little more so the butterfly could slip right out. The butterfly had a swollen body and very small wings. He watched the butterfly, thinking it would soon take flight. It didn't. The body was too big, the wings weren't developed.

He later found out that it was the struggle to squeeze through that little hole that God had intended for the fluid to be pressed out of the body into the wings, making them full, firm and able to fly. By decreasing the struggle he had caused that butterfly to never be able to fly.

I think sometimes God sees that struggle is necessary. Yes, change is hard but the struggle is absolutely essential to our lives. We all struggle, and God is willing to give us strength, but He's not going to snip the end of the cocoon. He knows that's part of our very character. We will value the character more if we have to struggle for it. That's an important aspect to our growth."

Gwen thought about the changes they'd all undergone and wondered....

Tyler's entire life had been a struggle. Would he be able to escape his autistic cocoon and fly into a new world? Would her prayers be answered?

Ernest's struggle was difficult to accept. She'd soon be losing him to Alzheimer's and no amount of urgency or desire could change that. Only a strong belief that a better life awaited him provided comfort.

She thought of her own struggles. Would she become stronger because of them? How would her life change? Would God continue to test and strengthen her for what lay ahead?

Pastor Williamson paused for a few moments. The congregation sat perfectly still, anxiously awaiting his final words.

"Let's ask ourselves these questions: What do we think about change? What's our attitude toward change? Are we making excuses? Are we putting it off? How deeply do we desire change?

Now the result of change, even though it is a struggle, is a life of joy and happiness. We can be thankful that Christ went before us, died for us and enables us. That's such an encouragement when we're thinking about change. But let's remember that it's a struggle that brings happiness in this life. It also brings a tremendous reward in the life to come.

Let us pray...."

The family waited in line with other parishioners to shake the reverend's hand. "Very inspiring sermon today. It certainly impacted my outlook on life," Gwen said sincerely. "We'll see you again next week."

CHAPTER 15

The family left the church spiritually enriched…and hungry.

As they headed for Seabones restaurant to meet Roger Hall for lunch, Tyler leaned his head back and coughed several times, drawing his mother's attention.

"Hon, are you okay?"

"Ye…yeah."

"You sure? We can go home if you want." Gwen glanced over at the struggling teen.

"I'm…I'm fine. Let's go. I know you're really looking forward to seeing Roger," he stated with a hint of sarcasm.

The reporter was waiting in the restaurant parking lot. Smiling from ear to ear, he approached to give her a quick hug. "Good to see you. How was church?"

"Very inspirational. Reverend Williamson delivered a wonderful sermon."

"I'm glad you enjoyed it." He paused before adding, "You guys hungry? We've got good timing. Doesn't look too busy yet."

Once again, Tyler began wheezing. "I think I need my inhaler."

Gwen searched her purse, shoved the device into his mouth and pushed. Once…twice.

The teen's breathing immediately eased as he leaned on the car.

"I knew you didn't feel well. Should've taken you home."

"Mom, don't worry. I…I don't want to ruin your lunch."

"Forget about lunch. You're much more important."

"Well, maybe we should go home." He purposely coughed.

"Roger, I'm sorry, but we can't stay. Tyler's not feeling well."

"Of course. I'll come with you."

"That's not necessary."

"It's not up for debate." His mind was set and he followed them to the lake house.

Tyler's manipulative plan had almost worked. He hadn't counted on Roger Hall going home with them.

* * * * * *

"Hon, do you want to go to your room and rest for a while?" Gwen asked.

"I'm feeling a lot better now. Think I'll just lay on the sofa and watch television. The Braves game'll be on soon."

Ernest pushed his glasses up the bridge of his nose. "I'm hungry. When we gonna eat?"

"Right now, Daddy. I'll fix everyone something."

"Oh, you don't have to worry about me," Roger said, rising and heading for the door. "I'll just get out of your hair."

"Don't be silly. It won't be as good as Seabones, but I guarantee you won't starve."

"I'll only stay if you let me help."

The teen rolled his eyes.

A warm, appreciative smile appeared on Gwen's face as Roger followed her to the kitchen and was put to work spreading mayonnaise on a slice of bread. "I thought Tyler was taking shots for his allergies."

"He is, but the doctor says it may take a while to start working."

Barry Johnston was working in his office and heard the family return early. He came upstairs and was surprised to find Roger Hall. The atmosphere immediately chilled as the men stared at each other for the first time since their meeting at the C.D.C.

"I believe you two have met," Gwen offered tentatively.

There was no handshake, only a slight nod of acknowledgment. "I thought you were going out to lunch," Johnston said.

"Tyler had another allergy attack so we came straight home."

His interest immediately piqued. A concerned anxiety was etched across the physician's face. "Is he all right?"

"He seems to be better now," Gwen answered.

"In light of this, you still decided to drop by for lunch, Mr. Hall?"

"I followed them back to make sure everything was okay. I have a strong interest in the family's welfare."

"I'm sure you do," Johnston stated bluntly while staring coldly at the unwelcome visitor.

"Can we fix you a sandwich too?" Gwen politely asked.

"No thanks, I'm fine. Don't want to intrude on your lunch." Again he glared at Roger Hall. "I'll just check on Tyler."

He went into the living room where the teen lay watching the baseball game. The announcers were analyzing an injury suffered by the opposing shortstop.

Tyler was stretched out on the couch with his fingers intertwined behind his head. "Drag the guy off the field and let's get on with the game," he mumbled angrily, lacking patience and compassion for the injured player.

"Did you say something?" Dr. Johnston asked.

"No," Tyler abruptly responded, still mad about the delay.

"What are you doing?"

"What does it look like? I'm watching the game."

"Who's playing?" Johnston asked, wanting to develop a rapport with the young man.

"Braves and Cardinals."

A slow motion replay of the incident moved across the screen. "Looks like it could be his knee," the doctor surmised.

"It's his A.C.L.," Tyler responded.

"You know about A.C.L. injuries?"

"It's a tear to the anterior cruciate ligament. The A.C.L. is one of the four main ligaments of the knee. It attaches to the femur and passes down through the knee joint to the front of the tibia. That's the key ligament holding both the upper and lower parts of the leg together."

"That's exactly right," the physician confirmed.

"A.C.L. injuries are fairly common among athletes."

They watched as the St. Louis shortstop was helped off the field.

"Always wished I could've played more sports as a youngster. Kind of regret it, feel like I missed something. How about you, Tyler? Ever play Little League?"

"No."

"That's a shame."

"Never cared much about it."

"You never wanted to play ball with the other children?"

"Not really, didn't fit in. Wasn't very good at it."

"And now? Do you ever wish...?"

"I wish a lot of things," Tyler rudely interrupted. "Being different stole my childhood and turned Mom into a nursemaid. Taking care of an autistic kid made her miss a lot too."

"I'm sure she'd disagree. Your mother loves you."

"I know she does but...."

"Lunch's ready, come and get it," Gwen called from the kitchen interrupting their conversation.

"Dr. Johnston, are you sure you won't join us?"

"Thanks anyway. You folks go ahead and enjoy your meal."

As he turned to leave, she asked, "Do you have a minute to talk privately while everyone's eating?"

"Absolutely. Let's go downstairs."

"I'll be back in a jiffy. You guys go ahead and start without me," she called to the others as she followed the physician to his office.

There, Gwen gathered her thoughts. "I'm sure you've noticed the change in Tyler."

"His communication skills seem to have improved tremendously."

"It's all happened so quickly."

"That's wonderful," he responded.

"You know he started feeling different right after his first allergy shot. This'll probably sound crazy, but is it possible there's something in them that's affected him?"

Barry Johnston wasn't surprised she'd made the connection. Now the question was, how should he handle it? *Should I try to reason with her? Who knows? The woman might be so grateful that she'd overlook my approach and appreciate Tyler's new life. Maybe she'll understand just how lucky he was to be chosen for the experiment.*

The physician couldn't take that chance. "I wish it was possible, Gwen. If so, there would be thousands of Autistics out there who'd be cured. However, I'm afraid it's not."

"But the timing, it's such a coincidence."

"That's exactly what it is. I'm sure you know there's no medication of any kind in an allergy shot, just minute amounts of allergens. An injection with absolutely no medicinal value can't possibly have a therapeutic effect."

"Then what's causing it?"

"I'm not a big believer in miracles, but if the boy continues to improve, well maybe it's just that." Johnston smiled. "Now go upstairs and enjoy your lunch with him."

Gwen stood quietly, mulling his comments. She'd always believed in the power of God to perform miracles. But for some reason, she remained unconvinced it was the only explanation for Tyler's new-found normalcy.

* * * * * *

Tyler claimed to be feeling better and wanted to attend the Lanier Baptist young adults meeting that evening. He was anxious to see Belinda again.

He nervously walked into the church's recreation hall carrying a plate of Rice Crispy treats. Several other teens were already there, milling around and enjoying the gathering.

A ping-pong table sat at one end of the room and a big screen television hung on the opposite wall. A table filled with pizza and snacks was off in the corner. Metal folding chairs were randomly scattered around, but almost everyone stood in small cliques talking among themselves. Some mingled from group to group, laughing and enjoying fellowship with their friends.

Tyler scanned the room for Belinda. Stepping out of his comfort zone wasn't easy. The scene was reminiscent of grammar school when he was left alone while the other kids played. He remained an outcast, unable to interact and socialize with his classmates. Back then, he didn't care. Now he did...and was terrified.

A pasty sweat formed in the palms of his hands and his heart raced. He nervously reached up to straighten his hair while balancing the plate of snacks against his body with the other hand.

Suddenly a voice called out, "Tyler, glad you could make it!" Belinda broke away from a small gathering and stepped toward him. The bubbly teenage girl was wearing a pair of jeans with a pale orange blouse.

A huge grin spread across his face as she approached.

"Why don't you put those on the table with the other snacks?"

She led him over and set the platter down next to some brownies. "They look great. Probably won't last long around this crowd."

"I just started eating them." Tyler added, "Never cared for them before."

"You're kidding me. How can anyone not like Rice Crispy Treats? I could eat them all day long."

"Always had Cheerios."

"Your Mom made Cheerio treats with melted butter and marshmallows?"

"Not exactly. Just plain Cheerios and milk."

Belinda chuckled. "Way too healthy for me."

"My tastes have been changing lately."

"C'mon and I'll introduce you to the rest of the group."

Tyler remained frozen, still nervous about meeting the others.

"C'mon, they won't bite. I promise." She reached out to grab his hand. Her warm touch was comforting and helped put him at ease.

With her encouragement he inched forward, his heart pounding harder with each step.

"Hey guys, this is Tyler Shealy. He'll be joining us tonight."

Tyler's eyes remained locked on Belinda as she led him around and introduced everyone, never releasing his hand.

The last group was standing next to the ping-pong table. "Tyler, this is Sara and Beth," pointing toward the two girls. "And that's Gray." She finally released her grasp and stepped over to lock arms with the tall, good-looking young man. "His family has a house out on Lake Lanier too. You guys are probably neighbors."

"Hey, Tyler. Glad to meet you," Gray said politely.

"Hel...hello," Tyler stuttered.

"Wanna play?" Gray reached down to pick up a paddle lying on the table.

"He's the best ping-pong player here." Belinda warned, "Nobody can beat him."

"No, I don't think so. Never played before."

"Are you sure? Don't you want to try?" Belinda urged.

"I'd rather not."

Once again she turned to Gray. "Wanna play me instead?"

"Sure, grab a paddle."

Suddenly, Tyler felt abandoned as she focused on the other teen. The two were soon consumed in their match and he stood by feeling awkward and left out.

Sara, one of the other girls stepped over and asked, "Are ya new to the community?"

"Yeah, uh...we just moved out from Atlanta."

"Must've been exciting."

"What?" His attention was still on Belinda, laughing and enjoying her match with Gray.

"Did ya like living in the city? Miss your friends?" she asked.

Tyler replied bluntly, "Didn't have any."

"Oh, okay." Tired of trying to make conversation, Sara finally gave up and left.

Once again, Tyler stood alone watching Belinda play ping pong. He only wanted to be with her. None of the others mattered.

"Wanna play again, Gray?" she asked after losing 11-0.

Now, the Savant was experiencing another human emotion. Jealousy. He spent the rest of the evening sitting by himself....while Belinda spent hers with Gray.

When Gwen picked him up, Tyler was upset and refused to talk about the gathering.

At home, he stalked off to his room shouting, "I'm not taking that job at the church. We were crazy to think it would ever work." He slammed the bedroom door behind him.

CHAPTER 16

"I'm leaving for a late supper," Dr. Johnston announced as he passed through the living room.

"I'll be glad to fix you something," Gwen offered while sitting on the couch holding her new laptop.

"I wouldn't hear of it. I impose too much now. Besides, looks like you're busy working."

Gwen finished researching another grant. Hopefully this one would be what he was looking for and prompt some new assignments. She forwarded the document to Johnston's printer. Instantly, a window popped up indicating the device was out of paper. She went downstairs to refill the tray so the document could print and be available for Johnston's review once he returned.

Passing through the laboratory, she once again thought about Tyler's improvement and how it coincided so perfectly with the injections. While Dr. Johnston denied any connection, it continued to nag her.

Curious, she approached the cabinets and opened a drawer where the allergy serum was kept. Dr. Johnston's handwriting was scrawled across the face of a box.

EXPERIMENTAL COMPOUND. SPECIMEN #2-TYLER SHEALY. MALE, 19 YR. AUTISTIC SAVANT.

Experimental? Specimen? Unsure what it meant, she picked the carton up and read it again. *Specimen #2...Tyler?* For several moments she tried to digest the implications. Then her hands began shaking, rattling the vials inside the box. The room spun and she leaned against the counter to maintain balance. *It can't be. This isn't allergy serum. What's he doing to my son? Pumping some strange substance into his body without my knowledge? Oh my God, is this why he's changing, because of some other drug?* she reasoned.

The past weeks flashed through her mind. Tyler's smiling face appeared as he described how different things felt, how the world seemed to slowly open up. Gwen stood motionless, stunned that some fiend was secretly using her son as a test animal. Her emotion continued to build as she placed the box back in the drawer. The woman stormed upstairs filled with anger and fear. "Tyler! Daddy!" she yelled in a frantic voice. "Come on, we're leaving this place right now."

"Mom, what is it? What's wrong?" Tyler asked coming down the hall from his room.

"Get in the car," Gwen ordered as she grabbed Ernest by the arm to lead him outside.

"Where're we going?"

"Away from here!"

They drove directly to Roger Hall's apartment.

Gwen knocked on the door.

"Well hello, what a nice surprise. Come in."

As the family entered the two bedroom apartment, Roger quickly noticed the tension in her face. "Is something wrong?"

"I'm sorry for barging in like this, but didn't know where else to go."

"What is it? Is everybody okay?"

She replied in a frightened tone, "It's Dr. Johnston."

"What about him?"

"Tyler, why don't you and Daddy sit down and watch television? I'd like to talk to Roger alone."

They stepped into the guest bedroom which doubled as the reporter's home office. The soft, muffled sounds of the T.V. penetrated the thin apartment walls.

"What'd Johnston do?" Hall demanded.

"You're probably going to say I'm crazy, but I think he's injecting Tyler with another drug. I don't believe there's allergy serum in those shots. It's something else, some other substance."

"What…what makes you say that?"

Tyler entered the small bedroom.

"Where's your granddaddy?"

"On the couch. He's fine," Tyler responded. "What's happening, Mom? You've been upset about something ever since we left the lake house. Never said a word on the drive over."

She embraced him. "Oh Tyler, I love you so much."

"I love you too but something's wrong. I've been lost all these years, not having a clue about the world around me. Now I'm finally alive. So please Mom, tell me. I can handle it."

Her voice began to crack, "Hon, you…you mean so much…so much to me, I couldn't bear if anything…anything happened to you."

"What are you talking about?"

Roger stood silently by.

"It's the allergy shots. We talked about how they might be impacting your behavior."

"Yeah, my condition began improving about the time I started taking them."

"We both wondered if maybe they were responsible."

"But you asked Dr. Johnston and he said it wasn't possible. Is there something else I should know?" Tyler probed.

Gwen looked away. How could she explain he might have been nothing more than an expendable specimen in a potentially dangerous experiment? He'd already been through so much and now this.

"Mom, please."

"Those shots you've been taking may not be for allergies. I think Dr. Johnston's been injecting you with something else, maybe some type of experimental drug."

"What? How could you possibly...?"

Roger Hall chimed in. "Let's not jump to any conclusions here. What proof do you have?"

"I was in the laboratory and found a box of vials with some strange notes about experimental compound and Tyler being a specimen. Lord it scared me."

"Are you sure? Maybe you misunderstood the label. You don't know what's in those vials and if Johnston was really using it on Tyler."

"No, but it makes sense. Don't you understand? His allergies haven't improved and he's been receiving the serum for weeks now."

The teen wiped his nose.

Roger shook his head. "They said it could take a while for the shots to work."

"The transformation began about the time Johnston started injecting him. He told me there wasn't any medication in the allergy shots and it couldn't be related. But what if there was something else in those vials? I'm calling the police. Let them investigate. What he did, or what I think he did, was illegal and dangerous. He used Tyler as a guinea pig."

"Hold on a minute. There's no use getting the police involved until we're certain," Roger offered, trying to calm the situation. "What if you're wrong? Then what? How's that going to impact your relationship with Johnston...and your job?"

"I don't care about that right now."

"Why don't you go back tomorrow and talk to him. I'll come along and maybe we can get to the bottom of all this."

Gwen paused to think. "Maybe we should go tonight. If it's true, we're better off finding out sooner than later. Who knows what that drug could be doing to Tyler?"

"Look, it's late," Roger reasoned. "Johnston's probably asleep by now."

"We'll wake him up."

"Gwen, I understand how angry you are...."

"No you don't. You can't. He may have injected something into my son's body not caring what it could do. If he did, I've got to know now!"

She reluctantly agreed not to involve the police for the time being. However, Gwen couldn't be dissuaded from confronting Johnston immediately.

* * * * * *

A quarter-moon lit the sky as the rental car's headlights beamed down the highway. Hard rock blared from the radio, keeping Manny's mind occupied while traveling the empty road. "Born in the U.S.A., I was born in the U.S.A…," the Puerto Rican sang along with Bruce Springsteen and the E Street Band. His Hispanic voice was woefully out of tune with the group that made the song a classic. "You 'n me, Bruce, we both be boss," he referenced the rock star's media persona.

A small duffle lay in the passenger's seat. Manny reached over and patted the bag which held a Colt .375 Magnum Python. "We both be boss," he repeated.

The automobile slowed as it approached the entrance to the secluded lake home. He turned into the driveway, immediately killing the headlights. The car crept along in the darkness until it reached the iron gate guarding the property. Remembering the code, Manny punched 2-2-6-2. After a sudden jolt the gate hummed open.

The rental with New Jersey plates proceeded through the barrier, stopping just inside as the gate swung shut behind it. Manny reached in the duffel bag for the Magnum revolver and a handful of cartridges. He loaded the weapon, tucked it securely inside the waistband of his jeans and slid the rest of the ammunition into his pocket.

The narrow entrance was covered by overhanging tree limbs shielding the moonlight. An army of chirping crickets broke the silence as the Latino walked toward the house's blackened silhouette.

At the door to the daylight basement, he turned the knob with a gloved hand. It was locked. The minor inconvenience was easily overcome as he lifted an elbow and with a quick but forceful jab, shattered a pane of glass. Manny paused to see if the sound had awoken anyone. The house remained dark and still. He reached through to unlatch the door and went inside.

Manny moved stealthily through the basement. Upon reaching the bedroom door, the intruder reached into his waistband to remove the revolver. He raised a closed fist and knocked.

Barry Johnston immediately sat up in bed, "Who...who is it? What do you want?"

There wasn't a response.

"Gwen, is that you?"

Another tap on the door.

"What the hell...?" Annoyed, Johnston crawled out of bed, his silk pajamas sliding effortlessly across the sheets.

Manny stepped away from the door as it cracked open.

"Gwen? Tyler? Who's there?"

"Guess 'gain, Doc."

"Manny! God damn it!" the man cursed angrily as he flipped the nearest light switch. His tone instantly softened upon seeing the .375 Magnum pointed at him. "I...I don't understand, what's...what's the meaning of this?"

"My friend here?" Manny waved the gun slightly. "Means you not in charge no more."

"In charge of what?"

"Dis project."

"Put the gun down. You're going to hurt somebody."

"Sorry Doc." He shook his head.

"Let's talk," Johnston pleaded.

"Already talk. You not hear."

The physician took a small step forward.

"Careful, Amigo," Manny warned.

Johnston stepped back, holding up both hands. "What do you want from me? The remaining compound? Is that what you're after?"

"My job to get rid'a friggin' fleas on dog and here de flea powder." He steadied the pistol.

Johnston stared at the gun as he raked a hand through his ruffled hair. "Did our mutual friend in New York put you up to this craziness?"

"Not friend no more. Pay real good to clean up dis mess."

Realizing the seriousness of his situation, Johnston tried to reason with the man. "You'll never get away with this. I don't care how much he's paying, you won't be able to enjoy it. Do you know what happens to convicted murderers?"

"Murderer!" The Puerto Rican laughed. "Doc, you kill Mexican woman, you murderer too."

"Don't do this. It's just not worth it."

"Hell yeah worth it! Risk 'n reward. Dat what you say. Bigger de friggin' risk, bigger reward. Tired of gettin' pissed on. Got nothin' now. Dis my chance and goin' take it."

"So you're just going to shoot me?"

"Not just you, Doc."

"You…you're planning to kill the entire family?"

"Not take de friggin' risk. All go. No big loss, 'specially old fool and idiot boy. Neither got life no way."

The room became deathly silent as the intruder's full intentions were revealed. Everyone would be eliminated.

"You're wrong about a lot of things, especially Tyler. He's changed. The compound works!"

"Sure it does," the Puerto Rican replied sarcastically.

There was no reasoning with him. All the hard work and sacrifice flashed before Johnston's eyes. The acknowledgement and recognition he'd craved were about to be snatched away.

Running out of options, Barry Johnston made a bold decision to salvage his legacy. He'd try to save the boy and then the knowledge of his clinical contribution could be preserved. In the end, he'd still be recognized. That's all he ever really wanted.

In a daring move he turned and darted toward the stairs. "Tyler! Get out!"

Two bullets from the Colt magnum immediately tore through the back of Barry Johnston's silk pajamas. The first pierced a lung dropping the fleeing physician to his knees while the second entered the right ventricle of his heart.

The hired killer then hurried upstairs and systematically went though each room anxious to finish the job. But no one else was home.

* * * * * *

Unable to persuade Gwen to wait until morning, Roger drove her back to Barry Johnston's home.

"Son of a bitch!" he cursed as another vehicle sped around a curve forcing him onto the shoulder. He struggled to maintain control and avoid a row of trees bordering the blacktop. Gwen gripped the arm rest, willing the car back onto the hard surface.

"Where in God's name was he going so fast and at this hour?" she asked, still a little shaken.

"Probably some drunk. You all right?"

"Yeah, I think so," she replied. "Don't miss the driveway, it's right up here."

"You're sure you want to do this now?"

"I really need to find out what's going on. If he gave Tyler something dangerous, then we might need to act quickly."

As they pulled down the driveway, Gwen exclaimed, "Good Lord, what's going on?" The entire house was aglow. Even the lights in the upstairs bedrooms were on.

They went inside and walked to the top of the stairs. "Dr. Johnston?" she called out. "Dr. Johnston, are you down there?"

No response.

"I know he's here, his car's outside."

"Gwen, he's probably asleep. It's late."

"With all these lights on? And frankly I don't care if he is, I'll wake him. I'm not leaving until I get some answers."

They started down the stairs. At the bottom, Gwen stopped cold. A hand flew to her mouth stifling a scream.

Barry Johnston lay face-down on the floor, a dark puddle surrounded his body. The fabric of his pajama top was drenched in red blood.

"Wait here." Roger cautiously searched the basement. Finally he returned and crouched over Johnston to feel for a pulse.

"Is…is he…dead?" Gwen asked.

"Yeah, I think so."

The nurse had witnessed death numerous times. However, seeing death in a nursing home was different than stumbling upon someone murdered in a home she'd left just hours before.

"We need to call the police." As Gwen reached for her cell, the woman's eyes traveled through the laboratory to the drawer where she'd found the box of vials. It was slightly ajar. She cautiously stepped over and opened it. "Oh my God, it's gone."

"What's gone?" Roger asked.

"The box of vials with Tyler's name on it. Someone took it."

She began to dial 9-1-1.

Roger snatched the phone. "Wait!"

"Hey!" she protested. "What're you doing?"

"Before you call anybody we need to decide what you're going to tell them."

"What are you talking about?"

"Think about it, Gwen. You claim Johnston's using your son in some bizarre experiment. Then tonight the sleazeball turns up dead." He paused. "How do you think that's going to look to the cops?"

"You mean they might think I…? But that's ridiculous! I've been with you most of the evening!"

"You don't have to convince me. It's the authorities who'll be looking for a motive. If the bastard was doing what you say, I think that gives you a pretty good one."

"I haven't done anything!"

"Look, innocent people go to jail every day. Your family needs you. Think about your dad and Tyler."

Was Roger right? Would the police really believe she'd killed Barry Johnston?

"We don't have a choice. There's a dead man lying in the basement. I have to call. Maybe the murderer is the same person who killed that Mexican woman. He needs to be stopped."

Gwen called 9-1-1 and notified the authorities that she'd come home and found Dr. Barry Johnston dead in his basement. The dispatcher assured her the police were on their way.

After she hung up, Roger grabbed her arm, "Come with me."

* * * * * *

While investigators snapped photographs and dusted for fingerprints, Gwen and Roger sat on the sofa and waited. A black man eventually walked up and introduced himself. "I'm Detective Randall Padgett from the Forsyth County Sheriff's Department. Now Mrs. Shealy, I know this is upsetting, but I need to ask you some questions."

She nodded.

"As I understand it you live here with Dr. Johnston, is that correct?"

"Yes that's right. My son and father also live here."

"And what was your relationship with Johnston?"

"What do you mean?"

"Were you personally or romantically involved?"

"Oh for God's sake, no!" she shouted. "I'm sorry. I didn't mean to…. He was my employer. I'm a nurse. This past summer he offered me a position as a research assistant."

Recalling his earlier interview with Dr. Johnston, the detective probed, "So, did you help the deceased conduct any experiments?"

Gwen hesitated, then replied, "No."

"How did you end up residing in the same house? Most people don't live with their boss," Padgett asserted.

"My circumstances are a little unique."

"How's that?"

"My son's disabled and Daddy has Alzheimer's, so I couldn't leave them alone. Dr. Johnston let us live in the upstairs portion of his house."

Padgett produced a pad and pencil from his pocket and scribbled some notes.

"I see. So where is your family now?"

Roger interjected, "They're at my place."

"Oh? And you are?"

"Name's Roger Hall. I'm a family friend."

"They spend a lot of time with you?"

"Some, we had dinner together tonight."

Detective Padgett scribbled more notes. "Where'd you go?"

"I'm sorry?"

"For dinner, where'd you go eat?"

"My apartment, I cooked."

Gwen broke back into the conversation. "Afterwards, Daddy fell asleep and rather than wake him, Roger kindly offered to let us stay there."

"So the two of you came back here? Why?"

"For some personal items."

"Like what?"

"To get some clothes and toiletries for everybody. My father also needs his medications. He takes them on a strict schedule," she explained with a glance toward Roger.

Another officer approached and whispered to Randall Padgett.

The detective stood. "Excuse me for just a minute."

As they waited, Gwen pressed her palms against her eyes. "I'm so nervous."

"Anybody would be, considering what we walked in on," Roger asserted.

"I don't like lying. I think we should tell the police the truth, everything."

"That's not a good idea."

Detective Padgett returned to the room. "Now where were we?"

The interview continued late into the night with both Gwen and Roger recounting how they'd come to get some overnight items and found Johnston in the basement. They reported the car that ran them off the road, but neither could describe it. No, they hadn't heard or seen anything unusual. No, nothing was missing...*except the vials.* No, she didn't know of any reason someone would want to harm the doctor...*except that he was injecting innocent people with an experimental drug.* Reluctantly, Gwen withheld those particular details from the police.

"We'll probably have some more questions over the next couple days," Detective Padgett stated.

"Please keep us informed as to your whereabouts."

They were finally allowed to gather their personal belongings including Budgie, the parakeet, and leave the lake house.

On the ride back, Gwen thought about the box stashed in the trunk. They had quickly searched the office and retrieved Dr. Johnston's laptop and files before the police arrived.

"Are you all right?" Roger asked.

"Not really."

"Try not to worry. We did the right thing."

"What now?" Gwen asked, scared and confused.

"Just sit tight. The authorities are all over it. They'll figure out who did this."

"But taking Dr. Johnston's computer and files...and keeping them from the police."

"We've already been through this. It's no use having the cops waste their time investigating you when the real killer is still out there. They should be directing all their resources elsewhere."

Gwen nodded but remained uncertain.

"Let's give them some time," Roger urged. "Everything will work out. Trust me."

CHAPTER 17

The prior night had been chaotic and sleepless, causing Roger Hall to struggle at work. What should he do next?

He needed some time to clear his mind and reaffirm his dedication to the project. He left the office early and drove to the nearby King Center, a memorial for Martin Luther King. There, he sat reverently in the car reflecting upon the message of the legendary civil rights leader....

"If you want to be important...wonderful.
If you want to be recognized...wonderful.
If you want to be great...wonderful.
But recognize that he who is greatest among you, shall be a
servant."

The inspirational words struck a chord as he'd also been indoctrinated to serve. Duty and responsibility rose above all else.

But now some unexpected events had surfaced to complicate matters. What was happening? Was he left out and not being informed by his superiors? Hall grabbed his cell phone.

"Hello, this is Roger Hall down in Atlanta."..."Can you tell me what in the hell is going on with Project Cerebral One?"..."Johnston's been murdered and you don't know what happened?"..."Well I need to talk to somebody who does. I told you he could be a problem."..."I still don't get it"…"Then how can we continue the tests?"…"I see, uh huh, okay."…"But"…"But"…"Yeah, I know my role, but this kind of shit wasn't part of the deal!"…"Hell yeah I'm concerned. We've got some lunatic out there killing people. Is that what this assignment's about?"…"I didn't think so, but it happened."…"I understand."…"Okay, I'll take care of it."…"Yeah, I'll keep you informed, but you've got to do the same. No more surprises!"…"I know the project's critical and I'm still committed. But it's not so damn important that people have to die."…"You heard me."…"That's right."…"Think about it. Somebody killed Johnston for a reason, and it could impact everyone connected to him, including me!"…"You damn sure better and fast."

A mother with two young children walked past on their way to a minivan parked several spaces away. A small boy stopped and curiously pointed at Roger Hall sitting alone in the car. "You come to see Reverend King?" he yelled.

"Hush up," the woman snapped, grabbing an arm to lead him away.

Hall ignored the minor distraction, continuing his phone conversation. "If that's what you want me to do."…"I'll need some more compound. What Johnston had in the lab was gone."…"Of course I'm sure. Unless he had it stashed somewhere."…"I don't know."…"That's fine. I'll watch him and we'll go from there."…"Yeah, I know we've got other alternatives."…"Don't worry about the woman, I'll handle her." Roger Hall ended the call.

The man masquerading as a newspaper reporter needed to uncover the mysteries surrounding Johnston's death. Who did it and why? The answers were vital for the success of Cerebral One. But something strange was happening and he needed to find out what.

He looked toward the Center and reflected once again about Martin Luther King's legacy. The man was a unique leader, striving for equal rights through a philosophy of non-violent, civil disobedience. Illogically Roger Hall felt his role in the project was similar. *I've got to do my part and get the job done,* he thought. *After all, I'm a servant of the people too.*

* * * * * *

Tyler sat cross-legged on the floor surfing the internet on his mom's laptop. His old desktop computer had been left at Dr. Johnston's lake house.

Roger sat on the couch watching the late news. The T.V. anchor began a segment on the gruesome murder of a physician living at Lake Lanier.

"What'd they say?" Gwen asked as she hurried from the small apartment kitchen.

"Sorry Mom, I was reading this article on the internet and...."

Roger threw his hand up indicating for everyone to be quiet.

"...respected physician's body was found in his Lake Lanier home. It's the second homicide in recent months and those living in the influential community are demanding answers from the authorities."

Tyler coughed to clear the mucus dripping down his throat. "Do they think the two murders...?"

"Ssshhh," Roger urged.

"...and the Sheriff's not releasing any more details until the investigation is complete, but we'll stay on top of this breaking story and let our viewers know of any new developments. Now, back to you...."

As the newscast segued to another less riveting piece, Tyler completed his thought. "Do they think they're related?"

"I don't know," Roger responded.

"Sure hope so."

"Why's that?"

"If not, then they've got two murderers to contend with."

"Roger, you worked the first case with that Hispanic woman. What's the newspaper's take on all this?" Gwen asked.

"Most of the guys believe they're somehow connected, just don't know how."

"Are you assigned to the story?"

He hesitated before replying, "It's my job."

"But I could be a suspect! How can you?"

"I know you didn't do it so there's not a problem. Besides, it'll help me keep on top of what the police find," Roger rationalized in an attempt to ease her mind.

"Why would someone want to kill Dr. Johnston?" Tyler asked.

Roger offered, "Could've been a burglary. You know there's a lot of money living on Lake Lanier, particularly around Eagle's Pointe. Mighty tempting target, especially in these times."

"That doesn't make sense. Nothing was taken," Gwen argued.

"Except for the compound." Tyler's focus immediately returned to the laptop, absorbing information with a ravenous intellect.

"He's right, Roger. Nothing else was missing. Dr. Johnston was murdered for that drug. That's got to be it. Somebody else knew about it and that's who killed him." The more Gwen thought, the more frightened she became. "Oh my God, the authorities aren't even aware it existed."

Roger tried to calm her. "Even if somebody knew about the drug, I'm not convinced it's worth killing for. If you believe the two murders are connected, how was that young woman involved? Let's not get ahead of ourselves."

"Well the more I think about it, the more I believe we should tell the police about the drug," She glanced in Tyler's direction, "and what Johnston was doing with it."

"Gwen, please. Are you also planning on telling them that… uh…it was used on your son without anyone's consent, possibly endangering his life? Talk about handing them a motive! How do you think they'll react to that?" He then added softly, "What's going to happen to your family if you end up in jail?"

Roger Hall's ultimate mission was to protect the anonymity of Project Cerebral One and to help ensure its success. He couldn't afford any additional intervention by the local authorities. For a lot of reasons the experiment was too important to be exposed and he was determined to make sure it wasn't.

"But I'm innocent, I had nothing to do with his death," she repeated.

"I know you didn't," Roger agreed. "But the police don't. Why take that risk and put yourself through all the scrutiny? I'm certain they'll find the real killer soon enough."

Was he right? Was she doing the right thing by withholding the information? Roger certainly thought so and he'd never misled her before. The man was her salvation. He'd given them a place to live. Although not comfortable with the arrangement, what choice did she have? No job, no home and very little money. She needed Roger Hall, but more importantly she trusted him.

"Oh God, I don't know what to do."

Playing on her faith, he added, "Just leave it in His hands and everything will work out, you'll see."

"Suppose you're right."

A loud squawk sounded from the corner of the room interrupting their conversation. Gwen draped a cloth across Budgie's cage to quiet the bird. She was surprised at the condition of the aviary. Tyler had always been meticulous about feeding the parakeet and keeping the cage clean. Lately those chores had been ignored and she constantly had to remind him. "Hon, you need to take care of Budgie's cage tomorrow."

Still engrossed in the laptop, he responded absently, "Okay."

"When are you going to bed?"

"In a minute," the teen replied.

"I made a pallet on the floor beside Granddaddy."

The elderly man had moved into the spare bedroom. Gwen would sleep in the master.

Roger stretched out on the couch and pulled a blanket over his chest.

"Is he going to bother you?" Gwen asked.

"Nope, not a bit. I can sleep through anything."

"I still feel bad about taking your bed."

"Not a problem. Sleep well."

After she'd retired for the night, Roger asked, "So what are you doing on there anyway, Tyler?"

"I'm researching the drug Dr. Johnston was using on me."

"Finding anything?"

"It's hard to determine the specific compound. It was probably produced by some chemical synthesis procedure in a laboratory."

"Synthesis? What's that?"

"Basic chemistry. In simple terms it's the manipulation of several existing compounds to create a series of reactions that could produce another chemical by-product...the new drug."

The teenager's response was comprehensive and logical. No choppy broken phrases were used.

"That's simple? Sounds awfully complicated to me."

"It depends. The process can be fairly easy like mixing two chemicals in a beaker or very complex, depending on the number of reactants and the reactions that occur."

"So Johnston could've created it in his basement," Roger said trying to mislead him about the drug's origin.

"I don't think so. He didn't have the equipment to complete the procedure. The process would've involved a more elaborate setting, like those at a government research institution or at a pharmaceutical company."

"Where do you think he got it?" Hall probed, hoping to discover what the young man suspected.

"I believe it was synthesized by a pharmaceutical company."

Throwing the blanket off to the side, Roger Hall popped up on the sofa. "What makes you say that?"

"Any drug company would have the facilities, materials and intellectual resources to conduct the experiments. For a chemical synthesis to be successful, it has to be reproducible and reliable. The process must also be replicated in different locations. All major pharmaceuticals have the ability to do it."

"You got all that by reading stuff on the internet?"

Tyler nodded. "It's all public information. You just have to look for it."

"That's amazing."

"As a matter of fact, I might even know which company's involved."

"But...but how?"

Tyler rubbed his eyes and coughed. "It's not too hard to figure out. All the pieces are there, just need to put them together."

"And you've done that, put it all together?"

"I believe so."

"Okay, so whose picture is on the puzzle?"

"Looks like Chemical, Biological & Genetic Research Incorporated. They're headquartered in New York City."

"C.B.G's one of the largest pharmaceutical companies in the nation," Roger stated.

"For now anyway. Based on their Annual Shareholders Report the company's in serious trouble. The auditors issued a Going Concern disclosure. According to their Security Exchange Commission filings, several key drugs go off patent soon. With nothing coming out of their R&D pipeline the company won't be able to survive very long without a major restructuring."

"So what? That doesn't really prove anything about the compound or that C.B.G. produced it," Roger countered, becoming more and more uncomfortable with the puzzle being pieced together by the teen.

"Maybe not, but their S.E.C. filings disclosed that the company had to pull a promising neurological compound from testing." He paused before adding, "The F.D.A. didn't approve their phase three clinical trial submission. Management was hoping it'd be their next blockbuster and sustain them until other products came out. That was a real blow to them."

"Still doesn't prove anything."

"From what I could find, that new compound was really special. It had some novel impact on neurological functioning by enhancing chemical synapses within the brain." Tyler paused again. "In simple terms, it was supposed to make people smarter."

"If it was such a wonder drug why'd they discontinue testing?" Roger pressed further.

"The compound wasn't considered safe. It had some serious side effects."

"Like what?"

"Like death," Tyler replied.

The room fell quiet as the two momentarily locked eyes.

The teenager concluded, "It has to be C.B.G. They must've provided the compound to Dr. Johnston. After their clinical trial was denied, the company was probably desperate and needed to find another way to prove the drug's worth, so they conspired with him to continue the experiments. C.B.G. needed additional data to help calibrate the dosage and prove the drug's safety before they could resubmit another trial to the F.D.A. That's when Johnston contacted Mom. He used her to get to me. I was a perfect candidate for testing."

The young man walked into the kitchen. "Do you have any Juicy Fruit in here?" he asked. "I need some gum. Some gum," he repeated.

"We can pick more up tomorrow."

"Yes, that'd be good, tomorrow morning."

Roger Hall lay back on the sofa. "I don't know. There's still a few missing pieces to your puzzle."

"Maybe so, but I've got this feeling," Tyler declared. He also had a feeling about Roger Hall.

* * * * * *

Gwen blinked several times focusing on the unfamiliar surroundings. The bedsprings creaked as she rolled over to peruse the room. A shaker style chest of drawers draped in a fine layer of dust sat in the corner of the master bedroom.

It was early, but she couldn't sleep. The new day was immediately consumed by worry and doubt as her world had totally changed. Her thoughts migrated to Tyler and the experimental drug. Would there be any future side-effects? The monster injecting him had been murdered, and by who? Should she have been more honest with the police investigating his death? Doubt kept gnawing away.

She rose and retrieved a robe from the closet. Inside, lying on the floor was the box with Dr. Johnson's laptop and hardcopy files. Why was Roger so adamant about retrieving them and not allowing the police to know or have access to the information?

Gwen reached down for the computer. Sitting back on the bed, she opened Excel and began searching the files. One near the top of the list caught her attention...CT—POTENTIAL. She moved the cursor and clicked on it.

A spreadsheet popped open revealing several columns of data.

- **Specimen Name**
- **Age**
- **Gender**
- **Compound**
- **Date**
- **Dosage**
- **Outcome—Efficacy**
- **Outcome—Safety**
- **Progress Notes**

There were only two specimen names listed—AG and TS. The initials TS obviously referred to Tyler, but who was AG?

Focusing on TS, she noted several weeks' entries, all with similar doses. The "Outcome" column indicated the specimen was progressing well.

There were far fewer entries for AG. The last one was only a short time before they'd moved to the lake house. There was also a wide disparity between dosages, significantly lower at first then increasing with each subsequent day. All were much higher than Tyler's. Finally her attention was drawn to the "Outcome" column, and more specifically to the very last entry. It simply read, "Trial Terminated—Specimen deceased".

A frightening shiver shot through the woman. The experimental drug was deadly. AG hadn't survived.

Gwen entered the living room where Roger was folding the blanket from his makeshift bed. "Morning. You're up early," he said

"Couldn't sleep." She took one end of the blanket and folded it toward him. "Roger, can I ask you a question?"

"Sure. What is it?"

"Dr. Johnston's laptop and files, why did you want to take them and keep them from the police?"

"We've been through this before."

"I know, but...but I've looked at some of his files..."

"You what?"

"I scanned through his computer files and read about his experiments on Tyler. There was another specimen too. I believe that one died."

"That's exactly what I was afraid of. That's why I took them."

"I don't understand. Why wouldn't we want the authorities to have that information? Wouldn't it prove that Johnston was illegally using these experimental drugs on humans?"

"Sure it would. But it'd also give them more reason than ever to believe you're involved in his murder. What a motive, an angry mother taking the law into her own hands."

"I still don't know. Hope we're doing the right thing here."

"It serves no purpose to turn them over. The man's dead. He can't hurt Tyler or anyone else now that he's gone. They'll only confuse the police and complicate their search for the real killer. It's best if we keep this to ourselves at this point. Let the investigation run its course."

"So what am I suppose to do in the meantime?"

"Just sit tight. Everything will be fine."

"Where am I going to stay? What am I going to do? I still need a way to support my family."

"Listen, you can stay here as long as you want."

"But we can't impose forever. I probably should go back to Golden Years and ask for my old position. If that works out, I can start looking for a place to live."

"Don't rush into anything. Just remember, there's still a murderer out there and we don't know what his motives are...or who he's after next. I think you're safer and better off living with me for a while. At least until this situation is resolved."

Hall reached over and gently grasped her hand. "Don't worry. I'm here for you," he promised.

CHAPTER 18

The investigation into the murder of Barry Johnston continued. Gwen and Roger were questioned again about the night of his death and both confirmed their original stories.

In addition to dealing with the police, Gwen made time to contact Golden Years and inquire about returning to her old position. Management graciously agreed to meet and discuss the matter. While content to live at Roger's apartment for the time being, she still needed a job.

"Tyler, I'm leaving for a bit. Are you okay staying here with Granddaddy?"

"We'll be fine."

"I won't be gone long."

"Pick up Juicy Fruit on way home. I need some gum. Some gum," Tyler repeated as she left for Golden Years.

Fortunately the administrator at the nursing home was receptive to rehiring her. "As soon as we have an opening, we'll give you a call," he promised.

On the drive home she stopped at a convenience store to buy some chewing gum. Before entering, she pulled out her cell and called the apartment.

Tyler finally picked up after several rings. "Hello?"

"Hey, it's Mom. How are you guys doing?"

"Okay. Everything's okay."

"Where's your granddaddy?"

No response.

"Tyler, where's your granddaddy?" she repeated, her voice rising slightly.

"Kitchen. Kitchen. In kitchen."

The halted speech and repetition was reminiscent of his Savant mannerisms. "Hon, are you…is everything all right?"

"I…I…think so."

Suddenly a deafening screech blasted over the phone. It was the piercing sound of a fire alarm.

"I'll be there in a few minutes. Take Granddaddy and get out of the apartment," she yelled, but the connection was lost.

Gwen raced to the apartment complex. Tyler and Ernest stood outside the door while several neighbors peered inside.

"What happened?" she yelled approaching the group.

A neighbor stepped forward. "The boy says something caught fire on the stove."

"Mom, there's no fire, not anymore."

Gwen surveyed the apartment. "Everything's fine," she informed the neighbors before herding Ernest and Tyler back inside. The old man plopped down on the couch and began watching television as if nothing had happened.

"Tyler, what…?"

"I'm not sure," he blurted out. "Let me think for a second."

A slight scent of smoke continued to linger in the kitchen. The faint haze wafted upward then disappeared. A trail of black ash was scattered across the countertop from the stove to the sink. Crumpled in the bottom of the stainless steel receptacle were the blackened remnants of a burnt kitchen towel.

Gwen looked toward the teen.

Tyler's forehead wrinkled. "We were in the living room watching T.V. I think the phone rang."

"I called and you sounded confused."

"I smelled smoke. When I looked around, Granddaddy… Granddaddy was gone. One minute he was on the couch and the next he wasn't."

A sickening dread began swelling inside Gwen.

"The alarm went off and I ran into the kitchen," Tyler continued. "He was standing at the stove and the towel was on fire. Granddaddy was just watching it burn." The young man's shoulders drooped. "I turned the stove off and threw the towel in the sink."

She put a comforting arm around him. "You did the right thing, Hon."

Tyler pushed her away. "What are you talking about? I was…I was supposed to watch him. He was my responsibility. The whole building could have burned down…burned down!"

"Calm down, everything's okay."

"The shots Dr. Johnston gave me are wearing off, aren't they? I lost focus." He looked into his mother's eyes. "It started a couple days ago. I've been feeling kind of strange. Drifting at times, just like before. I'm going back to the way I was. My Autism is returning, I can sense it."

"You don't know that."

"Yes I do," he said with conviction.

The smoke dissipated and the black ash from the burnt towel had been cleaned away, but despair still hovered over everyone except Ernest. "Tryin' to fry me up an egg," he'd explained. Moments later the event was erased from his memory. Wiped clean as if it never happened. That's how Alzheimer's works. The potentially catastrophic fire had slipped through his mind and evaporated, just like the smoke.

Roger returned that evening carrying two sacks of groceries. Gwen tossed a milk carton with an approaching expiration date and a block of fuzzy cheese into the trash can before putting away the items. "Roger, what am I going to do?"

"I don't know. We're lucky, today could have been disastrous."

She sadly turned away.

"I'm sorry," he immediately apologized.

"For what? Letting us live here and eat your food? You're giving up a bed and sleeping on the couch. You've been so supportive through this whole ordeal." She closed the refrigerator door, then buried her face in her hands.

His arms encircled the distraught woman. "It's going to be all right. We'll figure something out."

Tyler entered the kitchen and they immediately separated. "Did you tell him?"

"Tell me what" Roger asked.

"The shots are wearing off. I'm starting to revert."

"Are you sure?"

"No, he's not," Gwen quickly asserted.

"You don't know how I feel, Mom. I'm beginning to have short lapses. Mostly I'm okay, but at times I'm gone. I need to resume the shots."

"Absolutely not!" Gwen shouted.

Roger remained quiet.

"If I don't go back on the drug, I'll become a Savant again. Is that what you want?"

"I want you to live a long, full life. That drug could be dangerous. It could kill you and I'm not willing to take that chance."

An uncomfortable silence filled the room before the teenager countered, "Well I am. It's my life." There was no hostility in his voice. On the contrary, his words were spoken softly and compassionately.

Still, she was stunned by the defiance.

"I'm willing to take the risk, Mom. At least it gives me a chance. The way I see it, being autistic is worse than death."

"I don't want to argue. Besides, the drug's gone. There's no decision to be made."

"But what if I could get more?"

"That's enough!" She had to make him understand. His life was too precious to gamble on some mystery medication. But her pleading was useless. Tyler wasn't interested in caution. He was drowning and determined to grab hold of the lifeline Barry Johnston had tossed.

Despite her reservations there wasn't any denying the amazing change in Tyler. As much as she resisted, the fact remained that the drug worked.

* * * * * *

Each day, Tyler's abilities continued to deteriorate. Gwen was faced with the dilemma of having the family completely dependent on her, incapable of functioning on their own. Once again her life was solely dedicated to theirs.

Fortunately, Roger Hall was there for support. "How are you holding up?" he asked.

"I'm surviving."

"It's tough. You miss him, don't you?"

She sadly nodded.

"I know this isn't what you want to hear, but maybe you should reconsider."

"Reconsider what?"

"The drug."

"No!" she stated vehemently.

Roger remained calm. Somehow she had to be persuaded to allow Tyler back on the compound. Getting more of it wouldn't be a problem, he could handle that. But convincing Gwen might be tricky. It was imperative that he change her mind. The success of the project depended on it.

"I know how you feel about...."

"You don't have any idea how I feel. He's not your son."

"You're right, there's no way I could."

Tears sprang from her eyes. "I'm sorry. It's not your fault. You didn't move my family in with a total stranger. I'm to blame. I...I should've...been more careful," she sobbed.

He tried to console her. "No one could have foreseen this."

"But when Tyler started getting better so quickly, I should have known."

"It's hard to question something so wonderful."

"I wanted it so bad. Guess I overlooked the obvious," Gwen admitted. "It's my job to protect him and I failed."

Roger moved closer. "Don't let guilt cloud your judgment. You can't change what happened. Johnston was an ass, but a brilliant one. Look on the bright side, there weren't any problems, only positive results. Tyler did improve."

Gwen hesitated for a moment, then asked, "You think I'm wrong don't you?"

"It's not my place to say."

"Tell me. What do you think?"

The opportunity was right so Hall replied, "Maybe the drug isn't that dangerous. There didn't appear to be any side effects, and it did work. Just look at the change it made in him. He wants to continue the injections and I think you should consider his wishes."

She turned cold. "It doesn't matter what you or anyone else thinks. There isn't any more."

"Maybe, maybe not. Tyler was researching the drug on the internet and believes he knows who produces it. If he feels that strongly, maybe we should try and help him get it."

But his suggestion fell on deaf ears. "I refuse to put his life in danger and nothing anybody says is going to change my mind," she stubbornly stated and left the room.

Roger's shoulders slumped as he watched her leave. Minutes later he stepped outside to the parking lot and placed a call. "I tried and it didn't work. She's not budging"...."I realize the importance of the boy continuing."...."You're preaching to the choir. I'm on your side, remember?"...."No, time's not going to change anything. Her mind's made up."...."Believe me, she's adamant."...."So what do you want me to do?"...."Is that the only way?"...."I guess we have no choice if we want Cerebral One to succeed."...."Is he ready for the boy?"...."That soon? I got it."...."I'll be in touch."

That evening Tyler sat with the computer in his lap, chomping on a mouthful of Juicy Fruit gum. Every now and then he'd utter a count. "One thousand twenty-four...one thousand twenty-five...one thousand twenty-six."

Roger leaned against the stove watching Gwen sweep the kitchen floor. "Didn't you say your dad has a doctor's appointment tomorrow?"

"Yeah, at eleven o'clock. We won't be tying up the bathroom until you've already left."

"Actually, I've arranged to work from home tomorrow. Thought you might want to leave Tyler with me. Make it easier on everybody."

"That's awfully nice of you, but he can come with us. I hate to impose any more than we already have."

"Just thought I'd offer. Feel kind of bad about our argument. Maybe one of these days I'll learn to keep my mouth shut."

"I asked for your opinion and you gave it. Sorry I got so mad."

"Still, I had no right to question your decision. He's your son and I was out of line. Anyway, the offer stands. I'm going to be here, so you can leave him if you want."

Gwen pushed the crumbs from the floor into the dust pan. "Well, it would be a lot easier on him, that's for sure."

"Good, then it's settled. You tend to your dad. We'll just hang out while you're gone. Trust me, we'll be fine."

CHAPTER 19

It was a long morning at the doctor's office. Once the examination was complete the physician spoke with Gwen. "So your father's condition seems to be deteriorating?" he asked, paging through the medical chart.

"I've noticed a big change in the past month or two."

"Have you made any decisions about his ongoing care?"

"I'm still weighing my options."

"Will someone be with him during the day?"

"Uh...no, not really. My son's around now, but may not...not be... capable in the future," she stuttered.

"Placing a loved one in a nursing home is difficult, but there are some good facilities available."

"Yes I know. I've worked at one for years."

"Of course there's always in-home care," the doctor persisted. "Either way Mrs. Shealy, your father will need supervision. He can't be left alone. You'll have to make a decision soon."

On the drive back to the apartment, she reached across the seat to grasp Ernest's hand. *Things are such a mess,* she thought. *I'd give anything to be able to stay home and take care of him, but I have to make a living. Lord, help me. What should I do?*

Momentarily taking her eyes off the road, Gwen glanced at him. "I'm sorry, Daddy."

He stared blankly ahead, drifting along in an impenetrable world.

"I'm going to have to.... I've got to go back to work and you need.... I wish things were different."

Suddenly, Ernest squeezed her hand. "Me too."

The remainder of their journey home was sadly quiet.

"Roger? Tyler? Are you guys here?" Gwen called out as they entered the apartment.

They were gone.

She called Roger's cell. The rhythmic ring sounded six times before switching to voice mail.

"Hey, we're back from the doctor. Guess you guys decided to go out." She glanced at her watch. "Hope Tyler's behaving. Daddy'll probably take a nap. Think I'll do the same. See you when you get home. Bye."

She helped Ernest into bed. He placed his dentures in a cup on the nightstand, then closed his eyes mumbling, "Know what they say. Early to bed, early to rise, makes a man healthy, wealthy and wise."

Gwen wasn't buying it. Years of going to bed and getting up early hadn't bestowed health or wealth, and Alzheimer's had slowly stolen his wisdom.

Pushing aside the tough decisions that lay ahead, she left the room and sprawled out on the couch, quickly falling asleep.

When she awoke, Tyler still wasn't back. Again, she left a message on Roger's cell. "It's silly but I'm beginning to worry. I know you're capable of handling Tyler, but I can't imagine where you are. Oh well, I'm sure you'll be home soon. If you get this, please call me."

As she cracked the bedroom door to check on Ernest, he opened his eyes and blinked several times. "That you, Esther?"

"It's me. You've been asleep a while. Hungry? Want some supper?"

The old man rose and fumbled for his glasses and teeth, then shuffled toward the kitchen.

Ernest was soon slurping noodles from a soup bowl. A milky white moustache coated his upper lip. "Esther, I need some more milk," he mumbled to his deceased wife.

Another glass was placed in front of him. The man drank and burped loudly.

While Ernest was satisfied, Gwen wasn't. She was becoming nervous. Where in the world were they? She'd been calling for hours. Why wasn't Roger answering the phone? Maybe he just lost track of time. Or maybe his phone battery had died.

Roger Hall was one of the most thoughtful, caring individuals she'd ever known. He'd find another way to contact her. Something was wrong. What if they'd been in an accident? But if there'd been an accident someone would have notified her.

Maybe she should call the police. What would she say? Her friend and son were missing? She'd only left them that morning. Suddenly a chilling thought surfaced from a tiny seed, then flowered into full-blown panic. What if the fiend that murdered Johnston abducted them? No one knew the killer's motive or who he was after next. Was it possible the two events were connected? Gwen couldn't shake the unease. Something had to be done. She called a friend.

Latrisse, who worked at Golden Years answered. "Hey, Baby Girl! How in the world ya doin'? We ain't talked in a while."

"I'm sorry to bother you, but I've got a problem."

"Don't dare 'pologize. Ya can call on me any time'a day or night. Don't matter none."

"Tyler's gone and…." Gwen explained the situation. "I'm probably going to feel like an idiot when they walk in the door but I can't help it."

"What can I do?"

"I need somebody to stay with Daddy for a little while."

"I be off pretty soon. Just tell me how to git there."

As the sun dropped below the rooftops and engulfed the parking lot in shadows, the doorbell rang. Latrisse had arrived from work.

"I've got to go. Don't know how long I'll be…."

Waving off the explanation, Latrisse said, "Now don't worry 'bout nothin'. Just go take care'a business and find that boy."

Gwen dialed Directory Assistance. "City and state," the recording prompted.

"Cumming, Georgia."

"What listing?"

"Forsyth County Sheriff's Department."

* * * * * *

Gwen sat across from Detective Randall Padgett. He leaned back in the chair. "You're lucky to catch me. I was about to call it a day and head home. Now what can I do for you, Mrs. Shealy?"

"My son and Roger Hall are missing."

The detective sat up. "What do you mean?"

"This morning I left them together at the apartment and when I returned they were gone."

"I assume you tried to get in touch with Mr. Hall?"

"Of course I did," Gwen replied growing irritated. "I've been calling all afternoon."

"No answer?"

"At first the phone rang and rang. Then it started going directly to voicemail like it was turned off or something."

"Maybe it is."

"What?"

"Maybe it's turned off," Padgett simply stated.

"You don't understand. Roger would get in touch with me. He'd never leave this long with my son and not let me know where they are. He knows I'd be worried."

"But if his phone's dead...."

"He'd find another one. Something's wrong. They're in trouble, I just know it."

Detective Padgett sighed. "All right, you wait here. I'll check our accident reports. Mr. Hall driving his own car?"

"Yeah, it's a Honda Civic. I don't know the license plate number."

"That's all right. I'll find it. We'll run a check of all the area hospitals too. See if anyone matching their description was admitted."

"Oh my Lord!"

"Don't panic, Mrs. Shealy. It's just a precaution. Wait here, this may take a while."

The detective finally returned. "Good news. No accident involving Hall's car was reported and they haven't checked into any local hospitals."

"Where could they be?" she pleaded.

"Look, they're probably home by now. Why don't you try calling again?"

She called Roger's cell. "Directly to voicemail," she informed Padgett.

Next the apartment. "Hi, Latrisse. Have they shown up yet?"...."Okay. How's Daddy?".... "All right thanks. I'll let you know."

Gwen stared back at the detective. "What now?"

"How old's your son?"

"He's nineteen."

Padgett scratched his head. "Well, our hands are tied until tomorrow morning. We have to wait twenty-four hours before filing a missing person's report. I suggest you go home. Give me a call if you don't hear anything by then."

Gwen took in a deep breath, debating whether to recount the truth about Dr. Johnston's experiments. She'd initially withheld the information, afraid it would give the police a motive in his death, pointing them in her direction. That was no longer a concern. Now all she could think about was the possibility her son was in danger. If so, she'd sacrifice anything to get him back safe and sound.

"I don't know how or why, but their disappearance might be related to Johnston's murder."

"What makes you say that?"

"There...there're some things I need to tell you."

"What is it, Mrs. Shealy?"

"I believe Johnston lured us into his house and was injecting my son with some experimental drug."

"That's quite an allegation. How do you know all this?"

Gwen's head dropped as she confessed, "I went to his laboratory and found a box of vials marked 'Experimental Compound'. Tyler's name was on the box. He was listed as 'Specimen #2'."

"That implies there was a specimen #1. Any other boxes or names?" Padgett probed.

"I didn't notice any at the time."

"What'd you do then?"

"I left. Went to Roger Hall's apartment."

"You didn't confront Johnston?"

"No. He was gone. I was scared for my family. All I could think about was getting away from there."

The detective stood and walked over to stand directly in front of her. "But you went back to the house with Mr. Hall later that night. Did you plan revenge for what the doctor had done?"

Gwen shook her head adamantly. "No. See that's why I didn't tell you this in the first place. I figured you'd think I went back to kill him."

"Did you?"

"I didn't murder Barry Johnston."

"So this box of vials you discovered in Johnston's office, where is it now? Did you take it?"

"No."

He looked at Gwen skeptically. "Mrs. Shealy, my people went over that house with a fine-toothed comb. They didn't find any vials."

"Don't you get it? The vials were gone by the time we arrived that night. The killer must have taken them."

Padgett crossed his arms. "Why should I believe you? You lied to me before. How can I be sure you're being truthful now?"

"I've got more proof."

"What kind of proof?"

"Dr. Johnston's computer files. I've got his laptop."

"How'd you obtain his computer, Mrs. Shealy?"

"We took it before you arrived at the house that night."

"You what!"

"We were afraid if you knew about his experiments on my son, you'd think I killed him."

"So you stole his computer and withheld the evidence."

"There were some hardcopy folders too," she reluctantly added.

Detective Padgett took a deep breath. "Where are these items now?"

"At Roger Hall's apartment."

Padgett rolled down his shirt sleeves and buttoned the cuffs. "Okay, let's go. I'll follow you and take a look."

* * * * * *

Back at the apartment, Latrisse offered to stay the night.

"That's not necessary." Gwen insisted, "You've got to work tomorrow and it's already late."

"Listen here, Baby Girl. If ya need anythin', call me and I come'a runnin'. Hear?"

"Thanks. Don't know what I'd do without you."

"Sho ya don't want me to stay?" She peeked warily at the detective standing nearby.

"I'll be all right."

Reluctantly, Latrisse left the apartment.

Gwen turned her attention to Detective Padgett. She led him to the master bedroom and opened the closet door. Her clothes hung on one side. The faint smell of Roger's cologne clung to a dirty shirt lying in the clothes basket. A pair of dress shoes sat in the corner.

Otherwise, his side of the closet was empty.

Gwen stumbled backwards, raising a hand over her mouth.

"What is it? What's wrong?" the detective asked.

"Roger's clothes are gone, and…and the box with Johnston's computer and files is missing too," she added frantically.

Padgett stood by silently, scanning the closet with an inquisitive eye.

"I don't understand," she cried out hurrying to the guest bedroom where Ernest slept. Her mind raced with unthinkable accusations and rueful denials.

Detective Padgett followed closely behind.

The woman put a hand on the closet door, momentarily stopping, afraid to look inside. Finally she mustered the courage to open it, confirming her worst fears. Tyler's clothes were gone too. Several empty hangers swung from the rod. His Braves duffle bag was also missing from the top shelf. The only thing left was a shoebox stashed in the corner. "What's going on?" she cried out. "Where's my son?"

Ernest rolled over in bed. "What…who's there?" Startled and still half asleep, he didn't notice the police detective standing quietly at the door.

"It's…it's just me, Daddy," Gwen stuttered trying to regain control. "I'm sorry for waking you. Go back to sleep." She softly closed the door on her way out."

"Now do you believe me? They're gone! I'm telling you something's wrong."

"All right Mrs. Shealy, calm down. We'll put out an A.P.B. on them. I'll let you know if we hear anything."

Gwen watched helplessly as Detective Padgett left the apartment.

She then returned to the guest bedroom and tiptoed through the dark to retrieve Tyler's shoebox from the closet.

Ernest was still awake. "That you Gwenny?"

She sat next to him on the bed. "I'm scared, Daddy."

"Scared'a what? That mean ol' boogy man back? You 'fraid he's under your bed again? Don't you worry none. Your mama and me won't let nothin' bad happen to our little girl. We'll keep you safe."

"I wish you could. Things are such a mess."

"Don't fret none. Daddy's right here." Ernest patted her knee before finally drifting off, his hand resting limply on her leg.

Gwen got up and took the shoebox to the master bedroom. She opened it. The distinctive sweet smell of Juicy Fruit gum escaped. Detective Padgett's business card was lying on top. *Where did Tyler get this?* she wondered, setting it aside.

Along with stacks of baseball cards was a note. Gwen picked it up and began reading….

> *Dear Mom,*
>
> *First, let me say I love you more than anything in the world. The sacrifices you've made for me and Granddaddy are a testament to your goodness. There's no possible way I can ever thank you.*
>
> *The thing I feared most is happening. My Autism's coming back. Once again I'll be trapped inside a mind that won't allow a normal life.*
>
> *This is not what I want, Mom.*
>
> *When I'm gone, please help me.*
>
> *I know you're afraid of losing me. That's understandable. As my mother, taking a chance on something that might harm or even kill me isn't acceptable. But from my standpoint, this is worse than death.*
>
> *I'm begging you to find a way to get more. Let me come back and be your son again. My fate, as it always has been, is in your hands.*
>
> *Please remember Pastor Williamson's sermon. Change is hard. While you consider the consequences, don't ignore the possibilities.*
>
> *Your Angel,*
> *Tyler*

After tossing and turning half the night, Gwen finally succumbed to sleep with Tyler's letter still in her hand.

Sunlight eked through the blinds waking her late the next morning. She sprang from bed. *Daddy must be up by now.*

The door to his bedroom was still closed. Gwen flung it open causing a loud bang as it hit the doorstop.

Ernest lay motionless on the bed. The cup holding his dentures sat next to his glasses on the nightstand.

"Daddy?"

No response.

Again, "Daddy!"

Still no movement.

Gwen rushed over and pulled down the blanket. Ernest lay on his back. A peaceful look covered his old, wrinkled face. No confusion or fear, just tranquility.

She felt his cold wrist for a pulse. "Oh God no, not now. I can't take this. Daddy, please don't. Please!" Nothing could be done. The man was dead.

The phone rang and she stumbled to answer it.

"Hey there, Baby Girl. Just wonderin' if ya heard anythin' from...?" Latrisse stopped mid-sentence. "Ya still there?"

"Oh...oh Latrisse. Can you come over?" Gwen asked in a husky voice. "It's Daddy. He's...he's gone."

"He run off again?"

"No." A long pause ensued as she mustered the strength to reply. "He passed during the night."

* * * * * *

Ernest Eugene Shealy was laid to rest at the Veteran's Memorial Cemetery. Eight men from the local American Legion carried the casket to its final resting place as a handful of mourners stood quietly paying their respects. Reverend Williamson delivered a touching service. Afterwards, "Taps" was played to honor the passing of the Korean War Veteran.

Gwen placed a red carnation on the lid of the coffin then climbed into the passenger side of Latrisse's car holding a perfectly folded American flag in her lap.

Detective Randall Padgett, who'd attended the funeral, stepped up to the window. "Real sorry about your father, Mrs. Shealy."

"I'm going to miss him. He...he was a wonderful man."

"I'm sure he was."

"Any news?"

"I wish we had more information but…." The Detective shook his head.

"I just buried my father and my son's been missing for days. Please give me something to believe in."

"We're working on it. Talking to everybody who knew Roger Hall down at the newspaper." He paused and then asked, "Just how long have you known him?"

"A few months, why?"

"What do you know about him?"

She thought for a few moments. "Not much, other than he was a reporter for the A.J.C."

"Did you know he'd only worked there since March?"

CHAPTER 20

A small cabin overlooked the Mississippi River. Two men walked out onto a dirt pathway leading up the ragged hillside. Crooked hardwoods and a slew of tangled underbrush lined both sides of the narrow trail. An occasional tree root burrowed across the path, complicating their journey.

Squirrels darted back and forth in the trees above, ignoring the intruders maneuvering the bumpy incline. A few Cardinals were perched in the foliage, their brightly colored feathers camouflaged within the forest's early autumn colors. Only the bird's crisp, distinctive chirps exposed them.

One man carried a black satchel. "Should start seeing an improvement in the boy soon," he stated while taking short, deliberate steps up the uneven terrain.

"You're giving him the same dosage as Johnston, right?" Roger Hall asked, following closely behind. "You know he showed a remarkable change at that level before."

"Who's in charge here anyway?" the short stocky physician snapped back, raising a finger to point at Hall. "I've been injecting him with the same levels that were recorded in Johnston's files. I'll do my job. You just make sure the specimen's secure and doesn't give me any problems."

While only in his early fifties, Dr. Michaels left his medical career after losing several mal-practice lawsuits, all vigorously defended in court. Although he vehemently disagreed with the allegations of negligence, a jury saw it differently siding with the plaintiffs. No longer willing to pay the exceedingly high cost of malpractice insurance, the disillusioned and bitter physician decided to quit his practice when approached with a novel opportunity to conduct independent research, a role in which he'd be paid quite handsomely.

The men struggled up the hill, finally reaching the entrance to a cave. Over thousands of years a vast network of caverns had been created in the Illinois Basin. A combination of carbon dioxide and water had slowly seeped through crevices in the ground, dissolving the limestone and carving out giant holes in the surrounding hills.

The opening leading into the mountain was nearly a yard wide and stood about seven feet high, ample for an average man to pass through. A chain-link fence was securely anchored in front of the passageway guarding its access...and exit. The only way past the barrier was through a gate secured by a heavy padlock.

Dr. Michaels removed a key from his pocket to open the gate. He immediately flipped a switch to light a long, narrow passageway leading back into the bowels of the cavern. The men stepped forward through the tubular conduit. Its ragged sides were damp with moisture waiting to slither down the limestone wall. The air was cool and musty.

"How long are we going to keep him locked up like this?" Roger Hall asked, agitated at the conditions of the makeshift laboratory.

"As long as it takes to complete the experiment."

"I wasn't expecting him to be caged like an animal," Hall fired back.

"You don't like my laboratory, Mr. Hall? Granted it's not ideal, but we couldn't take any risks with the authorities. You know how the damn legal and regulatory systems work...let me clarify...don't work. They'd never allow these experiments to occur. No no, I couldn't take the chance anywhere else. This location is perfect. It's private and no one will ever know or interfere with my work here."

"It may be secluded, but do you have the infrastructure to properly conduct your experiments?"

"I've got everything that's needed. Our benefactor has equipped the cave to satisfy every possible requirement. There's full utility service along with several rooms to accommodate my work. The lab equipment was delivered and I had enough compound to get started. What else could you possibly ask for?"

"How about windows?"

"You may not appreciate the facility, but it's well suited for the project." The physician paused. "At least the boy doesn't have to be tied up. He's free to move around for the time being."

"For the time being?"

"As long as he doesn't demonstrate any violent behavior, I'll leave him alone. Usually Savants are extremely shy and timid so I'm not too worried. He's relatively safe to be around. If that changes I may need to consider some type of physical restraints. No no, can't afford to take any chances with the young man."

"Is that how you handled your first specimen, with restraints?"

"They were required, yes."

"From what I hear, your tests didn't turn out so well."

Dr. Michaels stopped in his tracks. "Just what did you hear, Mr. Hall?"

"That he died during your experiment."

"That's the price of knowledge. Let me remind you that scientific breakthroughs don't come cheaply."

"Does the price tag include the life of Tyler Shealy?"

Dr. Michaels thought for a moment. "I hope not but if it does… well, *C'est la vie*. The boy's sacrifice and the information obtained may help others."

"What if the experiments continue to fail? When does it all stop?"

"It'll never stop. Human research will continue as long as there are questions to be answered and benefits to be gained. That's just the way it is. If lives have to be lost in the process, so be it," the doctor replied in a cold, absolute tone.

Roger Hall stood motionless. The physician's philosophy sounded eerily like Barry Johnston's. The specimen held no value for them.

Only the advancement of medicine and their personal agendas mattered.

"Now if you don't mind, follow me," Michaels ordered.

The passageway led the men to a large open cavern. Strategically placed incandescent lighting fixtures provided a bright view of the space. The temperature remained cool, but tolerable.

Several rooms constructed of gray cement blocks lined one side of the cave. Three smaller tributaries branched off and led further back into the limestone mountain. Positioned against a relatively flat section of the cave wall were a metal desk and a long table stacked with folders. Shelves were built to accommodate the physician's files and other medical paraphernalia.

Still not satisfied with the earlier response about the cost of human experimentation, Roger Hall probed further. "So, you're just going to continue injecting the boy until he responds or you kill him, whichever comes first?"

"No no, that's not what I said, Mr. Hall. That's not what I said at all."

"Sure sounded like it."

"You're wrong, that's not the plan."

"Okay, clue me in. What exactly is the plan?"

Dr. Michaels walked to the desk and placed the black bag next to a small lamp. An uneasy frown etched across his face causing wrinkles to line his brow. "If the specimen doesn't show improvement soon, I'll need to increase the frequency and dosage."

"But isn't that more dangerous?"

"It could be, but we might have to try and see if he can tolerate it," Michaels replied. "Can't expect a different result if we continue the same course."

"Is that what happened with your first specimen? Did you keep increasing the dosage until...?"

"I don't have to defend my work to you, Mr. Hall," the physician interrupted. "If you're so concerned about the boy, here's the key. Why don't you go check on him while I prepare his meal?"

Roger Hall unlocked the door and entered the room. Tyler lay on a small cot next to the gray cement wall. A toilet and sink were installed nearby. A cold silence filled the space as the teenager stared blankly at the limestone ceiling.

"Hello, Tyler."

The teen slowly rolled toward Hall. His eyes were swollen and red from the moldy air. Slimy, green mucus dripped from his nose. "Go home. Go home. Want to go home," he repeated in a pathetic, pleading tone.

"I'm sorry, but we can't let you do that. Not yet anyway."

"Mom. Mom."

"Your mother's fine, don't worry about her. She's coming to see you soon, okay?" Hall lied, trying to comfort him.

"Why…why keep me here? Why here?"

"We're just trying to make you better like before. Do you remember?"

Tyler coughed and wiped his nose.

"Looks like those allergies are still bothering you."

The Savant remained quiet.

"Here. I brought you something." Roger Hall reached into his pocket and pulled out several packs of Juicy Fruit.

The young man took the gum then turned toward the wall.

"Listen, you probably can't understand." Hall paused to gather his thoughts. "Hopefully what we're doing will help you and a lot of others. I know that's a small consolation, but it's all I got. For what's it worth, I truly am sorry."

"Sorry. A sad or troubled feeling, showing or causing sorrow, a sign of pity or just mild regret," Tyler softly mumbled the definition from Webster's New World Dictionary, a book he'd previously read and memorized.

Roger Hall left the cell, disheartened by his condition.

Tyler rolled over and stared up at the ceiling. Unbeknownst to Hall, the teen's mind raced with a multitude of complete, logical thoughts.

He would continue to portray a Savant.

Since resuming the experimental drug, his extraordinary mental capabilities had returned. However to Dr. Michaels and Roger Hall, he purposely showed no significant reasoning ability. All the while, the young man was evaluating his situation and weighing the options.

How would he escape the earthen cell and return to his family? He agonized about their well-being. Were they all right? What had these monsters done to them?

Tyler also needed more compound or risk reverting back. He'd do anything necessary to obtain the serum. Absolutely anything.

Along with these thoughts, a new emotion emerged…revenge. A strange compulsive anger was gnawing inside. It was squarely focused on Roger Hall, the man who'd betrayed him. *How could you do this to me and my family? What kind of man are you? Deceitful liar! Two can play that game!* he vowed silently.

Click. Click. The door was unlocked again.

"Six hundred, forty-five miles. Six hundred, forty-five miles," Tyler continued the charade as he pushed a thin blanket away and sat up in bed. He wiped his nose with a damp sleeve. "Six hundred, forty-five miles."

Dr. Michaels stepped inside carrying a tray of food. He set the platter on a small table next to the cot. "Hello Tyler, I brought you some soup and crackers. He cautiously stepped away to gauge the young man's demeanor.

"Want to go home. Home. Six hundred forty-five miles." He momentarily developed eye contact with the physician before turning away.

The gesture went unnoticed by the normally perceptive doctor as he moved closer. "Talk to me, Tyler. What are you thinking?"

Tyler reached into his pocket to pull out a stick of Juicy Fruit gum. He peeled off the yellow wrapper and plunked the gum into his mouth. "Six hundred forty-five miles."

"Yes I know, miles home. But how're you feeling?"

Still no response as Tyler swayed back and forth on the bed.

Dr. Michaels asked in a loud, firm tone. "Listen here, I need an answer! You understand me?"

The teenager remained quiet, now chewing the gum at a feverish pace.

Becoming irritated, Michaels stepped forward and slapped him across the face. "Answer me!"

Tyler jerked back, then curled up on the bed with his arms wrapped firmly around his legs. Still chewing the gum, he muttered, "One hundred fifteen."

"What'd you say?"

"One hundred twenty one...one hundred twenty two...one hundred twenty three...." Tyler continued to chew the gum and count.

"Damn! The medication's still not having an impact." The physician stepped to the door. Before leaving, he turned and said, "Eat your soup. I'll be back later." Michaels walked out, locking the door behind him.

Tyler sat up and slid sideways toward the tray. Slimy noodles and tiny bits of chicken peeked through a thin film of yellow grease. After placing the wad of gum on the table, he grabbed the bowl and lifted it to his lips. The soup was room temperature, straight from a can, but it tasted good. A small packet of saltine crackers was devoured next. He reached for a plastic bottle of water to wash away the last remnants of saltines nestled between his teeth.

As Tyler unscrewed the top, he began to sway rhythmically back and forth. A hazy version of his mother slowly materialized within his autistic mind. She was dressed in black and alone.

"Mom?" he muttered.

The image sharpened. Where was she? What was she doing? Where was his grandfather?

As she came into full focus, Tyler saw her face lined with worry and wet with tears. He suddenly realized she was in a cemetery. Gwen was standing over a grave. Granddaddy's grave!

"No!" A choked scream erupted from the young man and the water bottle tumbled to the floor.

Suddenly, his head began to spin. *What's happening*, he wondered. *What's hap...?* He passed out, falling into a drug-induced sleep.

Michaels had laced the soup with a sedative.

The doctor returned a short while later carrying a small black bag. Tyler's sleeve was pushed up exposing his lower arm. The physician reached into the bag and pulled out a syringe filled with a clear liquid. He grabbed the teen's limp arm and injected the experimental drug into a vein.

"Hopefully increasing the dosage will make a difference," Michaels mumbled, thinking of the hefty bonus he'd receive if significant progress was made.

* * * * * *

Wearing a dark cashmere sweater, Dr. Michaels relaxed on the cabin porch, watching the Mississippi River gently flow by down below. The sky faded into a beautiful burnt orange as the day peacefully ended.

Roger Hall stepped out of the cabin, surprising him. "Mr. Hall, you startled me."

"Notice any changes yet?"

"No no, nothing new," Dr. Michaels confessed. "Can't understand it. I upped the dosage and it's still not having an impact."

"You already increased it? I thought you were going to wait a while longer, give the current level a chance. It worked for Johnston."

"Dr. Johnston's methods are of no concern to me. I'm running this trial." He reluctantly added, "I don't understand why the subject isn't responding. Maybe his body's built up some resistance to the compound and needs more frequent injections."

"Could keeping him locked up in a cave have an effect? Maybe the environment's causing some type of emotional strain, impacting his behavior. Is that possible?"

"Did you learn that in medical school?" Michaels asked sarcastically.

"Well, something's going on. All I know is it worked before. Saw it with my own two eyes."

"No no, it has nothing to do with the environment. If the compound worked before, it'll work again," the pudgy physician replied stubbornly.

"What if we give him some type of stimulus, you know, to pass the time? Maybe that would help him relax and allow the drug to do its thing. Being locked up in that cave with nothing to do would drive me crazy."

"What do you prescribe, Mr. Hall?"

"I drove across the river to Hannibal and picked up some books. Hang on a second, I'll be right back." Roger stepped inside the cabin and returned a few moments later with a small bag. 'The Mustard Seed Bookstore' was printed across the sack in whimsical, lopsided letters.

Dr. Michaels reached for the bag, pulling out two paperbacks. "Let's see what we have here. The Adventures of Tom Sawyer and The Adventures of Huckleberry Finn."

"Grabbed the first thing I saw. It was...."

"Here we are just a few miles from Hannibal, Missouri where Mark Twain grew up writing about caves like this one. Now you go out and buy two of his books for the boy's entertainment. Don't you find that ironic, Mr. Hall?"

"Call it what you want, but it couldn't hurt."

"I remember reading Tom Sawyer as a young lad. Didn't think too much of it," the doctor said.

"Why's that? It's an American classic."

"A young boy being able to fool a whole town into thinking he'd perished in a cave is preposterous. Who'd believe such a charade?"

"A lot of readers did," Hall countered.

"Well I'm not that naïve." Michaels jammed the books back inside the bag and relented. "Fine. I'll give them to the specimen, but it's not going to help."

The sun's dying rays slipped below the horizon leaving the secluded area shrouded in darkness. Only a small cadre of fireflies darting through the woods illuminated the night. A chorus of chirping insects serenaded the men, temporarily soothing the tension between them.

"I have to say Mr. Hall, you seem a little...soft...for this type of work. How in the world did you get hooked up in this operation?"

"What do you mean?"

"Pretty simple question I think. How'd you get involved? You're not a doctor, obviously no scientific background. Don't appear to have the backbone for making difficult decisions. What special talent do you bring to the table?"

Roger Hall remained calm. "No particular talent. Just needed a job and took advantage of an opportunity. Same as you."

"Same as me, huh? I don't think so. You seem to be much more informed. I don't even know who our benefactor is. I've been dealing with some middleman that won't divulge anything. Tell me, Mr. Hall, who's behind all this?"

"I don't know any more than you. I'm the caretaker, you're the physician. Difference in title and function. That's it."

"So you're being kept in the dark too?"

"Yeah."

"You certain about that?"

"Are you saying you don't believe me?"

"Just wondering if you're being totally honest."

Roger shrugged. "Think what you want."

"Well, I think you know more than you're saying."

"That's your privilege."

"Just how stupid do you think I am?" Dr. Michaels stated bluntly. "You brought the boy here from some other test site, right? Another physician, this Dr. Johnston, was performing the same type of experiments that I'd been conducting."

"So what's the big deal?"

"I was led to believe that I was the only physician involved. Imagine my surprise when they contacted me about continuing Johnston's work. Exactly what's going on? Nobody's told me shit about the scope of this project! Just how many tests sites are there?"

"Like I said before, I'm nothing more than a caretaker. I was told by my contact to bring the Savant to you. That's it. That's all I know. To tell you the truth, I figured you were more in the loop than me."

"Humph." The doctor shrugged and leaned back in the chair. "Oh well, suppose at the end of the day it doesn't matter how big the ship is or who's steering, just as long as I get paid at the end of the voyage."

"So you're doing this for the money, that's your motivation?"

"Mostly."

"Thought you doctors were supposed to be all holier-than-thou. Guess that oath you took doesn't mean squat."

"Don't dare judge me, Mr. Hall. There's nothing wrong with wanting to be wealthy. I put in my time. Went to med school thinking there'd be a payoff."

"There wasn't?"

"Could have been. I was a decent doctor on my way to retiring at a young age. Helped a lot of people during my career but that wasn't good enough. No no, the public expects miracles now-a-days and if things don't go exactly right, people blame you whether it's your fault or not. Then you get hit with some ridiculous law suit. Throw in an outrageous claim for punitive damages and you go broke defending your work. I finally realized there was a better way to make a difference in medicine and at the same time earn a buck."

"Aren't you guys supposed to believe in the sanctity of life? You don't care if innocent lives are lost?"

The physician took a deep breath. "I care. Loss of life is an unpleasant consequence, but if I don't participate in this research someone else will. In a perfect world, I'll get paid and some good will come from these experiments. In the end, everyone benefits."

"Everyone except Tyler Shealy," Roger added.

* * * * * *

The bedroom window was cracked open allowing the night's cool air to slip through and create a cozy sleeping environment. But Roger Hall couldn't sleep. He lay in bed pondering Dr. Michaels' motivation, and at the same time wondering about his own. His mind raced with doubts. More and more he questioned the project and his role in it. Were the benefits really worth the costs? How many lives would have to be lost? Was he doing the right thing supporting an initiative to develop an intellectually superior human being?

A quilt was pulled up around his neck. Its comforting warmth didn't lessen the chill running through his conflicted mind.

How many more people would he have to mislead? What about Gwen, a wonderful woman whose life had been turned upside down?

Her precious son had been abducted and placed in jeopardy. How could his actions be justified regardless of the potential benefits?

Hall's new cell phone began ringing. He grabbed it from the nightstand and searched for the "talk" button. The unfamiliar device was a replacement for the one discarded after taking Tyler and leaving Georgia.

"Hello, this is Roger Hall.".…"Don't worry about it, I wasn't asleep.".…"No, the Savant hasn't shown any progress yet. He was administered the same dosage as before but didn't respond.".…"Dr. Michaels doesn't know why but has increased the dosage to see if that'll have an impact.".…"Hold on I'm losing you. Wait a minute you're breaking up. Can you hear me?"

Roger Hall stumbled across the room hoping for better reception.

"Now, what were you saying?".…"Dr. Michaels?".…"Yeah, he has. Told him I didn't know any more than him.".…"Naturally he's curious but don't think he cares that much about it. All he's interested in is the money."

Hall reached over and gently pushed the window down to prevent any further drafts from entering the room.

"What?"…"Are you certain that's what needs to happen next?"… "But have you given him enough time?"…"Sounds like a death sentence for the Savant.".…"Is the pharmaceutical company on board with this?"…"Well, obviously nobody's told Michaels about the change in plans. Like I told you, he's still conducting the damn experiment.".…"Tomorrow, huh?"…"I'm not surprised. Can't imagine something like that would take place in a cave on some hillside in Illinois. Do you know where yet?"…"Some of the other test sites have to be better suited than this place…"I don't know about all this."… "Okay, okay.".…"I know what's at stake… "Yeah I'm still committed to Cerebral One but…."

Roger eventually disconnected and tossed the phone onto the nightstand. "Damn." He stared out the window at millions of stars dotting the sky and worried about the next phase of the project.

In order to properly test the experimental compound, four different evaluation sites had been covertly established around the country. Each had a separate physician and specimen group.

Unfortunately, none of the specimens had survived except for Tyler Shealy. Not only was he able to tolerate the experimental drug, but the nineteen year-old Savant had demonstrated some remarkable intellectual changes.

Why had he tolerated the compound while the others didn't? How was he different?

Similar to changing a drug's dosage, it was now time to change the project plan. In order to find the answers, different procedures were needed on the lone survivor.

The search for new specimens had been halted until more data was obtained. No other lives would be put at risk for now.

Tyler Shealy would be relocated to another secret laboratory for additional testing. This time it wouldn't involve the injection of an experimental drug. Instead it would encompass a series of brain scans and aggressive exploratory surgery to determine the physiological factors contributing to his tolerance of the drug. It would be extremely dangerous and risky, but it needed to be done. Once some answers were known, the project could continue as the new knowledge would be used to identify future, more appropriate specimens for testing.

Roger Hall had been ordered to escort Tyler to the new surgical site.

Early the next morning he awoke from an uneasy sleep. Passing through the cabin he noted that Dr. Michaels' bedroom door was open and his bed was made. The Mustard Seed Bookstore bag lay on the quilt. As he stepped out onto the porch, he also noticed the doctor's car was gone.

A cool morning breeze blew across the bluff toward the muddy Mississippi River. Roger zipped his jacket and stared at the slow-moving water. Once again he thought about Gwen, a single mother who selflessly sacrificed everything for her family. He'd never met anyone quite like her.

In the beginning his relationship with the woman was part of the job, only an ancillary component to be monitored. He'd conducted surveillance before and never gotten emotionally involved. But with Gwen, things eventually started to change. At first he remained focused, overlooking and suppressing his desires. Work was still the priority.

Now he felt differently. *I really miss her,* he agonized. The success of the project didn't seem as important. While logic reminded him of its ultimate goal and the benefit to the country, his heart questioned the cost. He'd lied and broken the family apart by putting her son in a dangerous situation, one that could potentially kill him. **What in God's name am I doing?** he wondered.

Roger's well-trained, pragmatic mind didn't surrender easily. *Look at the potential good that'll come from this. It's a matter of national security for God's sake! The project must succeed.*

His compassionate side argued, *Well, it's not succeeding. All the other subjects have died and Tyler's no longer responding. Face it, the experiment's failed.*

Don't give up so easily. It worked for a while. We're so close. The additional surgery will give us the answers we need.

So you're going to jeopardize him to find out why? Sacrifice his life for information that may or may not be of value?

What's wrong with you? All this time, you've been totally committed to the project. You knew what was involved and the risks. Something's going on. Is it the woman? Has she changed you?

Leave her out of it.

My sentiments exactly.

The internal debate was interrupted as Dr. Michaels pulled in the driveway.

"Out kind of early this morning," Roger called, looking down from the porch.

Michaels failed to acknowledge the greeting. Walking up the steps to the porch, he blurted out, "The sons of bitches are pulling the plug. The idiots are stopping my trial."

"What happened?"

"Met my contact across the river in Hannibal for breakfast. He informed me there'd be no more supplies coming. You'll be instructed to take the boy someplace else."

"Where?" Roger asked.

"He didn't say and I don't care." Michaels pounded his fist on the porch railing.

"Looks to me like you do."

"The only thing I'm concerned about is getting paid. They better not try to short me either. I did my part." Regaining some composure, he added, "Well it appears my involvement's over. The boy's your problem now." He started to walk away, then abruptly stopped. "Mr. Hall, you don't seem particularly surprised by all this. My gut still tells me you know more than you're letting on." The intuitive physician waited for a response. When none came, he walked away.

By day's end he'd cleared the cave laboratory, packed his clothes and left the cabin.

Roger Hall watched him drive away.

* * * * * *

The door was unlocked and opened but no one entered the room. Tyler waited a few seconds. Still nobody came in. He rose and walked slowly toward the opening, curious yet cautious. Roger Hall was standing outside holding a pack of Juicy Fruit gum.

"Come on out Tyler. Nothing to be afraid of."

I'm not scared, but you should be, he thought as the vision of his distraught mother standing over his grandfather's grave resurfaced.

Hall offered the chewing gum but Tyler remained still.

Laying the pack on the desk, Roger Hall stepped back. "All right, I'll just leave it here."

Tyler's eyes darted about the room eventually returning to the desktop. There along with the chewing gum was a lamp with a metal base, suitable for providing a lethal blow to the head. He slowly stepped over to pick up the gum, unwrapped a piece and popped it into his mouth.

The gum's sweet taste couldn't overcome the bitterness building inside. *Granddaddy's dead and Mom is dealing with it alone. Maybe things would be different if you hadn't betrayed us and brought me to this place.*

Roger's voice interrupted his thoughts. "I'm taking you back to Georgia. I made a mistake. Nothing I can do to change the past, but maybe I can help make things right going forward. Let's give your Mom a call and tell her you're coming home."

Hall was no longer committed to the project. His priorities had changed. "My good intentions weren't justified."

Good intentions? What's good about kidnapping and locking me in a cave like an animal? Well, my intentions are justified. Tyler picked up the lamp.

Hall didn't expect the Savant to understand. Whether from guilt or the prospect of building trust, he felt obligated to explain. "Thought I was part of a project that'd benefit our society. These experiments were supposed to expand the capability of the human intellect. Any of that make sense to you, Tyler?"

The young man's eyes squinted as he chewed faster. "Two hundred thirty-eight, two hundred thirty-nine, two hundred forty."

"I didn't think so."

With his anger and resentment growing, Tyler gripped the metal lamp feeling its cold hard surface in his hand. *Wait! Hall admitted to having knowledge about the experiments. Maybe he could help get more compound. He's certainly more valuable alive than dead.* Tyler's mind raced as he slowly set the lamp back on the desk.

"Let's go. It's time to get you home to your Mom."

"Six hundred forty-five miles." Tyler remained in character.

"What's six hundred forty five miles?"

"Home."

"Yeah, that sounds about right. And that's where we're going."

Suddenly Tyler ducked his head downward toward the floor.

Startled, Hall asked, "What's wrong, you all right?"

Still bent at the waist, the teenager looked up, his eyes darting from one side of the cave to the other. Just then a group of small black creatures erupted out of a passageway leading back into the hillside.

"Holy shit, what's that?" Hall exclaimed ducking for cover.

"Chiroptera," Tyler answered.

"Looks like bats to me."

"That's what Chiroptera are. Bats."

"You mean flying rats!" Hall shouted over the noise of their tiny flapping wings and unearthly screeching.

"Not really, but they are mammals. In fact they're the only mammals capable of sustaining flight. The name, Chiroptera, means *hand wing* in Greek."

"How…how'd you know they were coming? I didn't hear a thing until they were on us."

The teenager stood upright. "I felt their vibrations," he stated as the animals disappeared back into a tunnel.

Hall slowly raised his head. "Radar," he softly uttered. "I'll be damned."

"It's not that complicated, just simple sonar."

"Simple sonar, huh? And you can do it?"

"It's just processing sound waves, that's all," Tyler stated matter-of-factly.

"But how?"

"It involves a special focus, an intense concentration of one's senses. I could hear and feel them coming. Everyone has the ability, they just don't use it."

Roger suddenly recognized the unexpected metamorphosis in Tyler. The young man's speech pattern had changed again. His responses were structured and logical.

"Tyler, what…what the hell's going on? What happened to you?"

"It seems we both have the capacity for dishonesty."

"Wait…the drug…it worked after all," Roger stated incredulously.

"It's quite effective."

"It came on so quickly. Michaels was right. The increased dosage must have done the trick."

"Not really, I've been back for a while. Just didn't tell anyone."

"But why? Why the masquerade?"

"You've been at this deception game longer than me, why don't you start. What's your story, Roger?"

"My story doesn't matter, it's over. Time to start a new book."

"Not yet. We've got some unfinished business."

Roger Hall stared at the young man. "What unfinished business?"

"I can't go back to Georgia just yet."

"You don't want to go home to your Mom?"

"Of course I do." Tyler insisted. "But not like before. I want to return a complete person, someone who can reason and function."

"Well, look at yourself. You are. The compound's worked! You said so yourself."

"Only while I'm taking it. When the medication stops, I drift back." The young man's stare hardened. "I can't let that happen. For me to stay this way, I need the drug."

"We don't know that for a fact."

"Remember in Georgia when I was taken off the compound? I reverted. Then you brought me here and another regimen was started. Look at me now." He shook his head. "I'm not going back. That medication gives me life."

"But there's none here. Look around, it's gone. Michaels took it," Roger stated.

"There's got to be more somewhere."

"I don't...."

Tyler interrupted. "One thousand fifty-eight."

"What are you talking about now? One thousand fifty-eight what?"

"Miles."

"I don't understand."

"It's one thousand fifty-eight miles to New York City. That's where we can get the drug. C.B.G. is headquartered there and they're running the project. But then you already know that. You work for them, right Roger?"

"No, I'm not associated with the company. You're wrong about that."

"I don't believe you."

"I'm telling the truth. I don't work for C.B.G."

Tyler persisted, "Look, you owe me an explanation."

"Let's go home to your mom," Hall countered. "Then we'll talk and decide what to do next."

"Mom'll never agree. That's why I need to go to New York first."

"Well, maybe I can persuade her differently. There might be a way."

CHAPTER 21

Roger Hall unlocked the door and stepped into the apartment. Tyler followed closely behind. To their surprise an unexpected visitor was inside relaxing on the couch.

The young, dark-skinned man wore a gray sweat suit and donned a New York Yankee baseball cap. "Come in, Amigos. I waitin'."

"Who the hell are you?" Roger asked.

"I know who he is," Tyler interjected. "Name's Manny. Came to Dr. Johnston's lake house." The teen then noticed the expensive and familiar Cartier timepiece adorning the Latino's left wrist. "Nice watch. Where'd you get it?"

Manny's eyes narrowed. "Was gift from old Amigo."

"That belonged to Dr. Johnston."

"Look like Doc's experiment work." The Puerto Rican stood up. "Made retard real smart. Is too bad I waste him. Fool not listen. Had to do things his way."

Roger dropped his bag to the floor. "Where's Gwen?"

"Somewhere nice'n snug. Be fine long as you do what I say."

Moving forward, Roger threatened, "You son of a bitch...."

"Would not do," Manny warned, reaching underneath his sweatshirt to pull out a pistol.

Roger immediately stopped. "Don't do anything crazy."

"Up to you, Amigo."

"What do you want?"

"He wants to kill us, just like Dr. Johnston." Tyler turned to the Latino. "That's right, isn't it? You came to kill Mom and me, didn't you?"

Manny raised the gun threateningly. "S'posed to take care of that night. Time to finish de job."

"Who paid you to do this?" Roger demanded.

"Shut de hell up!"

The hair on the back of Hall's neck bristled. "Is C.B.G. behind this? Did they have you murder Johnston?"

"What you know 'bout company?"

Tyler interrupted. "Based on their S.E.C. filings they're in serious financial trouble. Several drugs are coming off patent and they don't have anything coming out of R&D to replace them. C.B.G.'s revenues are drying up and the market's worried about their viability. They may not be a going concern."

"What de hell you talkin' 'bout? Speak English."

"The company's going broke."

"You say dey go belly up? Bullshit! Dey one of biggest drug companies."

"Not for long," Tyler countered. "C.B.G. won't be able to sustain their infrastructure unless new drugs are introduced into the marketplace. Otherwise, they face some major cash flow issues and will have to restructure the business."

The bill of the Latino's baseball cap tilted slightly downward as he processed the information.

"It's true," Roger confirmed. "The company's in real trouble."

"But got new drug, de one Doc use. It work on him." Manny motioned toward the teen.

"Doesn't matter. It was never going to be released to the market. C.B.G. is probably going to be liquidated."

"Dey got friggin' money and I get some!" The .375 Magnum was now pointing directly at Hall's head. "You be dead while I lay on de beach with my bitches."

Tyler's attention was suddenly directed solely onto Roger. "What do you mean it was never going to reach the market?"

"It was going to be used…for other purposes."

"What other purposes?"

"Not now, Tyler."

"I want to know what's going on. If the drug works, it has to be made available to the public."

Roger Hall said nothing.

"Why wouldn't it?" the teen persisted.

Roger took a deep breath and exhaled slowly. "C.B.G.'s not running the project. The company may think so, but they're not."

"Then who is?"

Manny stood silently by, intently listening to their exchange.

"The Federal Government's driving this initiative. The pharmaceutical company is only the vehicle."

"What? How do you know this?"

"I'm not a reporter." Roger paused, contemplating the consequences of revealing his true background, but plowed ahead. I work for the Central Intelligence Agency."

Stunned, Tyler slowly repeated, "You work for the C.I.A.?"

"I'm involved in their Special Activities unit. It reports up through the Science and Technology Division."

"Holy shit, a friggin' G-man!" Manny exclaimed.

"That's right and you'd be well-advised to put down that gun. The government won't take the killing of one of its agents lightly. They'll hunt you down until you're brought to justice. Don't dig your hole any deeper," Roger warned.

The pistol remained pointed at the two hostages.

Despite the danger, Tyler was intent on getting some answers. "So why's the government involved with C.B.G. Pharmaceuticals? What've they got to do with drug development?"

"They became aware of the compound's potential after it was submitted to the Federal Drug Administration for approval."

"More government bureaucracy by de man," Manny taunted.

Roger continued. "The compound, NRC8890, demonstrated some remarkable capabilities, but unfortunately it also had some safety issues. Based on the initial testing, the F.D.A. had to deny the application and prohibited further development by C.B.G."

"If it's unsafe why did they allow the experiments? And if you're working for the C.I.A. why didn't you stop it?" Tyler asked.

"The F.D.A. did its job. However, they also saw tremendous potential in the compound and brought it to the attention of the C.I.A."

"But you say dey stop test 'cause not safe," Manny interjected.

All at once, Tyler understood. "They only stopped the official development of the drug. He works for the Special Activities Unit and I'm a special activity."

"So?" Manny was still confused.

"The C.I.A. valued the potential of the compound and wanted it for their agents involved in covert operations across the world. It's a brain-altering medication with the potential to enhance intellectual capacity. The government wanted to improve the tools in their arsenal. In other words, to enhance their agent's mental abilities."

"You mean for spyin' and shit?" Manny asked in awe.

"But the drug needed further testing. Isn't that right, Roger?"

He nodded. "The C.I.A. recognized its value and wanted to explore the possibilities."

The Latino looked at Tyler and smirked. "You nothin' but friggin' lab rat for de gov'ment."

"How many more experiments were conducted?" Tyler asked.

"There were four test sites established around the country," Roger admitted.

"What happened to the other subjects, or should we call them special activities too?"

"The others were unsuccessful. You were the only one that responded positively to the compound."

"You mean I'm the only one who survived. And you still let them do this to me?"

"I didn't realize the danger at first."

"Didn't realize the danger! It was an experimental drug. Even the F.D.A. wouldn't allow testing. How could you not know the risk? Admit it, you just didn't care about me."

"Yeah G-man, what de story?" Manny pushed, enjoying the hostility between them.

"Maybe I was blinded by ambition or just brain-washed into doing my job. Hell, I don't know. When you started to change, proving the compound really worked, everything seemed okay." He paused for a moment. "At the time I wasn't aware of the problems the other test sites were having."

"When did you realize I could die? At what point did it become clear that the drug could kill me?"

"Not until later. That's when I learned about the others and began to have doubts. Hey, regardless of what I've done, I'm not the monster you think. I worried about you and your mother. She's a wonderful person and I didn't want to deceive her. Just couldn't do it anymore."

"What about your job, your responsibilities to the C.I.A.?"

"The C.I.A.'s no longer my priority. You and Gwen are. That's why I brought you back to Georgia."

Manny entered the conversation. "Bad choice, Amigo."

Suddenly, Tyler began to shift from one foot to the other, all the while staring intently at the Puerto Rican. Finally, he blurted out in an elevated, concerned voice, "You have to release my mom from that car trunk. Please! I'm begging you."

A stunned look appeared on Manny's face as he lowered the Magnum. "What de...how...?"

"My mom. She's tied up in your trunk."

* * * * * *

Total darkness. The smell of gas fumes and dust clogged Gwen's nose as she struggled to breathe. Cramped in the car truck, her back ached. She was unable to stretch her arms and legs as both were bound tightly with duct tape. Another strip was wrapped around her mouth preventing cries for help.

What's happening? Why would Manny do such a thing? her tormented mind wondered. *Please, God. Help me.*

Her anxiety intensified. She was alone. There wasn't anyone left who cared or would even miss her. All hope was lost. Gwen surrendered to despair accepting her bleak fate. *Our Father who art in Heaven, hallowed be Thy name*.... The Lord's Prayer crept into her mind providing peace, temporarily soothing the misery.

But hope didn't return.

* * * * * *

"Where's the car? Please let her go," Tyler pleaded.

"Are you sure about this?" Roger uttered.

"Yes. It's what he's thinking."

"Is she all right?"

"I think so, for now at least." The boy's eyes glazed over as he thought about her lying helplessly in the dirty, locked space.

"What else is the bastard thinking?"

"He's worried about where he's going to dump our bodies. He doesn't want to leave any trail for the police."

"Shut up, Freak," Manny threatened. "What kind'a friggin' trick is dis?"

"The boy's not a freak. He's got some special talents."

"Don't matter none. Play circus act if want. I got de gun and you got problem."

Roger urged, "Now wait a minute. Think this through. Is it really worth killing innocent people just for a few dollars?"

"More than few, Amigo. Is worth it."

"I think you're missing a bigger opportunity here."

"What de hell you talk 'bout?"

"If it's money you're after, there's a better play."

"Shut your friggin' mouth. Just tryin' to save ass."

"That's right, I am. But this will benefit you too," Roger explained. "The Feds have more at stake than some pharmaceutical company running out of cash. The government's got deeper pockets."

"Go on," Manny relented.

"This entire operation and all the experiments are being orchestrated by the C.I.A. They can't afford to have it leaked to the public. They get criticized enough by the liberals already. Think about what this would do to their image and more importantly, future funding. Seems to me you've got some real leverage here. They'd probably pay a lot to keep this operation quiet."

"You out'a friggin' mind. De government not pay to keep quiet. Cheaper to put bullet through Puerto Rican head."

"Well, here's a news flash. That's exactly what's going to happen if you murder one of their agents. They'll never stop looking until they find you. You'll be a marked man," Roger threatened.

"Friggin' asshole," Manny yelled, agitated over the bleak picture being painted.

"Maybe there's another way," Tyler interjected.

"Let me handle this," Roger ordered.

"Shut up G-man, or I kill you now." Manny tipped the bill of his cap back. "Okay genius boy, what your plan?"

"It's simple. You just set us free and we all go our separate ways."

The Puerto Rican shook his head. "Bullshit, you friggin' crazy. Dat ain't no plan."

Tyler persisted. "Think about it. Just melt away. You won't have the government on your back for killing an agent. I'm sure he can get the C.I.A. to call off the dogs in return for your silence. No harm, no foul."

"What 'bout Doc? I still kill him."

"Collateral damage," Roger offered.

"What 'bout my money?"

"Can't have it all, Manny. Consider your freedom and the chance to live as payment. All in all, I'd say it's a fairly good deal. Beats dying."

The room fell silent as the Puerto Rican sorted through his alternatives. None were very appealing. Finally he concluded, "Already cut deal, stick to it."

"You're making a big mistake," Hall warned.

"Doc told 'bout risk and reward. Got nothin' now, not afraid to take chance. May be only one I get." Manny took a deep breath. "Enough of dis shit."

"Don't do this!" Roger Hall pleaded.

"Shut de…."

Suddenly, there was a tap on the door.

Manny lifted a finger to his lips warning them to remain quiet.

245

Ignoring him, Tyler boldly stepped forward.

"Get ass back…."

As the Savant calmly turned the knob, the Puerto Rican instinctively moved behind the half-opened door. His gun remained pointed at the teen.

A man wearing a Florida Marlins cap stood outside holding a large paper bag. A small heart-shaped birthmark was located just below his right earlobe.

"Delivery from Lin's Chinese. Somebody called for an order of Kung Pao chicken."

"Got de wrong place," Manny responded from behind the door.

The delivery man looked at the receipt stapled to the bag, then up at the number on the door. "Nope, don't think so, this is the right address."

"I say you got de wrong place. Get de hell out'a here!" Manny yelled.

Trying to peek around the half-opened door, the persistent delivery man replied, "Look, this is the address they gave me. Can't take it back, otherwise I'll have to pay out'a my own pocket. Gotta tell you, don't make enough for that."

He made direct eye contact with Tyler who began rocking side to side. The teen then stopped and deliberately eased the door wider allowing a partial view of the Latino.

Seeing the .375 Magnum, the delivery man began to stutter, "Ho…hold on here, Bud…Buddy. Don't, don't worry 'bout the…uh food. It's fr…free. I'll pay…pay for it."

Reaching into the sack with his right hand, the delivery man stated in a firm voice, "Just take it, free of charge."

Pop. Pop. Two gunshots pierced the paper bag as Manny fell to his knees, his eyes wide open and gazing straight ahead. A second later the Magnum dropped from his hand to the floor. The limp body collapsed face first onto the carpet. His tattooed arms lay neatly by his side.

The delivery man stepped over and kicked the gun away. "Are you all right?"

"I'm good," Roger replied. "You okay, Tyler?"

"Yeah."

"I'm Agent Shaun Ryan from the C.I.A.," he said reaching in his back pocket to pull out his credentials. "Everything's under control now."

Hall stared at the man's unique birthmark. "I'm Agent Roger Hall. I work with Special Activities."

"I know who you are. I'm also assigned to Cerebral One."

"What about my mom? Is she all right?" Tyler immediately asked.

"Don't worry, she's being tended to."

"When can I see her?"

"We'll get you together soon."

Relief swept across the teenager's face.

"By the way, you made my job a lot easier by opening that door wider. Really helped me get a lay of the land and see the suspect. It was almost like you knew what I needed."

"I did."

"What?"

"I knew you wanted me to open the door. It's what you were thinking."

CHAPTER 22

A slow but steady flow of vehicles exited the parking lot. Drivers maneuvered onto side streets and headed off to work. Many functioned on auto-pilot while staring blankly at the road ahead, their minds free of thought. Others focused on the tasks to be done during the new day. A variety of music and morning news blared from radios, competing for their attention.

Still wearing a nightshirt, Gwen sat at the kitchen counter sipping a cup of freshly-made coffee. She slid the barstool back and refilled the mug.

Her cell phone buzzed. "Hello."

"Gwen, it's Roger."

"What do you want?" she responded coldly.

"Just checking on you. Did you get moved into your new apartment okay?"

"Working on it."

"Anything I can do?"

"Try leaving us alone."

"Listen, what I did was wrong and nothing can change that." Roger took a deep breath. "I want to help you guys get back on your feet. Try to make things right."

"We'll manage without your help, thanks."

"For what's it worth, I went ahead and paid three month's rent on your apartment. Hopefully that'll give you a little time to find another job."

"I'll pay you back," Gwen offered curtly. She hated taking anything from the man but was desperate and needed it. There wasn't anyone else to fall back on.

He continued. "How're you doing after your ordeal with Manny? Being locked in that car trunk must've been horrible."

"If it weren't for Tyler…sometimes I wish I hadn't survived. It'd sure be a lot easier. That sounds awful, but it's the truth."

"I know it might seem that way, but things turned out all right didn't they?"

"All right? How can you say that?"

"Well, at least the police closed the case on Johnston."

"They're not questioning me anymore. That's all I care about. I just want this whole thing to be over. We've been through enough."

"Wish I could go back and change everything. All any of us can do is go forward." He paused then boldly asked, "Any chance for us?"

"How do you expect me to feel? What you did, lying to us and risking Tyler's life with that God-forsaken experiment…what do you want me to say? That I forgive you and everything's okay? My son could've died and still might because of this. Who knows if there're any future side effects."

"I've made a mess of things."

"Since you came into our lives, my whole world's changed." Her voice cracked with emotion. "I lost my job…my father…and heaven knows what lies ahead for Tyler."

Roger hesitated before asking, "How's he doing, any changes?"

"He seems to be all right so far."

"Any signs of reverting?"

"Not yet, but he's worried about it. Constantly talking about the drug and how he needs more. He's so afraid."

"Yeah, I know. Back in Illinois he asked me to help him get some."

"So what did you tell him?"

"Nothing. I put him off, but the fact is I may know a way."

"What? You can get more? How?"

"It's a little complicated." Roger cautioned, "The question is whether you want me to."

Gwen remained silent.

"Well, think about it. Call me if you do."

A blanket of sadness enveloped the woman. She reflected on the turns in her life. Abandoned by a husband and raising a Savant had been hard to overcome. Her parents became a support system. Then her mother died of breast cancer and Alzheimer's slowly took Ernest. Now Tyler faced an uncertain future. It'd been a difficult road with a heavy toll, but she'd sacrificed and pushed forward. *When does it all stop?* she wondered.

The winds of self pity eventually dissipated and a new breeze circulated. Thoughts of Roger Hall surfaced, the man she hated… or did she?

He was an intelligent, caring person genuinely interested in the family's well-being. He appeared to care for her too as they seemed to share a real connection.

But he'd betrayed them. How could she have been so wrong about him?

Maybe she wasn't. Roger had made some mistakes, but he seemed truly sorry. After all, he was only doing his job. Did he have a change of heart and recognize his mistakes? Maybe he does care.

And what if he did? The Christian way was to forgive. But could she?

The mechanical roar of a leaf blower penetrated the walls of the apartment as a maintenance man began his chore. The noise grew then subsided as he moved back and forth around the building.

Tyler stumbled slowly out of his bedroom wearing a pair of dark blue gym shorts and a white T-shirt. His hair was tangled wildly in all directions. He immediately walked to the counter and picked up a pack of gum, popping several pieces into his mouth.

"Morning, Hon."

"What's that idiot doing?"

"Who're you talking about? What idiot?"

"The one outside blowing leaves at this hour of the morning. Doesn't he realize people are still trying to sleep? What an ass!"

"Tyler please, your language. And it's not that early."

"The people who run this place should know better! They promised quiet and peaceful accommodations for their residents. We were told that when you signed the lease. This kind of annoyance is unreasonable. Technically they're in breach of contract. At a minimum they could be charged with false advertising. We should complain to management." He began chewing the gum harder and faster.

"Calm down. You're overreacting. It's not a big deal. You needed to get up anyway."

"Not only is it disturbing anyone trying to sleep, but it's inefficient as hell. There's dew on the ground and the leaves are wet. They're heavy and stick together. It takes more time and uses additional fuel. It's ludicrous. All they have to do is wait an hour or two until the dew dries and everything's quicker and cheaper."

Tyler's rant continued for several minutes. He eventually calmed down, feeling ashamed for his actions. "I'm sorry, Mom."

"Sometimes we're all a little cranky when we first get up." She walked over and hugged him.

"You know what?" He sniffed. "Blowing leaves early in the morning may not be such a bad thing."

"Why's that?" she asked taking a box of cereal from the cupboard.

"The moisture keeps the dust and pollen down. Sure better for my allergies." The nineteen year-old sat at the counter.

"See, there's always a silver lining if you just look for it."

His mood unpredictably shifted again. "Not always. There's no silver lining living as a Savant."

"Please don't start."

"It's true. I can't be that way anymore."

"I'll always love you regardless."

"But how would you like to be like that? You wouldn't and I don't want to either."

The roar of the blower grew louder, temporarily filling the apartment and drowning their conversation. The mechanical rumble soon subsided as the custodian moved away from the building.

When the noise softened, Gwen responded, "You've got a lot to offer."

He replied in a calm but firm voice, "I'd rather die."

"Tyler! Don't ever say that!"

"It's true. I've got to get the drug before it's too late."

"Maybe you don't need it. You've been fine. Maybe the effects are permanent now."

"I can't just wait and see."

"What choice do you have?"

"I can go to the company that makes it. Chemical, Biological & Genetic Research Incorporated."

"Even if they agree to supply it, the drug's dangerous. It's still experimental and could...."

"Don't care. I'll take that chance."

"Please don't. I'm begging you!"

"I'm sorry, but I have to. I'm going to contact C.B.G. Got nothing to lose."

"What if they deny knowledge of the drug?"

"I'll make them tell me the truth," Tyler countered stubbornly.

"Why would they give it to you? What if they just say no, then what?"

Tyler threw up his hands in frustration. "I don't know! Maybe I can set up a lab and produce it myself. There's a lot of technical information available on the internet. The chemical agents and reactants are available. With time, I can probably synthesize the compound. May take a little trial and error, but I'll replicate it." The young man paused for a few moments, then added, "If I have enough time."

"How will you know if you've reproduced the exact compound and it actually works?" Gwen asked, afraid of the answer.

"Look, I refuse to give up without trying something." Hard and unyielding determination was carved into his face.

The roar of the leaf blower returned as Gwen walked to her bedroom and closed the door, refusing to debate the issue further. She then took the cell phone from her pocket....

* * * * * *

The Monte Carlo meandered slowly through the rolling hills of Veteran's Memorial Cemetery. Marble and granite headstones blanketed the grounds with only a few trees breaking the monotony. A colorful smattering of red, orange and yellow leaves dressed their branches, waiting to be stripped by the hands of autumn.

The car slowed and pulled off to the side. Gwen and Tyler got out and began walking through the army of markers. About fifty yards in they stopped. At their feet lay a plain granite gravestone...ERNEST EUGENE SHEALY.

"God rest his soul," Gwen softly muttered.

"Mom, what...or who...do you think this soul is?"

In a slightly elevated tone, she replied, "It's your Granddaddy. His spirit's with God. The Bible says his human body will turn to dust, but his heart and soul will live forever. Tyler, you should know that!"

"I loved Granddaddy, but he's dead and gone. His life's over."

"That's not true! Your Granddaddy's an angel in Heaven."

An obstinate Tyler pointed at the burial site. "He's buried right here. His remains are decomposing just like everything else that's ever lived and died."

"His earthly body but not his soul," Gwen challenged.

"Who is God and where's Heaven anyway? Neither exists! Mankind wasn't created by this fictional character, Mom. The human species evolved over millions of years."

"Stop it! You weren't raised that way."

"That's right, I was raised as a Savant. I never had the ability to believe in anything."

The teen's erratic personality shifted again as his mood softened.

"I'm sorry, Mom. Hate to upset you especially at Granddaddy's grave. I don't know what's happening. I just say things without

253

thinking." In an effort to console her, the teen added, "Maybe there are such things as angels. Who knows for sure? Anything's possible, I guess."

"God does work miracles," Gwen added, confirming her belief.

"Some believe we can return to life. According to the Hindu religion, souls are reincarnated after death. Maybe they are." Tyler looked directly into his mother's eyes. "Regardless of what you believe or what really happens, I feel we'll see each other again."

"I know," she replied. "We'll meet in heaven."

"Or later in this life."

Looking down at the headstone she replied, "I just couldn't bear to lose you now."

"I don't want to lose me either. Don't you understand the drug will keep that from happening."

Their attention was suddenly drawn to an approaching vehicle. It pulled off the road and parked directly behind their Monte Carlo. Roger Hall got out and walked toward them.

"What's he doing here?" Tyler asked angrily. He spit out his gum then immediately reached into his pocket for more.

"I called and asked him to meet us."

"Why? He's a lying conniver and can't be trusted. I never want to see him again."

"I know how you feel."

"So why'd you have him come?"

As Roger approached, Gwen softly answered, "He may be able to help you."

"Like he helped before? When he was holding me hostage, I asked for his help but didn't get it."

Roger stopped a few feet away.

"Thanks for coming," Gwen said.

"Thanks for kidnapping and locking me in a cave," Tyler angrily added.

Hall ignored the barb. "I see they got your Dad's headstone up. He was a good man."

"What would you know about being a good man, you...?" Tyler curled his hands into fists and stepped threateningly toward him.

"Tyler! Stop it! What's happening to you?" Gwen said, moving between the two.

"It's all right. Don't blame him, he's got a right to feel that way. I've done some terrible things."

"That's no excuse. He should know better."

"And you should know better than to trust him," Tyler growled through clenched teeth.

Attempting to break the tension, Roger quickly interjected, "You needed to talk to me, Gwen?"

The woman took a deep breath. Her eyes were distant.

Immediately, Tyler began rocking back and forth while staring at her.

A cool breeze blew the woman's hair back as her thoughts were invaded by the teen. An eerie silence hovered as they stood next to the gravesite.

He stopped swaying and turned to Roger Hall. "Is it true? You can get more of the drug? How? Tell me!"

"Gwen, is that what you wanted to talk about?" Roger asked, disregarding the teenager's demand.

"I don't know. Oh Lord, help me," she pleaded.

"Why do you need help from some hyped-up religious character? I'm your son. Why don't you listen to me?"

"I love you more than anything, but I'm terrified of what it could do to you."

"And I'm terrified of what I'll become without it. I know what I want! And I don't want to become a Savant again."

"Hey, talking that way hurts your mother."

"You have the nerve to lecture me about hurting my mom?" He turned to her. "I'm going to get the drug one way or another whether you like it or not. I already told you, if the pharmaceutical company won't provide it, I'll try to reproduce it."

"That's going to take specialized equipment, the right chemicals and time. Let's be realistic, Tyler, you don't have any of them," Roger warned.

A flock of blackbirds circled the cemetery causing a shadowy footprint to slide across the ground. They eventually landed in a nearby tree peppering its colorful leaves with their ominous dark feathers.

"Somehow I've got to get more."

Finally Gwen gave in. "If your mind's made up, there's not much I can do."

"How can you get it?" the teen demanded.

Roger responded, "C.B.G.'s going to have to be persuaded. They'll never admit anything about the compound, let alone voluntarily give you any. That's just not going to happen. So you can mark that notion off your list."

"How do we persuade them?"

"It's simple. We have leverage."

Gwen spoke up. "What leverage could we possibly have?"

With a dull flutter, the cadre of blackbirds left their perches and darted back into the sky.

"Let's just say C.B.G. will do about anything to protect their interest in the marketplace. We're in a good position here."

Tyler interjected, "So you're going to threaten them? A powerful pharmaceutical giant isn't going to take kindly to that."

"I prefer to think of it as negotiating. Besides, we have an ally on our side. The company's not going to put up much of a fight against the C.I.A. The agency is very good at applying pressure."

"Blackmail," Tyler muttered. "Once a conniver, always a conniver."

"I don't understand." Gwen stated.

Tyler astutely reasoned, "With the Feds pushing, they'll be forced to provide the compound."

"How's that possible?"

"They won't have a choice. The government's ultimately responsible for reviewing any new drugs submitted by the company. Without their approval, no new medications will ever be released to the marketplace. That would be a death sentence for C.B.G."

"He's right. So, do you want my help or not?" Roger asked.

All eyes were now focused on Gwen. After a few tense moments, she reluctantly nodded agreement as her shoulders drooped downward.

"How soon will you have it?" the teen eagerly asked.

"It may take a few days. You guys sit tight. I'll get back to you," Roger promised.

As he drove away, Tyler started toward the Monte Carlo. "Let's go."

"I'll be there shortly." Gwen remained at the gravesite for several minutes praying for her father...and that she'd made the right decision.

*　*　*　*　*　*

On the ride home Tyler asked, "Do you really think he can do it?"

She stared ahead at the highway and shrugged. "I wouldn't get my hopes up, Hon. Can't imagine him having that much pull."

"Not pull, Mom...push. Roger's a schemer, a master manipulator. He's going to force them into it."

"Don't be so judgmental. Roger's admitted his mistakes. He's trying to make amends. God forgives people and we should too."

"Maybe you can forgive him after what he did. I can't."

"Tyler, he was wrong, but people change. Deep down he's a decent person. I can see it in him."

"You need to take off those religious blinders and see the man for who he really is. I don't know what you're hoping for, but he's no saint."

"He's trying to help you. I think his intentions are good."

"Believe me, I know how the man thinks. Saw him in action at the cave. He pretended to care but didn't. He can't be trusted." Tyler looked out the window at the passing landscape. "You know what? Whether I trust him or not, if he can get the drug then it doesn't matter. We just need to keep our eyes and minds open, and our hearts out of it."

"Doesn't seem right using blackmail to get something," Gwen persisted, shaking her head. "Wish there was another way."

"It doesn't matter how I get it. I'd rather die than revert."

"And you might. The compound...may...may kill you," she stuttered, fighting back the tears.

"Without it I'm dead anyway."

"Quit saying that! I just lost Daddy."

"You lost Granddaddy a while ago. Alzheimer's took him long before he died."

"That's not true. He was always with me." She reached up to brush away a tear. "Just…just know that re…regardless of what happens, whether you go back…back to the way you were or stay like…like this, my love for you doesn't change."

The teenager rolled the window down and with a mighty blow, spit out a huge wad of chewing gum. He put in another piece.

The two sat quietly as they continued their journey home. The colorful autumn countryside gradually slipped away as they approached their apartment.

Tyler peeked over at his mother who stared at the road ahead. His jaws began milling the gum, faster and faster. Now intently focused on her, the teen's shoulders swayed slightly from side to side while absorbing her thoughts.

What am I going to do? I know he wants this, but I'm so afraid of losing him. Should I go behind his back and talk to Roger, tell him not to pursue it any further? He'd stop if I asked him.

Maybe I should just forbid him. Can I do that? I know it's his life to live and his decision to make, but he's only a boy, my baby boy. Does he really know what's best?

What am I talking about? He's a man. I don't have any right.

I don't care whether he's a Savant or the smartest man in the world. It makes no difference, just as long as he's alive.

Tyler continued to rock as beads of sweat dampened his face, all the while stealing her secrets.

It was good to see Roger today. I know he's done some bad things, made some mistakes, but we all have. He's only human and deserves forgiveness, right? Deep down I think he's a decent man. It's just something about him. Roger was good to us for a while and I believe he can be again. He cares for me.

I've sacrificed for my family, done the best I know how. I'm not complaining because I was blessed to have them. But I've got to live too. Is it wrong to want more? Is it wrong for me to feel this way? Am I being selfish, thinking only of me? I'm so confused.

Not certain how it'd work between Roger and me anyway. Tyler certainly hasn't forgiven him and probably never will regardless of what happens. No use getting my hopes up. Guess it just wasn't meant to be, me and Roger.

Oh God, help me endure all this.

Tyler stopped rocking. Her emotions struck a nerve with the young man. All this time he'd selfishly focused on his feelings and never considered hers. What about her needs? Hadn't she been through enough?

"You've been quiet. What've you been thinking about?" he asked.

"Oh...just about Daddy."

He knew she was lying.

"I miss him a lot. He was a good father."

"What was my dad like?"

Gwen was surprised but determined to be honest. "We got married young and were happy for a while. He was smart and ambitious but had a restless vein, always wanting more."

"Is that a bad thing, Mom?"

"Absolutely not. In fact, it was one of his traits that attracted me. For a young woman from the rural hills of Georgia, he was sure exciting to be around."

"You two sound like a good fit."

"We were at first, but things just didn't work out. We didn't have a whole lot. Then after you came along...he just...uh...well he left."

"Do you miss him?"

Gwen paused for a moment and then responded, "Not anymore."

"Am I like him, any similar characteristics?"

"Yeah, you're both very handsome."

"Mom, would you like to get married again?"

"Nope. I'm done with marrying. Don't need it. You're all the family I want."

Tyler looked away, knowing she was lying again.

Finally they arrived back at the apartment. She tossed her bag in the chair. "Can I fix you a snack, Hon?"

"Okay," Tyler replied walking toward his bedroom.

"I'll let you know when it's ready," she yelled as he closed the door.

The bedroom walls were dingy white and void of the baseball paraphernalia that had always adorned his room. The carpet, which had been shampooed in an attempt to clean the stains left by previous tenants, was matted and still reflected years of abuse. A single window provided a mundane view of the parking lot.

Tyler plopped down on the bed and reflected upon their meeting with Roger Hall. Even though he didn't trust or like the man, his plan to use the C.I.A. to extort compound from the pharmaceutical company was certainly more feasible than any other options.

Closing his eyes, Tyler listened to his mom rattle around in the kitchen. Did she really care for Roger Hall? How could she, after what he'd done? Was she really that lonely and unhappy?

"Your sandwich is ready," she called out.

Waiting on the counter was a glass of milk along with a ham and cheese sandwich.

"I've got some chocolate chip cookies when you're finished," she offered.

The teen picked up the sandwich and took a big bite.

"How is it?"

"Good," Tyler mumbled.

"I'll fix another if you want it."

"No thanks, I'm all right." He swallowed and asked, "You aren't eating?"

"I'm not hungry right now." She ran a kitchen towel over the countertop.

"Anything wrong?"

"Just thinking about Roger's idea."

"I know how you feel about things, Mom. You've made it real clear."

"You're fine without the drug," she said stubbornly. "You might not…." Gwen swallowed. "What's so wrong with the way we were anyway?"

"Let's not fool ourselves. Things weren't that great."

"How can you say that?"

"It's true. I'm just able to admit it and you can't!" His voice rose. "C'mon Mom. Be honest for once!"

"You see what it's doing to you! You never talked to me like that before."

"I see more than you know." He pushed the plate away. "I know you're not as happy as you claim."

"And watching you die from some experimental drug will help? Losing the only family I have left and not being able to do anything about it?"

Tyler's emotions continued to swing uncontrollably as he slapped the counter in anger. "It's not about you! I'm sick and tired of being deprived a life. Can we please think about what I want, about my happiness for once?" he unfairly shot back.

Feeling the sting of his words, Gwen picked up the empty plate and placed it in the sink. She reached into a cabinet for a bag of Chips Ahoy cookies and slid it across the counter.

A red-faced Tyler snatched the cookies and retreated to his bedroom. A shameful ache built inside. How could he have said those things to his mother? After all she'd done, all the sacrifices? How could he be so mean? He looked at the bare wall separating their rooms wishing he could take everything back.

What's happening to me? he agonized. *Is this what life feels like? Is it supposed to hurt so much and be this hard?*

CHAPTER 23

The jet landed at Reagan National. Roger Hall grabbed his carry-on from the overhead compartment and exited the aircraft. After leaving the terminal he hailed a taxi for the short ride to Langley, Virginia where the headquarters for the Central Intelligence Agency was located.

He entered the lobby of the mammoth complex. Like so many times before, he paused to reflect upon a granite seal embedded in the floor. The emblem measured sixteen feet in diameter. An eagle's head was positioned atop a shield with a sixteen-point compass in its center. Written around the Seal's circular borders were the words "Central Intelligence Agency—United States of America."

Roger rode the elevator to the third floor. Cavernous hallways lined with a multitude of office doors extended in both directions. He started down the tiled corridor, eerily quiet given the volume of staff occupying the administrative space.

Hall's mind raced, anticipating his impending meeting with the Deputy Director of Special Activities. His long-standing career with the C.I.A. was coming to an end. An odd mixture of emotions battled within as he approached the corner office. The sadness for leaving a job he'd held for so many years was buffered by resentment.

He'd labored within the agency, slowly progressing into more responsible roles. But the opportunities and promotions never came fast enough for the overly-ambitious agent. At times he became frustrated for never reaching the level he deserved.

Hall operated within the Special Activities Unit of the Science and Technology Division. The covert function would deny knowledge of an initiative and the personnel involved if exposed. His last assignment was no exception. He'd supported a project designed to enhance human intelligence by developing a new drug which could unlock the vast capacities of the brain, making C.I.A. operatives superior. While extremely controversial and risky, the project was strategically important and assigned a very high priority.

But events hadn't gone as planned for the Agency or Roger Hall. Circumstances had changed as some unexpected relationships had evolved.

He softly tapped on the Deputy Director's door then entered.

"Hello Brent, how've you been?"

"Roger," the man simply replied without standing to shake hands. "Please have a seat."

He was dressed in a pristine blue striped suit with a fashionable burgundy tie. A matching handkerchief was neatly tucked into its breast pocket. His desk was barren with the exception of a telephone and a few manila folders neatly stacked on one corner. A laptop sat on a credenza directly behind him. He turned to close the screen, preventing any information from being exposed.

"How long you been with the agency?" the Deputy Director asked.

"It'll be twenty-six years next June. I came right after college. It's the only job I've ever had."

"Quite a career."

"Yeah, it's been a journey."

"Know what you mean. I started twelve years ago after finishing my law degree at Georgetown. It's the only place that's ever written me a paycheck," the much younger man confirmed.

The comment infuriated Hall. He had twice the experience and yet reported to this undeserving hot-shot lawyer who was continually promoted because of his elite background...and his father's connections inside the Beltway.

"Sorry to see things end this way after so much time."

"It is what it is," Roger stated simply.

"By breaking protocol you didn't leave the Agency much wiggle room in the matter."

Roger Hall sat stoically without replying.

"So tell me, what happened? You've been around long enough to know better. Why'd you break ranks?"

"I violated rule number one. Got personally involved."

The Deputy Director's tone changed. "Well, we've had to abort Cerebral One because of all the damn screw-ups. It's a real shame. The project could've paid great dividends for our country."

"Possibly. But at the end of the day, you'd probably end up having to add a few more names on the North Wall." Roger referred to the C.I.A.'s Memorial Wall located in the main lobby. The Wall of Ninety Stars stood as a silent memorial to the men and women who'd given their lives in the line of duty. Below the Memorial Wall was a glass-encased book with the names of fifty-five individuals. The names of another thirty-five remained a secret, commemorated only by a star in the book.

"Excuse me?" the Deputy Director asked.

"The compound's not safe. It's already killed all the test subjects except for that Shealy kid and the jury's still out on him."

"That's just the point. The jury is still out on the compound too, but now we won't get a verdict because the project's terminated. We'll never know if he could've tolerated the drug or what the benefits could have been. And those other subjects you mentioned? Well, thanks to you, they died in vain."

"Maybe the Agency should put their names on the Wall," Roger Hall stated sarcastically.

Not amused, the Deputy Director shook his head.

Hall added, "If not theirs, then the names of all the C.I.A. agents that could die using the drug."

"You're missing the point."

"Okay Brent, what is the point?"

The Deputy Director sat back in his chair and took a deep breath. "If the project would've proceeded, then maybe, just maybe we could've unlocked the drug's secrets. With more testing we may have been able to determine who could tolerate the drug and the exact chemical structure and dosage to make it both effective and safe. Don't you understand the advantage our agents would have gotten by using it? Think about our national security and the lives that could have been saved." He leaned forward, placing his forearms on the desk to make a final point. "I'm not certain the Wall's big enough for all their names."

Slightly defiant, Roger Hall countered, "Even if the initiative continued, there's no guarantee the drug would work. The lives of those test subjects are a hefty price for failure."

"A small cost for the potential benefit."

"Why don't you tell that to Gwen Shealy?"

"Obviously there's no need to debate the issue any further, Roger. It's clear you and the Agency are on different pages. We're no longer compatible. Why don't we just finish what we set out to do?"

Hall's mind raced with thoughts of the past twenty-six years with the C.I.A. He was ambitious and worked hard to succeed, continually looking for the next promotion. However those opportunities never seemed to materialize. Hall reflected upon many of the assignments, their unique objectives and eventual outcomes. While most were successful, others weren't. In the end his efforts had made a difference. He'd diligently supported the Agency and helped the country. No matter what lay ahead, Roger Hall remained proud of his contributions.

In a final attempt to salvage his career, he asked, "Brent, is there anything I can do to correct course, have the Agency reconsider its decision?"

"I'm sorry, but the damage is done and it's time to part ways. Your tenure here is over."

After years of service, Roger Hall's career with the C.I.A. came to an abrupt and unceremonious end.

He'd always placed the Agency's goals over his own, never allowing personal desires to interfere with the job…until now. With nothing more to lose he made his final play. "Before I go, there's one more thing I'd like to discuss with you."

"Make it quick."

"Even though Cerebral One's been terminated, some risks remain."

"You still worried about the safety issues?"

"I'm talking about something bigger."

"Okay, what do you see that we haven't already considered?"

This time Roger Hall leaned forward. "The risk of information leaks to the public and the negative impact it could have on the Agency's reputation. You know people don't always understand or agree with our tactics, especially when it comes to killing innocent people. We certainly wouldn't want the details to leak out, now would we?"

The Central Intelligence Agency served as the nation's first line of defense. Its primary mission was to collect information and conduct covert actions to achieve U.S. policy objectives. Both men knew it was imperative that these initiatives remain secretive as outside knowledge would put the safety of its agents in jeopardy.

While the Agency supported national security and ultimately the American people, their methods were sometimes controversial and potentially misunderstood. The C.I.A. valued their operating environment and would do anything to preserve it.

And now Roger Hall held an arrow pointing directly toward this Achilles Heel.

An uneasy quiet dominated the room as the men stared at one another.

The Deputy Director took a deep breath, opened a desk drawer and pulled out a small leather pouch. "Mind if I smoke?"

"No, go ahead. Doesn't bother me."

He retrieved his expensive Ascorti pipe and lit up. An aromatic, cherry-scented smoke soon drifted up, circling his perfectly combed hair. "They don't condone smoking at the headquarters building but I just can't resist. Know it's bad for me, but I really enjoy it. Takes the edge off."

"I guess we all have our vises."

"The Shealy woman yours? Hope she's worth it. Cost you a career."

Roger countered, "Whether we like it or not, she may cost both of us."

"What exactly are you getting at?"

"As one might expect, Mrs. Shealy became very, very angry once she found out about the project and the danger we put her son in."

"And who do we have to thank for that?" the Deputy Director stated in a hard, purposeful tone.

Ignoring him, Hall continued, "Like I said, she's extremely upset and threatening to get the media involved. Can't you just see yourself being interviewed by one of those '60 Minutes' reporters? You know spending federal dollars on an illegal activity sets her up as a potential relator in a whistleblower case too." Roger chuckled. "Wouldn't that play out well with the general public, not to mention the brass up the ladder?"

"Why are you telling me this?"

"Because there might be a way to avoid this messy little situation."

The Deputy Director replied, "I'm listening. Go on."

"Mrs. Shealy's a fine woman, but it's going to be tough caring for a Savant, especially on her meager salary. She's going to need some help."

"Help, huh?"

"Yes. I believe the Agency's in a position to provide some assistance."

"And in return?"

"Everybody goes their separate ways while knowledge of the project stays buried downstairs in the Agency's file room."

The Deputy Director rose from his chair and stepped over to a nearby window mulling his options. He took a long drag from the pipe stem, inhaling the satisfying nicotine fix before blowing its smoky remnants into the room. Finally he turned and responded, "All right Mr. Hall, how much does she want?"

CHAPTER 24

"Mom, heard…heard anything from Roger?"

"No, for the ump-teenth time."

"It's been five…five days since we talked at the cemetery. We should've heard something…heard something by now."

"Be patient. Said he'd get back to us. Give him some time."

"Don't have time, need drug now," Tyler persisted. The change in his speech was dramatic.

"Okay Hon, I'll give him a call," she relented as the teen popped in another piece of gum.

After several rings, she lowered the cell phone with a perplexed look on her face.

"What…what's wrong, Mom?"

"That's odd. His new number's been disconnected too."

"Maybe you dialed wrong. Try…try again."

Gwen redialed. "The number's no longer in use," she confirmed.

"I knew he couldn't…couldn't be trusted!"

"There's got to be a logical explanation."

Tyler began pacing. "Now…now what?"

"Everything's going to be fine. We'll go over to his apartment tomorrow and talk to him."

The teenager froze in his tracks. "Let's go now. Go now."

"First thing in the morning, I promise. Tomorrow's Saturday, he'll be home."

Tyler grabbed the laptop and went to his bedroom.

Time was running out. Without getting additional injections he'd be helpless to push for more. His fate now lay in the hands of Roger Hall, a C.I.A. agent trained in the art of deception.

The teenager pulled up a blank Word document and began typing.

Friday, October 28
Will turn twenty next birthday. Past nineteen years have been empty. Mad at what I missed. Determined to salvage rest of life. Have to.

He named the file "LIFE'S TO LIVE" and saved it.

Tyler closed the blinds, lay down and willed morning to arrive quickly. But he remained awake. Outside, a car door slammed. A couple with a young child laughed and chatted as they walked to their apartment.

Just before surrendering to sleep, Tyler's final thoughts were of a normal life with his own family.

"Come outside. I'll teach you how to catch and throw a ball, Son."

"I don't know, Dad. I ain't real good."

"Neither am I so we'll learn together."

The little boy reluctantly agreed and went outside to play catch with his father.

As the two gently tossed the ball back and forth, a sense of pride overwhelmed the man. He was so proud and loved the boy more than anything in the world, no matter what.

Although the lad tried to please his father, he just couldn't catch the ball.

"Keep your eye on it. Watch it all the way in," the man suggested as the ball whizzed by the boy's outstretched glove and fell to the ground.

Whether a natural lack of coordination or just plain fear of the ball, he couldn't seem to catch on. After trying for a short while he begged to quit. "I can't do it. Please, let's go back inside."

"Okay, you did great. I'm proud of you. We'll play again another time."

"Now we can watch T.V.," the child replied, relieved that he didn't have to play catch anymore.

"I got a better idea. Why don't we read one of your books? Your teacher says you need to read more."

"Oh Dad," the boy whined. "I don't wanna."

"Just for a little bit."

Once inside they grabbed a book and sat together on the couch. "I'll read a page and then you can read one to me."

The first page had a picture of a tree with a doghouse underneath. On the opposite side in bold print was a short sentence. "The oak tree was big and green." The man read out loud, then reached down and turned the page. "Your turn."

The youngster struggled with the words, unable to make out the short phrase.

"Sound it out Son, you can do it. What's that first letter?"

The child became frustrated and his eyes began to swell with tears.

"It's a 'D'. What sound does a 'D' make?"

"Da...da...da."

"That's right, good job."

"That second letter's an 'O'. What sound does it make?"

No response from the little boy.

"D...O...G. Dog." *The man spelled the word then answered.*

The child reached down and slammed the book shut, upset that he wasn't able to read. "I can't do it, I can't do it." *He stormed off, into his room.*

The man followed, finding the lad on the floor with an opened coloring book. A host of multi-color crayons were strewn around.

Although none of his colorings were within the lines, they were still beautiful. He loved him unconditionally.

"You're doing a great job, Son."

"Thanks."

"You having a good time?"

"Yup."

"I'll go get your bath ready. Back in a minute."

He returned shortly. "Go get in while the water's warm. I'll clean up and be there in a few minutes."

The boy scampered away while the man rounded up the crayons and neatly placed them back into their box.

Tyler then headed to the bathroom to bathe his son.

He was shocked to find the young boy lying motionless, face down in the water.

Tyler shot up in bed, awakened by the horrible nightmare. "Son!" he cried out. Cold sweat dampened his clothes.

When the alarm sounded at 6:40 a.m., the prior night's dream was still replaying in his mind. He now understood a parent's unconditional love for their child. The young man knew how much his mother cared and worried. He also realized her sacrifice in allowing him to take the risk, regardless of her own feelings and concerns. A tinge of guilt crept into his soul, knowing what he was putting her through.

Tyler rose and compulsively made the bed before neatly laying out a pair of jeans and a white T-shirt on the spread. Next he brushed his teeth, dressed and hurried out to make sure his mother was awake and ready.

Saturday morning traffic was light, making for a quick drive. As they approached the complex, Gwen asked nervously, "Hon, are you sure about this?"

"Ye…ye…yes."

Their minds and hearts were finally reconciled.

Tyler was determined to get more drug. It was his only chance at a normal life.

Although recognizing the danger, Gwen reluctantly succumbed to his wishes. As much as it pained her, at the end of the day it was his decision to make. It was his life to live, not hers. She had to let go.

At Roger's apartment, she softly knocked on the door.

"Harder...harder, Mom. Can't hear you."

She knocked again, this time with more force.

No response from inside.

Tyler's shoulders slumped. "Now what? I...need to talk...talk to him. Now what?"

"Maybe he's still sleeping."

The teen pounded on the door. "Roger Hall. Roger Hall. Get up," he yelled.

"Hush Tyler. It's still early. People are trying to sleep."

"Don't care. Need...need to see Roger Hall."

Gwen reached into her purse and pulled out a key chain. "I'll get us in. I've still got a key to his apartment."

She unlocked and slowly opened the door. "Roger? Anybody home?"

They stepped inside then froze in their tracks.

The air was stagnant and the entire apartment was vacant. Totally empty. No furniture, no food in the kitchen, no clothes in the closet... and no Roger Hall. Even the carpet stained by Manny's blood had been replaced.

* * * * * *

Tyler snatched Gwen's cell phone from the kitchen table and went to his bedroom. There he retrieved his shoebox and removed a small business card. The teen punched in the number and waited for an answer.

"This is Padgett."

Tyler gripped the phone tightly and read from the card. "Detective Randall Padgett? Forsyth County Sheriff's Department? 687-414-0776?"

"Speaking."

"Can't trust Roger Hall. Bad."

"What?" Padgett asked. "Who is this?"

"Roger Hall bad....Bad man."

"Look, I don't know who...."

The phone went dead.

273

Tyler then grabbed his mom's laptop, opened the Word document from the prior evening and began another entry.

Saturday, October 29

Come to conclusion. Will not get drug. Will revert to prior existence.

Rather die. Going back to Savant is sterile life. Read Webster's dictionary and still remember. According to it, life is "the physical, mental and spiritual experiences that constitute a person's existence." Savant not a whole person. Only have physical aspect, an empty body. Don't want to live like that.

Mom sees different. Relieved not to worry about me taking drug. She loves me, doesn't want to take risk. Rather have as Savant than not at all. After dream, I understand.

If not around would she pursue new life? Mom still young woman. I'm holding back. Who would want someone with me? Who would want that albatross around neck?

Two alternatives. Live life I don't want and burden Mom, or end now.

Would be easy. Bathroom cabinet full of Granddaddy's pills. Painless and quick, go to sleep and never wake up.

Not hard decision. Only option that's best for both. Know is right thing, but scared. Don't think can do it.

Don't have courage.

Tyler's final ember of hope was fading away.

* * * * * *

Over the next several weeks, his condition deteriorated further. Most effects of the experimental compound had melted away. The Savant sat cross-legged on the couch and Googled the Atlanta Braves, compulsively reading every site listed.

Gwen leaned over and kissed the teen's cheek. "I'm getting tired. Time for bed."

"Okay. Go to bed…okay." He continued to stare at the computer.

"I love you," she said warmly.

Looking up, Tyler uncharacteristically made eye contact.

"You okay, Hon?"

After a long pause, he finally responded, "I'm...I'm sorry."

"Sorry? Sorry for what?"

"Hurting...hurting you."

"You haven't hurt me. That's nonsense."

The Savant replied in a surprisingly firm tone, "I will."

"You'd never hurt me," Gwen said softly. "It's late. You should go to bed too. I'll see you in the morning."

"Yes, see again. Remember, I'm your...your angel."

"You sure are, Hon. You'll always be my angel."

Once she'd left the room, Tyler opened the apartment window. He approached Budgie's immaculately clean cage and reached in to gently grasp the bird. Leaning out into the cool, dark air, he relaxed his fingers and in a flutter of colorful feathers, the parakeet flew out into the night. "Go Budgie. You're free...free of cage. No cage. No more."

He then grabbed the laptop and went into the bedroom. Sitting at the desk, he opened Word and scrolled down to "Life's to Live."

After reading the two prior postings, Tyler added a third very brief entry.

Sunday, November 19
I found the courage.

He turned the computer off and sat for several minutes, staring blankly at the floor. Eventually the young man rose and headed into the bathroom. There, he opened a cabinet drawer full of his granddaddy's unused prescription medications.

The mirror reflected a determined nineteen-year-old man twisting the caps off several bottles.

The young Savant wouldn't see his twentieth birthday.

CHAPTER 25

The pilot's voice came over the intercom. "Folks, we've begun our initial descent into Panama City. As you can see, it's a clear day with a ground temperature of 28 degrees Celsius or 82 Fahrenheit. With no unexpected delays we should be touching down in about twenty minutes. Hope you've enjoyed your flight today. Thanks for flying with us and we'll see you on the ground."

The attendants began collecting cups, newspapers and other trash from tray tables. Procrastinators unbuckled their seat belts and hurried to the restroom one last time before landing. The passenger in seat 3B stretched his legs and removed the ear buds channeling soft tones of Beethoven. Traveling in first class, he finished the chardonnay from his crystal wine glass and handed it to the pretty flight attendant.

"Thank you," the woman stated, smiling briefly while discreetly glancing ahead to the next row.

Just as the pilot promised, the plane landed without delay and taxied to Gate 11 of the small airport. Passenger 3B gathered his carry-on and headed for the exit, feeling genuinely sorry for the poor saps back in coach. He'd been there many times before.

The flight attendant bid goodbye as he stepped outside into the bright Caribbean sunlight, then down the metal stairs to the tarmac. He entered the small terminal building and followed the signs to immigration. A uniformed man behind the desk waved passenger

3B forward, asking for his passport. "Why you visiting Panama, Mr. Carlton?" he asked with a Spanish accent.

"Well, actually I'm not just visiting. I...uh...I live here now."

Brad Carlton's passport was stamped and handed back. "I see. Is this first time to enter Panama as resident?"

"Yes it is."

"What type of residency, por favor?"

"I have a 'person of means' visa." He presented it to the immigration officer.

"As you know, Mr. Carlton, you must have purchased property or have sufficient funds deposited in one of our banks."

"I have both. My home's in Boca del Toro."

"Ahh, a beautiful place, Señor."

Carlton presented the appropriate paperwork. After several moments the immigration officer smiled and handed the documents back. "Thank you very much, Mr. Carlton. Welcome home."

* * * * *

The property at Boca del Toro was incredible, just as the real estate agent promised. Brad Carlton had contacted her with all the requirements. She'd taken care of everything.

The house sat forty yards from the high-tide mark of the warm Caribbean ocean. Mature palm trees surrounding the structure bent slightly in the soft breeze. Beautiful native plants and flowers dotted the immaculate grounds. The private beach was covered with white powder sand, tiny seashells and the occasional sea crab. Two woven hammocks swung gently back and forth under a small thatch hut. At the water's edge a wooden pier extended out into the clear turquoise ocean. A twenty-five foot catamaran was tethered at the end.

Carlton turned to look at the moderately-sized house. White plantation-style architecture beckoned him onto a full-length veranda. He walked up the steps inhaling the subtle fragrance of island jasmine and gardenias. The glistening white porch was furnished with comfortable wicker chairs covered by overstuffed pillows that faced the beautiful Caribbean. The ceiling of the veranda was equipped with three giant fans rotating slowly, just enough to enhance the ocean breeze. Pocket doors were slid open making the main living quarters part of the outdoor setting. Local hardwoods polished to a subtle shine adorned the floors and were softened by large rugs and tropical themed furniture.

A huge basket of papayas, bananas, pineapple, guava, tangerines and pomegranates sat next to a bottle of Dom Perignon chilling in a sterling silver ice bucket. Brad Carlton picked up the handwritten note tucked carefully between two tangerines.

> *Welcome to your new home. Please accept this small token of my appreciation. The refrigerator is stocked and there are clean linens in the bathrooms. Hope you enjoy it here.*

It was a lovely housewarming gift from the agent who'd sold him the property.

Taking his only bag to the master bedroom, Carlton quickly unpacked and slipped into a pair of shorts. He threw a thick towel over his bare shoulder and headed out.

Carlton grabbed two beers from the refrigerator, nestling them into the ice alongside the champagne. With the bucket of libations in hand, he jaunted down the steps toward the powdery sand.

He placed the bucket between the two hammocks, then lay down to relax beneath the tropical sun.

"Hey! What a beach bum!" a buttery voice called out. A shapely figure clad in a bikini walked toward him. She had aged well. As their eyes met, both broke into broad smiles. Her pace quickened until the couple joined, embracing underneath the thatched roof of the beach hut.

"Been here long?" the woman asked.

He glanced down at the Cartier watch on his left wrist. "Just got here. Drink?"

"You bet."

Carlton righted a glass on the tiny table between the hammocks. He popped the cork of Dom Perignon and poured the bubbly beverage.

"You're not going to join me?" the woman asked brushing strands of windblown hair from her face.

"I'm more the beer type. You know that."

"That's right. You never could stand to drink anything but P.B.R. in college."

"The cheapest thing I could get. I'm a little more refined these days," he said, twisting the top off a Cerveza. "Let's have a toast. To new beginnings," Carlton offered, raising his bottle to tap the woman's champagne glass.

The couple took a quick dip in the ocean before returning to their hammocks. The soft, soothing sounds of tumbling waves filled the air as they relaxed on the private beach.

"Assume you didn't have any trouble at immigration," she said.

"I'm here aren't I?"

"No problems back in the States?"

"I took care of everything." He raised his head. "What are you so worried about anyway? You're not involved."

The woman looked away.

"Hey, I didn't mean it that way."

She turned to face him again. "I care about you, so I am involved."

"You're right, I'm sorry. I just meant you can't be legally connected to any of this. I made sure of it."

"Good."

Carlton continued to try and make amends. "Look, I took care of everything. All my accounts have been closed, checking, credit cards." He paused. "Frequent flyer, library card."

Jenny finally cracked a smile.

"The money's all been transferred under different names. It's clean and safely deposited in the Banco Nacional de Panama account."

Sitting up, she refilled her glass with champagne. "You never told me how you managed to get all the paperwork done so quickly."

"Piece of cake. Let's just say I have a lot of contacts. Believe me, if you have enough money and know the right people, you can get just about anything done."

Carlton drained the beer and popped the top off a second. Icy cold water dripped from the bottle onto his bare chest. "The hard part was getting the money, now that was tough."

Jenny rose from the hammock and adeptly gathered her disheveled hair into a pony tail at the nape of her neck. "I'm going up to the house for a minute, need to use the bathroom. Can I bring you anything, Roger?"

"Don't call me that anymore. I'm Brad Carlton now. And yeah, grab me another beer."

He watched closely as his college girlfriend walked barefoot through the sand, eventually disappearing inside the house. *Damn, she still looks good after all these years.*

Roger Hall then closed his eyes, thinking about Gwen. *Need to quit worrying. Time to move on.*

Easier said than done. His actions weren't something to be proud of, but the money was too tempting to pass up. With the demise of his career, the timing was perfect. So he'd justified his actions and manipulated Gwen Shealy and the system to get what he wanted, a chance at a new life. Screw the fact it was illegal and he was on the run, hiding for the rest of his life. The risk was worth it. Hell, he'd been taking risks his entire career with the C.I.A. and had absolutely nothing to show for it. Now he did. A second life to live.

CHAPTER 26

Overhead, the sky was an ominous gray. Thunderheads tumbled over each other threatening to unleash a torrent of rain. Gwen stood beside the freshly turned ground. Her green eyes were dull, lacking the spark of life. Dark circles underlined their sadness. The hollows of her cheeks were sunken, resembling someone beaten and starved into submission. The corners of her mouth sloped downward. Tears tumbled out, funneling along tiny facial crevices before dripping onto her blouse.

"I miss you, Tyler. I'm all alone now," she spoke softly while kneeling next to his gravesite.

Suddenly the heavens opened and a downpour erupted. Gwen stood to leave. Her legs were numb. She stumbled back to the car planning to wait out the storm, but the rain persisted. Finally she gave up and drove to Lanier Baptist Church. Worn wiper blades scraped across the windshield making visibility even worse.

The torrent eventually subsided and she made her way inside the sanctuary. Despite the day's darkness, several stained glass windows allowed some light in.

Her damp clothes clung tightly and caused the grieving woman to shiver. She walked down the aisle toward the altar, her wet sneakers squishing with each step. At the pedestal, Gwen lit two candles. Then she sat down in a nearby pew, folded her hands and began praying.

A screeching hinge echoed through the chamber as Reverend Williamson entered through a side door. He gently took her hand. "How you doing, Gwen?"

"Not well. I'm struggling to understand everything, but it's hard."

"You're shivering." He disappeared and soon returned with a black choir robe. "Here you go. This here's all I could find. Put it around you." He draped it over her shoulders. "There now, that should help."

Her empty eyes stared back. "Nothing's going to help."

"I know it seems that way, but God'll get you through this troubling time. He hears you. I promise."

The reverend glanced toward a cross hanging above the pulpit. Jesus was nailed helplessly to it. He then bowed his head. "Oh Lord we pray you provide this woman the strength to shoulder the unspeakable tragedy that's fallen on her...."

When finished, he asked, "Is there anything I can do?"

"You can tell me why this happened. Can you do that?"

How could he explain something so tragic? The woman had given everything to her family. She raised an autistic son and took in her ailing father. Now she was expected to deal with their deaths, all within a month. It was almost too much to ask.

"We shouldn't question God's will," was his only reply.

"I never have before, Reverend. You once gave a sermon about change and human struggles. I've struggled a lot in my life and have always accepted it as God's will, but this makes me doubt my faith."

"The church will be here for you. If there's anything you need, anything at all, just let me know."

The chill subsided and her matted, snarled hair began to dry. Gwen stood to leave, allowing the robe to drop to the floor. Making no attempt to pick it up, she turned and headed toward the door. "I'm going home. There's a lot to do."

Williamson followed. "Do you have any family or friends close by?"

"I'll be fine."

"God be with you," he offered as she stepped out into the cool air.

Back at the apartment, Gwen had just changed into dry clothes when a knock sounded at the door. She looked through the peep hole and saw two well-groomed men in dark suits. "Can I help you?" she called out.

They both presented official-looking shields. "C.I.A. Mrs. Shealy, we need to speak with you."

For God's sake, after all that's happened, what now? Gwen wondered.

She opened the door and stepped aside, allowing the men to enter.

"We'd like to talk to you about Roger Hall."

"What about him?"

"When was the last time you spoke with him, Ma'am?"

"It's been several weeks."

The agents looked around the room, assessing every detail of the modest apartment. One asked, "No phone calls, emails, letters? No contact whatsoever?"

"No. He didn't even attend my son's…my son's funeral."

"We're sorry to hear that, Ma'am."

Gwen momentarily drifted away. *Why didn't he come? I know he cared for us, I just know it. Where was he?*

She composed herself. "Is Roger okay? Did something happen to him? Is that why you're here?"

The agents ignored her inquiry. "The last time you saw Mr. Hall, was there an exchange of money?"

"Excuse me?"

"Did he give you any money?"

"Money? For what?"

"Ma'am, we'd really appreciate if you'd just answer the question."

"No, there was no money exchanged. He paid my apartment rent for a few months. Other than that I've never taken anything from him. I wouldn't."

"I don't mean to insult you, Mrs. Shealy, but I'm not talking about rent money. What I'm referring to is a very large sum. Millions of dollars."

"Millions of...? Oh my God, no. Roger didn't have that kind of cash."

An agent reached forward to take her arm, gently guiding her to a chair. "I think you better sit down, Ma'am."

* * * * * *

Gwen emptied a packet of Splenda into her coffee and watched the tiny crystals dissolve into the abyss. Steam floated upward as her tongue touched the scalding brew. After blowing several times, she carefully took a sip. It was hot but tolerable.

The apartment was totally quiet. She was alone.

Her eyes traveled to the empty aviary sitting in the corner. What had happened to the bird? She'd awoken that terrible morning to find the door of Budgie's cage open and Tyler lying on his bed. Both were gone.

Gwen headed toward the bathroom where she stripped and stepped into the shower. A mist formed as a pounding stream of hot water shot out turning her pink from the onslaught. She rubbed a bar of soap over every inch of her skin. The soapy water dripped down the contours of her body, then into the drain.

Several minutes passed and the warmth was slowly replaced by a flow of icy wet needles. Shivering, she turned the water off and grabbed a towel.

Gwen retrieved a pair of jeans and a blouse. Spying the picture of Tyler on top of the dresser caused her heart to fill with an overwhelming grief.

I've got to pull out of this. There has to be a reason. God must have a plan for me.

She bravely walked down the hallway and entered Tyler's room for the first time since his death. The bed was unmade and still rumpled from that awful morning. Gwen pulled the comforter up and smoothed it over the pillows. She opened the closet and took his Braves jacket from a hanger. Holding it close, she sucked in the smell of her son.

A laptop computer sat on the desk. Sticking out from underneath was an envelope with "MOM" written on it.

Her heart froze. When the emotional barriers melted away, she opened the letter and read....

22-14-16-30-28 PB 8

You never believed in playing lottery. Said it was tax on stupid. But have to this one time. You sacrificed for me and Granddaddy. Now my chance to do something for you. Purchase ticket for Powerball drawing on November 25th. Pick numbers above. Won't worry again.

Small thing compared to what you gave. Maybe will make life better. You deserve it.

Always remember, life's to live.

Will see you again.

Your angel,
Tyler

Gwen read the message several times, tearing up remembering Tyler's aversion to odd numbers. All the lottery numbers were even.

She glanced at the calendar next to the computer. November 25th was circled. "That's tomorrow," she mumbled.

But it was difficult to wrap her mind around tomorrow. She was struggling just to get through today.

CHAPTER 27

FIVE YEARS LATER

"Happy anniversary, Babe. Does it seem like we've been married three years?"

"Heavens no." Gwen smiled lovingly at her husband as she reached across the table to gently touch his hand. "It's been wonderful. And so are you, Bob."

"I was lucky to find you. Never thought I'd feel this way again." The man had lost his first wife in a car accident twenty years earlier and had been left alone to raise two daughters. Both were now grown and married with families of their own.

He'd met Gwen when she'd come to him for financial advice, and their relationship blossomed into a mid-life romance.

The upscale restaurant was fairly busy. Most of the tables, covered in white linens with expensive silverware and china settings, were occupied. Their waiter approached. "Was everything to your satisfaction?"

Bob replied, "Dinner was great, thank you."

"Can I get you some coffee or maybe one of our fine desserts?"

"On no, nothing for me. I'm stuffed," Gwen responded politely. "Everything was lovely."

"I think we're finished. Just the check please," Bob stated.

"Very well, Sir. I'll be right back." The waiter turned and left the table.

"Do you have a busy day tomorrow?" she asked.

"Not too bad. Just a couple of accounts I want to review." Bob added, "The market's been so volatile lately. Don't want my clients to be hurt by any more companies in trouble."

"You mean like C.B.G.?"

"Yeah, I was lucky on that one. Got most of my investors out before the company filed Chapter 7 liquidation."

"You're good at what you do. But you don't need to work anymore. Take a day off. We've got enough money."

"Oh I don't know, guess I still enjoy it. Besides, *we* don't have enough money. *You* do."

"That's crazy. I've told you, it's ours now."

He smiled. "I know. Suppose I need to stay busy."

"We just spent two weeks in Rome. That didn't keep you busy enough?"

"Can't travel all the time." He then joked, "Besides, you'd probably get sick of me hanging around home. I'm only trying to save our marriage."

"Bob, you know better than that. The fact is you're just trying to get away from me, aren't you?"

They both chuckled enjoying the playful banter.

"What about you, Babe? Any plans for tomorrow?"

"Well, since you're working, I'll probably go down to Scottish Rite and spend some time." Scottish Rite was one of the largest children's hospitals in the Atlanta area. The facility treated everyone from toddlers with broken arms to teens undergoing chemotherapy regiments.

"You really like volunteering there, don't you?"

"Yeah, my heart goes out to some of the children, especially those who…." Gwen didn't finish the thought.

This time the man reached for her hand, providing a warm, understanding touch.

The waiter returned and laid the bill on the corner of the table. "Hope you enjoyed your meal. Thanks for dining with us this evening."

The couple left the restaurant and returned to their expensive home in an exclusive gated community. Even after all this time, Gwen couldn't believe she really lived there.

"Good to be home," Bob commented as they pulled into the driveway.

When she didn't respond he asked, "You okay, Babe?"

"Hmm? Oh sure, I'm fine. Just thinking."

"About?"

"The past I guess." As he turned off the car engine, she shook the melancholy feelings. "Have I thanked you lately for my anniversary present?" Gwen ran her fingers over the diamond bracelet.

"Not in the last hour."

"Well thank you. Now let's go inside. I'm ready for bed."

He said slyly, "Me too. I want to get my anniversary present."

The next morning, Bob went downstairs where the smell of bacon filled the air. "You don't have to get up and do this every day." He kissed her cheek. "I could've fixed a bowl of cereal or something."

"Nonsense. You're not eating cereal for breakfast as long as I'm around. No more Cheerios," she stated firmly, referring to her previous morning ritual with Tyler.

"I don't need to be eating anything after that meal we had last night."

"Well, try. Otherwise you'll be starving by lunchtime."

The man smiled and shook his head. "You're too good to me."

They sat down and enjoyed breakfast together. Afterwards he gave her another peck on the cheek and left for his office. "I love you," he stated walking out the door.

Gwen was living a charmed life, a big change from years past. She was financially secure with more money than she'd ever need, and sharing it with a wonderful man who adored her. Yet there still remained a hole in her heart, one that hadn't mended with time.

Before leaving for Scottish Rite, Gwen checked her email and Facebook page. A new picture of Latrisse sitting at a slot machine in

Las Vegas had been posted. Gwen smiled thinking of her dear friend. *Sure glad she's putting that money I gave her to good use.*

When she eventually arrived at the hospital, the admissions office was crowded as usual.

It was a somber place where parents nervously waited as helplessness and anxiety battled with faith and hope. One by one they were eventually called to answer questions and complete a mountain of paperwork to admit their ailing child.

As a volunteer, Gwen performed a host of tasks to assist the admissions clerks in their duties. She also roamed the waiting room and spoke with the families, answering questions and providing comforting words as they waited.

"The restrooms are out the door and down the hall on your right."…."It shouldn't be much longer."…."Can I get you something to drink while you wait?"

Other times, saying the right thing wasn't as easy. Worried expressions on parents' faces signaled their agonizing concern. "The staff here does a wonderful job."…."Your child will be fine."…."God bless you." Sometimes her words helped, sometimes they didn't.

As she handed out magazines, a security officer entered the waiting room with a small boy in tow. The child wore a white T-shirt and his shoes were untied. His shoelaces flapped against the floor as he walked along.

"'Scuse me folks, but we found this young'n wanderin' the hallways early this mornin' and we're tryin' to locate his parents." The officer paused for a response.

The room fell silent as people looked curiously at the child with curly, blond hair and green eyes. Some shook their heads and murmured to each other, but no one acknowledged the lad.

Gwen slowly made her way to the officer. "May I speak to him?"

"Who're you, Ma'am? You know the boy?"

"I'm sorry, no. I'm just a volunteer here at the hospital." She stared at the child. "Is it all right?"

"Yes Ma'am, go 'head. But I doubt you get much. No one's got a word out'a him."

She knelt down and spoke softly. "Hello there. You remind me of my little boy."

The youngster immediately looked away avoiding eye contact.

"What's your name, Hon?"

No response.

The security officer spoke up. "That's what he does. Won't look at nobody. Just looks 'way like that. Nobody knows nothin' 'bout him. Like he just 'ppeared out'a thin air."

"Surely his parents wouldn't have just dropped him off…left him here alone."

"Don't know, Ma'am. We contacted the police and Protective Services. So far, nothin's come back. It's a real mystery."

Gwen tried once again to talk to the child. "You're sure a handsome young man." She smiled and slowly reached out to pat his shoulder.

The boy immediately jerked away.

"I'm not going to hurt you. I bet your mom and dad are worried sick about you. We'll find them. What's your name?"

The child remained silent. Then he suddenly looked up and began pointing toward the ceiling. His finger moved slowly through the air as if counting the white corrugated tiles.

"How old are you, Hon?" Gwen persisted, trying desperately to connect with him.

"He 'ppears to be four or five," the security officer interjected.

She never took her eyes from the boy. "What'll happen if you can't locate his parents?"

"Don't know. Guess he'll be turned over to Protective Services." The man leaned close to Gwen.

"Even if they find 'em, don't know what'll happen. 'Specially if they just left the boy. State don't look too kindly on child 'bandonment. Might decide to take him into custody anyway. Too bad, but happens all the time."

She urged the youngster, "Please. Tell me where you live."

The young boy stopped pointing at the ceiling tiles and lowered his arm. He looked around curiously, his head jerking from side to side. Then he finally said, "Live."

Gwen and the officer exchanged glances. Encouraged by the response, she said, "Yes, that's right. Where do you live?"

For the first time he looked directly into her green eyes. "Life's to live."

Stunned, Gwen fell to her knees. "Oh my God! Wha...what'd you say?"

The youngster unexpectedly reached out to grasp her hand.

"Life's...to...live," the boy repeated with an angelic smile. "Remember?"

About the Author

Sherry Snelgrove lives in Atlanta with her husband and two college-aged children. Her third book, Life's Two Live, was completed in 2011.